He raised his fist for another strik[...]
roughly behind his back as he w[...]
unconscious body. He spat on the [...]
the rain. Sizemore looked dead, but Nick wasn't that lucky.

"Let's away with you, Nicky. That's enough now."

He hadn't expected the priest to come. He swallowed the
need to throw himself into the man's arms. Stood taller. This
man was more a father to him than a man of God. "He killed
her, Father." His knuckles started to sting, but it wasn't even
close to the pain ripping through his heart.

"And he'll have to live with that, won't he?" Father Mike
propelled Nick along the gravel path.

"He doesn't have to live with it." The cold air hurt his lungs
as Nick inhaled. It made him realize just how much he'd
sobered up, and how little he had left to lose.

The priest grabbed him by the shoulders and shook him.
"Chrissie left you, son." Father Mike spoke words no one else
had dared utter. "It's in God's hands now."

Grief fused Nick to the ground. Chrissie had left him, but he
had loved her, and she hadn't deserved to die like that. No
one deserved to die like that.

He stared at Sizemore over Father Mike's shoulders. It didn't
matter how long it took. He was going to make that murderer
pay for what he'd done to his wife.

TONI ANDERSON

was born and raised in the U.K. and now lives in the harsh but beautiful Canadian prairies with her husband and two children.

Formerly a marine and fish biologist, she unfortunately lives about as far from the ocean as physically possible. She escapes by writing romantic mystery and suspense stories set in some of the incredible places she's been privileged enough to visit.

Readers can find her all over the internet, even though she's supposed to be working on her next novel. For more information about Toni, please visit http://tonianderson.shawwebspace.ca/.

TONI ANDERSON

SEA OF SUSPICION

CARINA
PRESS™

For my late sister-in-law,

Helen Sarah Margaret Beddow,
Nov 14, 1964 to July 15, 2004,

whose life was cut tragically short by multiple sclerosis

and

All past occupants of the Gatty Marine Lab.

Recycling programs
for this product may
not exist in your area.

ISBN-13: 978-0-373-06247-8

SEA OF SUSPICION

Copyright © 2010 by Toni Anderson

SEA OF SUSPICION

Acknowledgments

Many people helped make this book possible.

Thanks for early critiques from the wonderful Kathy Altman, Kim Daniel, Judith Rochelle and Laurie Wood. Your patience is outstanding. Thanks to Loreth Anne White for being there on good days and bad. And thanks to my editor, Deborah Nemeth, and the team at Carina Press who got out the polish and made this story shine.

Although I lived in St. Andrews for many years, I never had cause to visit the police station until I was given a tour by James Steel of Fife Constabulary. I am indebted to him for the time he took to show me around and answer my questions. I used artistic license when writing this story, but all mistakes are mine.

A fellow member of the Kiss of Death Chapter of RWA helped me with the Portuguese language — again all mistakes are mine.

The biggest acknowledgment of all has to go to my husband and two children, who put up with my intense distraction when writing and who always keep the faith. I love you!

PROLOGUE

NICK STUMBLED. He was drunk and if Chrissie hadn't been dead, she'd have been furious. Raindrops splashed off gravestones, stirring up the smell of freshly dug earth and crushed grass. Dougie caught his arm and jerked him upright.

Good man, Dougie.

His parents-in-law stared into the rectangular pit with reddened eyes and strained mouths. Chrissie's mother, Emily, sobbed as though her heart was being ripped from her throat with a grappling hook. Chrissie's dad braced his wife with an arm around her waist. Wet hair hung limply around the woman's shoulders and she looked as if she'd aged a year for every day Chrissie had been dead.

Nick's fault.

Emily sank to her knees and her husband followed, holding on grimly as if fearing she'd end up in that muddy grave with her daughter. Nick frowned. He was the one who was supposed to be howling. Beneath his alcohol-soaked despair a small kernel of envy knotted his gut. Emily's grief bespoke an agony deeper than his, as if she was being physically tortured while they all stood by and watched. He looked away.

It *hurt* to watch a mother's grief. It hurt almost as much as losing the woman you'd pledged your life to.

His fault.

If he'd paid more attention, buried his pride, *this*

would never have happened. The muscles in his throat worked, but were so sore he felt as though he'd drunk paint stripper rather than single malt. Unconsciously he took a step forward. Automatically Dougie tightened his grip on the back of Nick's jacket and held him in place.

Good man, Dougie.

Emily and Peter's remaining daughter watched him with big, rounded eyes. Ten years old, but no one was paying her any attention. She looked exactly like photographs of Chrissie at that age. Dark ringlets, bright eyes that glittered like stars when she laughed and stabbed like knives when she was mad. The kid searched his face for a glimmer of comfort, and a tiny drowning part of his brain wanted to reach out to her. But guilt paralyzed his heart like a lightning shock. He had no experience with comfort and less with guilt.

The crowd stirred and suddenly all eyes were on him. Nick felt their expectation and pity. Dougie nudged him forward and Nick held out his hand for dirt, as if he'd buried a thousand wives and knew exactly what to do. The thick clod of earth hit Chrissie's ornate casket and he made a silent vow to his dead wife. Despite the whisky in his bloodstream, pain was beginning to seep back into his brain. Dougie put an arm around his shoulders and guided him toward the outer wall of the ruins. People started to drift away.

"Are you all right?" Dougie asked.

Nick looked at his friend, truth exposed in his eyes.

No. He wasn't all right. He'd failed and God was paying him back.

Nobody came to offer condolences. He and Dougie stood awhile, just the two of them, Dougie rolling a ciggie while Nick sat on some other poor bastard's tomb. The rain battered the marble and soaked through the arse of his trousers. Silently Dougie handed him the cigarette, watching him with somber brown eyes. Cold seeped into Nick's flesh and the pewter storm clouds brought a heavy dullness that matched the throb in his head. But he didn't want to leave. Not yet.

He took out his hipflask and shook it. *Damn.* Empty. He stuffed it back in his pocket. "I need a drink."

Turning to leave, he saw Chrissie's Ph.D. supervisor standing over her open grave. Tears ran down the man's cheeks, mixing with the rain. And suddenly there was nothing but pain. It drew a sharp knife over Nick's every thought, savaged each breath, lanced each cell like a septic boil.

"Nick…" Dougie warned.

But it was too late. The numbness had exploded into rage. Nick ran to Jake Sizemore and slammed his fist into the man's jaw. "You bastard. You bloody, fucking, bastard."

Sizemore went down, slipping on the wet grass, and Nick was on him, pounding, pounding. His one good suit was plastered in mud, his wedding shoes slipping on the rain-drenched earth, but he didn't stop. Sizemore fought, his arms fending off a really good uppercut.

"You killed her. You fucking killed her!" Nick shouted.

"No, I'm sorry. I didn't mean for this to happen. I loved her." Sizemore twisted, grabbed one of Nick's wrists with both hands, straining away as far as he could.

There were no words to describe the hatred that fueled Nick. Every bad thing, every evil act twisted inside him until *he* became the avenger, *he* became fury, *he* lusted to kill. He slammed his fist into Jake's face, splitting skin, drawing blood. And Nick hit him again.

Again. Unable to stop. Fought off Dougie, who tried to drag him away. Finally Sizemore's eyes rolled back in his head and Nick hit him again.

He raised his fist for another strike only to have it dragged roughly behind his back as he was hauled off Sizemore's unconscious body. He spat on the man who lay bleeding in the rain. Sizemore looked dead, but Nick wasn't that lucky.

"Let's away with you, Nicky, that's enough now."

He hadn't expected the priest to come. He swallowed the need to throw himself into the man's arms. Stood taller. This man was more a father to him than a man of God. "He killed her, Father." His knuckles started to sting, but it wasn't even close to the pain ripping through his heart.

"And he'll have to live with that, won't he?" Father Mike propelled Nick along the gravel path.

"He doesn't have to live with it." The cold air hurt his lungs as Nick inhaled. It made him realize just how much he'd sobered up, and how little he had left to lose.

The priest grabbed him by the shoulders and shook him. "Chrissie left you, son." Father Mike spoke words no one else had dared utter. "It's in God's hands now."

Grief fused Nick to the ground. Chrissie had left him, but he had loved her, and she hadn't deserved to die like that. No one deserved to die like that.

He stared at Sizemore over Father Mike's shoulders. It didn't matter how long it took. He was going to make the murderous sonofabitch pay for what he'd done to his wife.

CHAPTER ONE

RAFAEL DOMENICI, A GORGEOUS Brazilian post-grad student, followed her into her office. His English wasn't perfect but sure beat the heck out of her Portuguese. Susie took off her lab coat and hung it on the back of the door, uncomfortably aware of the young man's eyes following every muscle movement with the desire to touch.

It would be flattering if it wasn't so darned awkward.

"Just leave those on the desk, please, Rafael. And I'll need your literature review before I go home this afternoon." That should cure his adoration and remind him who was boss.

He didn't move. The young god just stared at her with bedroom eyes and ridiculously long lashes. Not a single line of age on that perfect face. He was twenty-two years old and had more sexuality in one little finger than most men accumulated in a lifetime.

There was a time when Susie Cooper had been comfortable flirting with gorgeous men. Not anymore. She'd once used her looks as a weapon and had been smashed into emotional spare parts for her effort. She was looking for other things now…commitment, family, kids. Ignoring Rafael's puppy-dog gaze, she sat in her chair, mechanical and biological joints creaking as she leaned forward to reactivate her computer.

Finally she sent him a tight smile of dismissal but rather than quenching the smoldering passion in his gaze, he laughed and pushed away from her desk.

"*Obrigado*, Dr. Cooper. I see you later, maybe for a drink in the pub?"

Dream on, little boy.

At that moment her other student, Lily Heathcote, appeared in the doorway and gave Rafael a hostile look. Lily was a local girl but if she was intimidated by her cosmopolitan coworker, it didn't show. Impatiently, the petite girl tapped lacquered fingernails against the doorjamb as the Brazilian angled around her, careful not to touch. A sly smile touched Lily's painted lips even though her eyes never left Susie's.

Always eccentric, today Lily was dressed in skintight leopard-print pants and a faded Cure T-shirt that had once been the color of eggplant. But beneath the layers of heavy makeup, weird clothes and incongruous blond braids sticking out like handlebars from above her ears, Lily was a nice, intelligent girl, whom Susie liked a lot. Rafael should have been attracted to his bright young peer, but maybe he only went for older women. That thought depressed the heck out of Susie.

Thirty-six wasn't old, though it was starting to feel like it. She stared at a photograph on her desk of her friend Dela Ortiz. Dela had died of an air embolism six months ago while they'd been diving off Fraser Island in Australia. She hadn't made it to thirty-five.

"You should do what I did," Lily interrupted Susie's reverie even as she leaned back to check out Rafael's butt.

Susie didn't pretend to misunderstand. She'd love to know how a girl like Lily handled guys like Rafael Domenici.

"What did you do?" Curious, Susie picked up her coffee, took a swallow of the cold, bitter brew.

"I put my hand on his dick and told him to let me know when the patch kicked in."

Susie spurted coffee all over her papers and reports. Trying not to laugh, she tore off blue lab tissue she kept in her drawer for emergencies—right next to the cookies—and dabbed at the brown splotches. "In the States, supervisors aren't quite that *hands-on*," she commented dryly.

She'd only worked at this prestigious marine laboratory for one short month, but she needed to deal with her handsome pain-in-the-butt Romeo before he did or said something unprofessional. God knew, she didn't want false rumors dogging her career. It was bad enough dealing with the fallout from her mother's political machinations, even if Scotland was thousands of miles from Washington.

"Does he look at every woman like he wants to—" Susie broke off. It was a totally unsuitable question to ask one of his peers.

"Like he wants to lay you down and lick you from the soles of your feet to the inner recesses of your mind? Too bloody right he does." Lily took a few steps into the room. "He gives the same look to everyone with a vagina, including Mabel."

Mabel was the hunchbacked retirement-age cleaning lady. A lovely woman, sure…

Lily crossed her arms in a belligerent pose. "He's an arrogant wee shite." Lab harmony sure was off to a smooth start. "Not that you're not hot," she assured Susie belatedly, biting her purple-painted lips as if it had just occurred to her she might have said the wrong thing.

Susie didn't care if she was hot or not. "I just need a way to get him to treat me like his boss and not a potential—" She broke off with a grimace. This was not how she'd imagined her supervisor-student relations would go.

Lily flashed a grin, cocked a hip. "Well, I told you my secret and it worked for me. You could pretend to have a *really* big boyfriend." She wiggled her eyebrows then her bottom jaw dropped as she checked the time. "Hell. I have to go. I've got a hot lunch date."

And with that she rushed over, dumped her proposal on Susie's overflowing desk, and dashed out of the room.

Susie mumbled to herself, "'Here's my report, Dr. Cooper. Gee, thanks, Lily.'" But her attention was captured by a man climbing the concrete steps outside her windows. It hadn't been much of a view until now. He was tall, long-legged, had quarterback shoulders and was clad in head-to-toe black leather with two motorcycle helmets hooked carelessly over one arm. Sweaty blond hair twisted into untidy tufts on his head, and she glimpsed a harsh unsmiling profile. Everything about him screamed pure animalistic male. No simpering eyelashes for him.

She pressed cold hands to her neck. And then he turned. Captured her gaze unerringly, assessing her through the glass with fierce green eyes.

The corner of his lips twitched before his attention shot back to the main entrance where Lily bounded out, clutching her knapsack and coat in one arm, throwing the other around his neck and giving him a big kiss on the cheek. Unwanted jealousy scratched Susie's insides.

Oblivious, Lily threw her a wave, chatting animatedly to her "hot lunch date." Susie pretended to concentrate on her computer screen, but not before she noted the slow sardonic grin sent in her direction from the man who towered over her diminutive student. Hot enough to scorch flesh.

The raw power of the 865 cc air-cooled twin cylinder Triumph Thruxton vibrated through his bones, the noise from the engine a deep-throated roar. Nick eased his weight to the right to take a bend in the road, hard left for the chicane, perfect control on the well-balanced machine. Lily gripped his waist, nails digging hard enough to score the leather, but as long as she didn't fall off he didn't care.

Barely slowing, he turned off the main road, down the secluded lane leading to her cottage. He slowed the bike to a gentle crawl, tires crunching softly over the gravel. Pulling to a stop, he put his foot on the ground and kicked down the stand.

Lily jumped off and dashed up the steps to the kitchen door, tearing off her helmet.

"Mom. Mom. Nick's here!" She gave him a cheeky grin, this woman-child who hid her resemblance to her long-dead sister beneath fancy dress and war paint.

He remembered Lily the day of his wife's funeral. Ten years old—black coat, black hair, blue eyes, arsenic-white skin—the perfect miniature incarnation of his wife, Chrissie. He'd wanted to reach out to that child, but he'd had nothing to offer.

The front door opened and a woman who looked much older than her sixty-odd years hurried down the steps, unsteady on her feet. A feeling of dread fingered his heart. He curved his mouth into an easy half smile and swallowed the rough sensation of suffocation. "Emily."

From the distance in the woman's blue eyes, he knew he'd left it too long. Again. He'd stretched their relationship as thin as he dared. Lily chatted, mortaring the wounds, bandaging the blows left by tragedy.

He stepped toward Emily and opened his arms, shame burning through him when the old woman sank into his embrace like a soft, frail dove. He squeezed her gently, held her away so he could examine the new wrinkles engraved on her skin.

"How are you, Em?"

She sniffed and blinked as if hoping to hide the redness of her eyes. Odd, considering grief was the thing she lived for. Her fingers plucked her cardigan.

"It's always difficult this time of year." She frowned at him, her bottom lip reproachful. "I thought you'd forgotten."

Regret and remorse cut to the bone like a butcher's blade. Old pain twisted in his chest until he could barely breathe.

The twelfth anniversary of Chrissie's death.

The twelfth anniversary of his wife's murder.

"I never forget, Em."

"He's still out there." Her eyes bulged, her hands clawed his sleeve. "Waltzing around like nothing happened, like she didn't even exist." Vehemence infused the words with hatred, juxtaposed against such soft features. "All these years and the police never caught him. You promised me, Nick! You promised he'd be punished."

He hugged Emily's shoulders and they turned to walk inside. Into a house full of memories he didn't want to remember and she didn't want to forget. She started sobbing. All these years, and her grief was still as fresh as it had been the day they'd stood in the rain and buried her other daughter.

It didn't matter what it took. He was going to bring the bastard who'd killed his wife to justice. And now he knew exactly how he was going to do it.

CHAPTER TWO

THE LECTURE THEATRE WAS DARK, the room sickeningly hot. Susie took a sip of water. Restless noises told her the students were finished and she flipped to a new slide that everyone began reverently copying.

"Now I want to show you an example of synchronous, mass and epidemic reproduction among broadcast-spawning marine invertebrates, otherwise known as coral reefs." She flicked to photographs she'd taken during her last post-doc position in Australia. Bright purple sea fans, translucent tunicates, orange sea stars dazzling against bone-white staghorn coral.

"In Australia's Great Barrier Reef, five different reefs—stretching more than five hundred kilometers— spawn over the same few nights between the full and last moon in late spring." She lifted her voice, trying to drive imaginations, to instill the magic of this immense biological event. "More than one hundred different animal species release eggs and sperm into the ocean over the same few days."

It never failed to amaze Susie how organisms that couldn't talk, text or date managed to get it together for one big humongous ejaculation to continue the species. There was no parental care with coral reefs. No tangled web of family drama.

A bead of perspiration rolled the length of her spine and soaked into the band of her pants. "That's all for today, folks. Any questions?"

As she flicked off the computer and accidentally plunged them into total darkness, a voice called from the back of the room.

"What about the effects of global warming?"

Susie tightened her lips as she searched for the light switch, her fingers getting snagged in the projector cable. She wished she could see because she didn't recognize the voice. It was an important topic. "Climate change could have a catastrophic effect on marine systems. Some research suggests it already has—"

"So how do you feel about your mother's poor record on environmental issues, given she's announced she's thinking of running for her party's nomination?"

Susie's lungs felt as if they'd solidified in her chest. Her mother had *what?* Her breath finally came out as a hiss. She found the light switch and flicked it on. Zeroed in on a thickly built man in an argyle sweater sitting at the back, his camera poised in one hand, pen in the other.

The British gutter press.

"Are you a student enrolled in this class, sir?" Her New England accent was suddenly as harsh as the Scottish weather. The journalist shifted, not at all perturbed, and she realized he was gearing up for more questions. She retrieved her flash drive and picked up her notes.

"Did you get this position at St. Andrews because of your mother's influence in Washington?"

Susie narrowed her eyes. She'd worked long and hard for this position and no one was going to say she'd got it through nepotism. But she reined in her reaction because a reaction was exactly what the slimeball wanted.

"See you next week, guys. This class is over." And she stalked up the stairs, stopping at the back row.

"If you enter my classroom again, sir—" she stabbed

a finger toward the journalist's chest, well aware of all her students' eyes on her "—I will call security." She stormed past him and out of the lecture hall.

Back in her office, she closed the door and put in a call to Senator Darcy Cooper. All she got was an aide who said her mother was currently in a television studio giving an interview and she'd pass on the message ASAP. Susie hung up and tried her father, but got bumped straight to voicemail. He was probably on the golf course getting in a quick nine holes before court.

She stood and paced.

Every detail of her mother's background would be raked over, every detail of Susie's background dug into like trash. Susie cradled her face in her hands.

What was it about the woman who'd carried her in her body for nine months that trapped them in this adversarial relationship? Why wasn't love enough? The phone rang and she grabbed the receiver. "Susie Cooper."

"Susie." It was Darcy Cooper. "I've been trying to reach you all morning." Her mother's voice was smooth as political silk. "This time difference is inconvenient, although the U.K. is better than Australia, I suppose."

"Maybe when you're *president* you can dictate time, Mother, but I don't think the Brits are going to like it." Susie tapped her short fingernails on the desk.

"Ah."

"Yes. *Ah*." Susie's fingers stopped tapping, poised over the hardwood. "Is it true?"

"That I've announced I'm *thinking* of putting my hat in the ring for the Democratic nomination?" The pause had a quality of calculation. "Yes."

"And I get to hear this from a reporter?" Susie dropped her head to the desk, pulling out her headband, running her fingers over her skull. "Why, Mom? Why would you do this to me?"

"Not everything is about you, missy." Her mother's tone took on a self-righteous indignation Susie loathed.

Her insides felt as if they'd dissolve into jelly. Thirty seconds talking to her mother and she was fifteen years old again. But she couldn't pretend everything was okay. Her mother's decision to make a bid for the most powerful position in the western world brought everything Susie didn't dare think about rushing back into focus.

"What about…?"

"An old friend of yours died last week and you can be damn sure *he* never told anyone about it."

Clayton was dead? Susie gripped the handset tighter. She didn't know how to feel about that. She'd loved him once. Stupid teenage love, but love nonetheless. Silence crossed the void filled with seven thousand days' worth of sorrow. Her mother's laugh was a fresh blow to an old wound.

"So it's over. All taken care of. Don't mention the subject *ever* again."

Nerveless fingers dropped the phone back into its cradle. Shame and regret boiled inside her until they crammed her pores and poured out of her body like tears. Her airway felt constricted and she couldn't breathe. She sank to her knees trying to force air in and out of her lungs. Slowly, steadily, her heartbeat eased back to normal.

Normal? Ha!

There was nothing *normal* about Susie's life. Nothing *normal* about losing her dive buddy, nothing *normal* about her mother running for president and nothing *normal* about seducing her mother's mentor when she was fifteen years old and stupid.

The phone rang with shrill demand. Still shaking, she pushed out her office door to head for the seafront, but the sight of a little girl examining a map of the world brought her to an abrupt halt. The child, dressed in a denim tunic covered in pink appliqué flowers, turned to stare at her with big blue eyes.

And there it was.

Everything Susie wanted. Everything she'd abandoned.

The little girl's eyes bugged and she waddled back to her daddy, a colleague, who sent Susie a distracted smile as he rifled through his mail.

"How you doing, Susie?"

She fixed a brilliant smile on her face as the little girl clawed her daddy's trousers, hiding from the crazy lady. "I'm just great." And if that wasn't the biggest, fattest lie in the universe, she'd eat her own liver.

THE WEEK HAD BEEN A BITCH and it wasn't finished with him yet. The barman served him straight away. Two pints of pale ale. If ever there was a day he deserved a beer...

Nick put the drinks on the table, went to the jukebox, choosing the Dixie Chicks' "Not Ready to Make Nice" and "Satisfaction" by the Stones. He took the bench seat facing the door, set his back to the wall and waited.

Ewan McKnight sat opposite. His shoulders sagged as he raised his glass to his lips and sipped. "I've got half an hour before I need to get home."

Nick met his partner's gaze before they both looked away. Ewan's home life sucked. Not that the man wanted pity. It wouldn't help. The only thing that would help was a cure for multiple sclerosis, which went far beyond Nick's limited medical capabilities.

He knew what it was like to lose someone you loved, but at least he had someone to blame for Chrissie's death. He just hadn't proved it yet.

"Made my bed..." the Chicks crooned and in walked Professor Jake Sizemore along with the woman Nick had caught checking him out that morning. Lily's Ph.D. supervisor, a newly arrived Yank with long blond hair and a perfect oval face. Nick allowed a smile to bend the edges of his lips as he watched her head to the bar closely followed by a horde of alcohol-deprived biologists from the Gatty Marine Lab. All these years and they still followed the same ritual, at the same watering hole.

Pain shot into his skull from clenching his jaw so hard.

"What?" Ewan glanced over his shoulder and gave a gusty sigh as he saw Jake Sizemore. "One of these days he's going to sue you for harassment."

Nick shrugged. Twelve years. He stared into his beer as a drop of perspiration rolled down his temple. Twelve *long* years. And there wasn't a day he didn't wish he could go back and do things differently. Because if he had, maybe Chrissie would have stayed and the tragedy of her death wouldn't shadow every single step he took.

His gaze veered to Dr. Susie Cooper. Tall, slim, self-contained in an aloof way that usually turned him off. But Lily was taken with her new boss and the kid wasn't easy to impress. Neither was he.

Dr. Cooper picked up a half pint of lager and took a swallow, the pale perfection of her throat rippling delicately. She wasn't just pretty. She had that moneyed, sophisticated quality. The Grace Kelly of marine biologists, compared to Jake Sizemore's Hannibal Lecter.

But there was nothing relaxed about her. Her shoulders were rigid. The arm not holding her beer was pressed stiffly over her waist, clawed fingers clutching her hip. She didn't seem to be aware that half the men in the bar were ogling her in that fitted white blouse you could just see the outline of lacy lingerie beneath and clingy black trousers that hugged a first-class ass. She wasn't his type, and yet something about her made him ache.

Too long without sex.

He shifted uncomfortably. Tired-looking postgrads milled around, dressed in worn-out jeans and ugly sweaters, ubiquitous in their affection of cheap beer and the Friday night buzz. More than a decade ago Christina walked in the same door having put in an eighty-hour week for less than you got on the dole.

Nick stripped off the top layer of his beer mat, eyeing tonight's crowd. A dark-haired, smooth-faced Latino brushed Dr. Cooper's shoulder and she adjusted her position away from him with a pinch-lipped smile. Then she jerked slightly, her eyes flaring as if she'd received a shock.

Narrow-eyed, Nick assessed the guy, noted the lanky build and the boyish head of curls. Figured he must be the student Lily had told him about, the kid who'd been strutting around the Gatty pulling anything with a pulse. Maybe Dr. Cooper liked getting it on with younger men. Wouldn't be the first time a lecturer had done a little extra-curricular activity.

The Rolling Stones' signature guitar beat came on the jukebox, and a nasty kind of happiness crept into Nick's lungs. He expelled it in a smile. Cautiously, like a snake scenting danger, Jake Sizemore turned his head to flick a look around the bar. Did he remember today was the anniversary of Chrissie's death? Nick raised his glass when he caught the man's eye, but Jake spun away.

"You're playing with fire, pardner." Ewan's lips quirked.

"I can't help it." Nick smiled back, but his heart wasn't in the banter. He wasn't interested in anything except revenge. And Susie Cooper.

Curious, Ewan glanced behind him and Nick noticed his colleague's gaze slide around Susie's figure and coil around her ass like a whip. Not that he could blame the man. Ewan hadn't had sex in years and wasn't likely to get any this year or next. Solitaire didn't count.

Jake Sizemore put his hand on Susie's arm and everything inside Nick sharpened to a fine point. Susie retreated an inch, breaking the contact, and though she smiled politely at the murdering bastard, she didn't look happy about the invasion of her personal space.

Grace Kelly wasn't anything like Chrissie had been. Nick took a big swallow of beer and forced the ale down as the tension in his throat increased. Chrissie had been warm and vivacious until her Ph.D. supervisor had gotten his claws into her. After that, their marriage had turned gray and ugly, floundering as she'd withdrawn and dedicated herself to her research. When she'd confessed to an affair with Sizemore, Nick had kicked her out, and twelve years ago today she'd been hauled up in a South African fisherman's net, dead.

An accident, the South African authorities had declared. How else could you classify being attacked by sharks?

Twelve years of hatred made each chamber of his

heart contract harder, building in intensity. Chrissie's short life had been wasted. Their marriage and love turned into an empty mockery of the vows they'd made. Had she been conscious? Desperate? Frightened? Had she begged for her life in the moments before that first predator had dragged her beneath the surface, thrashing and twisting?

Most days it was the *not* knowing that picked at his brain like a dirty finger scratching a scab.

Nick held his hand steady, forced himself to pick up the glass without his fingers shaking. Alcohol raced down his throat and sweat heated his back. All he wanted was to toss the glass through the nearest window, or better yet, into Jake Sizemore's face. But that wasn't who he was anymore. That scared, violent little boy had vanished years ago.

Nick stared at Susie, who suddenly returned his gaze with a defiant blue glare that told him she'd been aware of his regard the whole time. He held back a smile. Something about her piqued his interest. And that was a damned shame.

"Who's the bird?" Ewan drained his glass, popping it on the beer mat with a look of regret as he wiped foam off his lips.

Nick shrugged as if he didn't care, finished his own pint and collected both glasses, never dropping the woman's gaze. "New lecturer in the Gatty."

"You're not going to—"

"Oh yes, I am." He had plans for Susie Cooper.

He climbed to his feet as Ewan rolled his eyes. Nick placed the empty pint glasses on the bar, passed close enough to Professor Jake Sizemore to smell the fear.

He nodded to Susie, giving her just the hint of a smile. He knew the nuances of body language and recognized the reluctant attraction in her gaze. She tilted her head slightly, watched him from under her lashes. He was careful not to touch Sizemore as he moved through the crowd, but his fingers brushed Susie's elbow and the connection exploded through his body like a blast of gunfire.

TRACY GOOD WALKED ALONG the seafront and looked up at the Gatty's brightly illuminated windows. Just a few hours ago that lovely new Brazilian student had gone down on her in the library where anyone could have barged in.

Oh, my. Her eyes crossed at the memory.

The waves crashed on the beach, rolling backward with the pull of the tide. She shivered. She liked him. Liked the way his eyes sparkled as he'd watched her from his knees. Liked the way he'd given her an orgasm but hadn't wanted anything in return. Even now her body hummed with delicious little zings of leftover pleasure.

Ditching her virginity at twenty-three had been an enlightening experience. She'd discovered being bad was a damn sight more satisfying than being good had ever been. A year later, the sex was better than ever.

A seagull gave a raucous cry from the rooftop and made her jump. It was only early evening, but the sun had gone down hours ago.

She stifled a yawn. Long days running samples and crunching data had left her low on sleep and lacking in energy. And so what if she was one of the few sad souls back in the lab on a Friday night? Not everyone could afford to go out drinking every weekend and she had experiments to do, a Ph.D. to submit. A job to find…

She bit her lip. Her money ran out in three months' time and she didn't have anything lined up yet.

She inserted her keycard into the electronic lock and shoved at the heavy glass door. With dragging feet she skirted the scattered chairs of the coffee room then made her way along the corridor, up the stairs, to the tiny space she called an office.

There, she dug into her pocket for her keys.

"Tracy." Her supervisor, Professor Jake Sizemore, called out behind her. Startled, she jumped. She'd seen him leave for the pub at 5 p.m. and hadn't expected him back on a Friday night. He held up a finger. "I need a word."

"Yes, sir." She opened her door and threw her bag beside her laptop, some of the contents spilling onto the counter.

Jake followed her in and shut the door behind him. He grabbed her shoulders, his thumbs digging into the hollows of her collarbones as his tongue dove hard into her mouth. No hours of sweet-talk or half bottle of gin required. Not anymore. She pulled him to her to bring him deeper into her mouth. He tasted of warm beer and peanuts.

He'd taught her all about sex. Taught her the power of passion. Jake-the-snake might not be prime, but he had what she wanted and was extremely knowledgeable around the female body. His hands dragged up her skirt, exposing the black lace thong she'd changed into when she'd gone home for supper.

Jake was fully aroused against her. She smiled, enjoying what she did to her supervisor. And men in general. But today she needed something else.

"Let me get the condom." His voice and hands were shaking.

"Not yet." Tracy had a plan. She rubbed her palm over his erection and slowly slid down his zipper. She reached into his pants, wrapped her fingers around him and squeezed. Jake's eyes rolled back in his head.

She dropped to her knees, grinning as Jake flung out a hand to steady himself and then asked rather desperately, "Is the door locked?"

She giggled as Jake fell back against the door. Blocking entrance for anyone unfortunate enough to cross their paths tonight. Pulling his pants farther down, she ran her tongue slowly over him the way he'd shown her. Except now she was the one in control.

"Oh Jesus. Oh God, yes." He dug his fingers into her hair, forcing her to take him deeper. She could feel the tension growing in his body as she built the rhythm. He started to moan and she pulled away. No way was he getting off until she got what she wanted.

She stood and he pushed her roughly against the door, his lips wet and ravenous on hers, his tongue touching the roof of her mouth. She tore herself from his grasp and slipped out of her jacket and tossed it on the side. A pencil fell to the floor, the only sound in the room except for the harsh bellow of their breathing. Jake kicked off his pants, unbuttoned his shirt, his eyes burning with an absolute focus on sex.

"What do you want, Jake?" She scraped a long fingernail over the length of him.

"Jesus, Jesus! Ow!" He flinched, cupping himself.

She knew he liked a little pain. Loved it. She slowly—very slowly—unbuttoned her blouse, and he went stone still. Her breasts were her most impressive asset and Rafael hadn't even seen them yet. The thought made her hot. It wasn't Jake-the-snake she visualized when she slipped out of her plain white blouse, revealing a black lacy bra that offered up her breasts like an erotic fantasy.

Jake reached over and pinned her upper arm, holding her still when she would have removed her lingerie. "You have the most amazing tits." And then he lowered his lips to one nipple, laving it through the scratchy lace, which felt more incredible than she'd imagined. She moaned, not having to pretend to enjoy it, but knowing he'd never leave his wife no matter how fantastic the sex.

"Tell me what you want, Jake," she purred. She kept her thighs clamped together, making him work for it.

Jake's fingers dug so hard into her hips it hurt. "I want *you*, Tracy. I want to have you every way I know and then I want to fuck you all over again."

Tracy held his gaze, her lips slightly open in sultry invitation. "And what will you give me if I let you?" After a lifetime of poverty she had finally figured out how to climb out of the gutter. She kissed him, deep and long, her hand stroking over him just enough to keep him on the edge, but not enough to make him come.

"Anything." Jake's voice was ragged, his breath hot against her ear. "A job, references, a vacation, whatever the hell you want."

"A job first." She pushed him away. Unbuttoned her skirt and let it drop. Why waste the full effect of fabulous lingerie? She hopped up on the narrow bench and swung her legs playfully. He couldn't take his eyes off the dark lace triangle nestled between her legs. She wriggled out of her panties, found the condom, ripped open the foil packet and crooked her finger. He groaned as she rolled the cold rubber over his hot length. "And the best fucking reference you've ever written."

She sucked in a breath as he thrust deep inside.

It hurt for a moment, but she didn't complain. She'd pushed him as far as she dared and got exactly what she'd hoped for. The pain morphed into dark pleasure and she squirmed against him, urging him on, panting, begging, fighting to take more of him.

"I'm gonna fuck you, Tracy girl. I'm gonna fuck you good," he growled quietly against her throat.

Yes.

The coil of ecstasy unraveled inside her and a scream escaped as she started to come. Jake smothered her mouth with his hand. She couldn't breathe, but the pleasure intensified and she didn't give a damn. And finally he came with a vicious growl that tore from his throat.

Still pulsing deep inside her, he rested his forehead against hers. "I'll give you the best fucking reference in the world." And then he started laughing.

She tucked a sweaty lock of hair behind her ear and then started laughing, too. Because she'd got exactly what she wanted. Out of the corner of her eye she could see her little voice-activated digital recorder sitting on the countertop, and the light that said it was recording glowed ruby red.

CHAPTER THREE

IT WAS SATURDAY MORNING and Susie was on her hands and knees in her office, unpacking boxes. She swiped the back of her hand over her forehead. Why the hell had she brought so much junk with her?

A hand touched her shoulder and she whirled around. "Oh my god, Jake! You scared me."

Her boss laughed. "Sorry, I saw your light on when I came in." He nodded across the concrete steps that led to the main entrance just outside her window. "I thought I'd stop by and see how my newest member of staff was settling in."

"I'm doing great, thanks." She smiled up at him and climbed to her feet. "Just making sure I have all my lecture notes for next week."

"Of course." He cleared his throat and averted his eyes. "I don't want to bother you with rumor or gossip—" she braced herself for some comment about her mother "—but a couple of faculty members have objected to your light lecture load for the first two years."

Her eyes widened and she blinked at him. She hated conflict of any kind and went out of her way to be nice to others. She sighed. It wasn't her best quality. "You said the university was getting a good deal. Particularly when I agreed to start teaching immediately—"

"Don't worry, Susie." He wrapped a beefy arm around her shoulders and gave her a squeeze. She squirmed, uncomfortable with the intimacy, but he gave her a daz-zlingly white smile. "I made it quite clear to them that you are a first-class researcher who'll be a huge asset to this department. Especially now."

She'd have to be deaf and blind to miss the subtext in that statement. Damn. She pulled away, unease swirl-ing in her belly.

"Anyway, I dealt with the matter and it's all sorted now." A slight frown dented his brow.

She rubbed her arms and pressed her lips together. She was allowing personal feelings to affect her profes-sionalism. "Thank you, Jake."

"Oh, and I've got something else to show you." A fleetingly handsome expression touched his features. "Follow me."

She hurried after him, their footsteps echoing through the empty building. He headed through the old Victorian part of the marine lab, down the stairs into the deserted basement. Jake paused opposite the ladies' room and smiled at her expectantly.

"What is it?" she asked when the silence stretched and nothing happened.

He gave her a conspirator's wink. "Don't ask me how many strings I pulled to organize this so quickly, but—" he put his hand on a big metal door opposite and swung it open "—I got you allocated a Constant Temperature room all to yourself."

A thrill of excitement shot through her as she stepped inside the enclosed space. The air smelled cold and stale as a crypt but she inhaled gratefully. The room was stacked full to bursting with old aquaria, broken PVC pipes and moldy tubing. Jake stepped in behind her and she squeezed through the junk to make more room.

"There's seawater and freshwater outlets." He pointed to the taps.

"This is fantastic, Jake." This was exactly what she needed to start breeding octopi and build her research program. She picked up a PVC joint she might be able to salvage. Tossed it into a relatively sound fiberglass tank. Whoever had claimed this room previously hadn't used it for anything except growing penicillin. It was going to take a lot of scrubbing and hard work to get this space up to standard, but no one said the life of a marine biology professor was easy or glamorous. "Thanks so much."

"You're welcome."

She turned to face him and felt a flash of apprehension because he was standing close and she was squeezed tight into a corner. A shudder of revulsion passed through her as his stare dropped hungrily to her breasts. No wonder his wife had looked at her with such jaded resignation when they'd been introduced last week.

Jake's cell phone rang, breaking the awkward moment and he excused himself. Susie raised her eyes to the heavens. Why couldn't life be simple for a change?

Eight hours later, she was washing lettuce in her friend Leanne's kitchen. Leanne also worked at St. Andrews University and had married a lecturer in the computing department. They'd been best buddies since post-grad days at the University of Miami, where Leanne majored in psychology, Susie in marine biology. They'd hooked up in the sub-aqua club. It was Leanne who'd told Susie about the job vacancy here.

Susie's eyes misted and she grabbed her friend in a tight embrace. "I can't believe I'm here, with you. That we live in the same country, let alone the same continent."

"I love you too, Blondie." Leanne hugged her back using only her elbows, a baton of garlic bread in each hand. "Now get back to work."

After the awful period following Dela's death in Australia, life was finally beginning to feel good again. And tomorrow Susie promised herself a day off. She'd explore the coastal path, absorb the scent of the sea and the pale blush of the endless sandy beaches. Leanne put the loaves on the side and began grating cheese in time to U2's "Beautiful Day." Her short dark hair gave her the appearance of a manic imp.

"So who's coming to dinner?" Susie asked.

"Just a couple of friends." From beneath inky lashes Leanne flicked a glance that Susie didn't quite trust.

"You're not trying to set me up again, are you?"

Leanne affected a nonchalant shrug and Susie scrunched up her nose in exasperation.

"I invited Gray," Leanne began quickly. "You met him at the wedding. A girlfriend from Psychology, and Dougie's best friend, who does happen to be single, but—"

"Leanne!"

"You don't have to make out with him, just chat over a fabulous dinner of boiled lobster—"

Susie raised her chin and sniffed. "My octopi eat lobster."

Leanne tucked in her chin and made her mouth into a tiny *o*. "Too good for lobster now, are you?" she teased with her Midwest drawl. "How about triple chocolate mousse? Your octopi eat that too?"

Susie laughed and shook her head. "Not if I get there first."

They shared an addict's grin before Leanne grew serious. "I see Washington is hitting the headlines again." Washington. D.C. Darcy Cooper. Their codename for her power-crazed mother.

Susie's smile vanished. She shook the lettuce forcefully to remove the worst of the water and dried it off as best she could with a paper towel. "Don't you have a salad spinner? I thought people only got married to get salad spinners."

Leanne's eyes turned soft. "Susie, it's me. You don't have to pretend."

Susie licked bone-dry lips. "I know, but for one night I'd like to pretend my mother doesn't want to conquer the world." They exchanged a look, knowledge and friendship tangible.

The kitchen door flew open, the wind smacking it against the inside wall with a crash. Susie dropped the colander in the sink, shock stealing the moisture from her mouth. There, filling the portal, having to dip his head beneath the lintel, was Lily's boyfriend, the same guy who'd stared at her in the bar last night.

If the devil was blond, he was standing ten feet away in Leanne's kitchen.

"Nick! I haven't seen you in ages." Leanne bounced toward the tall, sharp-featured man and threw her arms around him and gave him a noisy lip-smack. Susie's stomach bottomed out.

"Get your hands off my wife." Dougie ducked through the door and shoved a case of beer into the guy's side before grabbing Leanne and bending her over his arm for a passionate kiss.

Susie averted her gaze and inadvertently caught Nick's.

It wasn't just the packaging that made him attractive. It was the sharp features and intelligent eyes that emanated risk like the Big Bad Wolf checking out Little Red Riding Hood on that wooded trail.

But no matter how tempting he looked, Susie did not want to get gobbled up.

Heat rose in her cheeks as his eyes swept her bare feet, her tight jeans and the big Mickey Mouse transfer plastered to her T-shirt. She crossed her arms.

Amusement crinkled the corners of his eyes as he noted her response.

"If you two lovebirds have finished, I'm waiting for an introduction to your guest." His eyes pierced her. She'd thought nothing could be more unsettling than that soul-hunting gaze, but his voice... He wasn't Scottish. English perhaps, some northern city with a regional accent she couldn't place, but his *voice*. It was deep and smooth and strong, with the power of wind shaping granite and as warm as the summer sun sinking deep inside her like some magical spell that spun music into gold.

"I bumped into Nick in the offy, gave him a ride out." Dougie, six-foot-four of adorable dark-eyed male, crossed over to Susie and gave her a squeeze. "How's my favorite bridesmaid?"

She snorted. "Your only bridesmaid. What's an *offy*?" She tensed as Nick came toward her, wondering how best to deal with the man. The guy was Lily's boyfriend, but he made her intensely aware of every part of her body and every possible escape route.

"What you'd call a liquor store." Nick pushed aside the garlic bread, slid the box of beer and wine onto the counter next to Susie. Their shoulders brushed, but she didn't flinch. She forced herself to remain still even though he was invading her personal space. He gifted her with a half smile when she didn't flee.

Dangerous and pushy.

Leanne's eyes sparkled. "Dr. Susie Cooper, meet Detective Inspector Nick Archer. Susie and I go way back. She just got a lectureship at the Gatty."

"You're a *cop?*" Susie knew her mouth was hanging open, but she couldn't believe Nick Archer was anything peaceable or law-abiding.

His quick smile told her she'd made a common mistake. People must often figure him for a bad boy, a renegade, whereas apparently the opposite was true—he was a twenty-first century knight. Still, he emitted hazard like a pheromone, and instinct told her Nick Archer would be ruthless at getting what he wanted. Poor Lily.

Yeah, right. Lily ate policemen for breakfast.

He inclined his head. "At your service, Dr. Cooper." His eyes drifted over Mickey Mouse's ears, letting her know exactly the sort of service he had in mind.

"How's Lily?" she asked pointedly, conscious of the effort it took to hold his gaze. She wasn't falling for the charm or pretending she didn't know he already had a girlfriend.

The kitchen suddenly felt as though it had been dropped into liquid nitrogen. Every particle of oxygen was sucked out of her lungs by the rapid chill.

Leanne slapped herself on the forehead, at the same time rescuing the cheese sauce she'd made for the lobster thermidor. "I forgot you two had a connection." Leanne wasn't paying a whole lot of attention to dynamics; she was now looking for a corkscrew. "You're getting a taxi home, by the way, unless you want a sleepover." She waved vaguely over at Susie, or it could have been Nick, or both.

"A connection?" Susie frowned.

"Lily is Nick's sister-in-law, or I should say…" Leanne paused, looking uncomfortable, a rare thing for the self-confident girl who'd grown up dirt-poor and desperate. "*Former* sister-in-law?"

Rays of light cut oblique angles through the old farmhouse window and highlighted tense skin around Nick's mouth. When he spoke, there was an odd glint in his eyes that was more complex than sorrow. "Lily was the flower girl at our wedding."

"You're divorced?"

"My wife is dead."

Oh, crap. Susie blinded herself with the sunset rather than look at him. "I'm sorry." Discovering Nick Archer was a widower shifted her perspective like a handbrake on black ice. She'd just assumed he and Lily were lovers. Jeez.

He picked up two beers from the box, tossed one to Dougie before opening his and taking a deep swallow. When he came up for air, he said, "It happened a long time ago." Then shrugged, each movement carefully staged to look as if he didn't give a damn, but the tendons in the back of his hand jutted through the skin and his smile was scalpel sharp.

Leanne looked up from where she had the wine bottle braced between her knees and the silence screamed with tension.

"So who won the football?" Nick asked Dougie, spinning the beer-cap into the recycling bin before striding into the den followed by a miserable-looking Dougie.

Susie pulled a face at Leanne, then rescued the salad, dumping it into a waiting bowl. "Sorry."

"How were you supposed to know?" Leanne popped the cork on the bottle and put the wine on the counter beside the glasses.

"Dougie told me what happened when we first met." Leanne kept her voice low so the men wouldn't hear them gossiping. "Lily's sister, I don't even know her name, was one of Jake Sizemore's Ph.D. students. She got killed by sharks doing fieldwork off the coast of South Africa when Dougie and Nick were both post-grads."

That explained the sense of seething hostility she'd felt aimed toward her boss in the bar yesterday.

"It must have been awful. Can you imagine?" Moisture gathered in the corner of Leanne's eye.

Susie was mortified by how badly she'd misjudged Nick Archer, and how badly she'd wanted to misjudge him.

"I couldn't bear the thought of losing Dougie." A tear ran down Leanne's cheek, but she scrubbed it away. "I don't know what's wrong with me. I'm so emotional these days." There was a pause. "You don't think I'm pregnant, do you?"

Envy made Susie's insides twist, but she pushed away the ugly emotion and peered at Leanne's ultra-skinny frame.

"You'd know better than me. Have you had unprotected sex in the last six months?" She wiggled her brows as Leanne mentally tallied the probability of being pregnant.

"Oh, *yeah*. As often as possible!" Leanne pushed the wine to the back of the counter, wet tears spiking her lashes. "Looks like we're on the wagon until I know for sure."

"Not me. Hey, give me that!" Susie grabbed a glass,

poured herself a healthy dose of red wine and took a fortifying gulp. If she couldn't be pregnant she could at least enjoy the benefits of being not pregnant. And numb the grief.

Leanne faked annoyance, the skin between her eyebrows crinkling even as her eyes shone. "How can you not support me during my *maybe* pregnancy?"

"When you find out for sure I'll consider it. Although you being over-emotional isn't exactly proof." Susie snickered. Despite her brains and street smarts, Leanne was a soft touch. "Anyway, *you* get to have sex whenever you want with a gorgeous man who loves you. No way I'm giving up alcohol as well as abstaining from sex."

It took a moment but Leanne and Susie grinned at each other.

"And if I'm going to be nice to Nick Archer, I need something stronger than OJ." Susie took another swallow of wine, absorbing the alcohol across her tongue, aware the nice convenient barrier to her attraction had been swept away like a stick over Niagara Falls.

Nick Archer was *not* the type of man Susie wanted to get involved with. She was done with bad boys. She was going to fall in love with a nice, easygoing man and have a comfortable, relaxed relationship and make babies. She was done with wild and destructive, no matter how good looking.

"If you drink lots of wine maybe you won't have to abstain from sex." Leanne jiggled her brows.

Knowing any reaction would be willfully misconstrued, Susie shrugged noncommittally, but Leanne wasn't put off.

"Here—" Leanne grabbed the bottle, tipped it into Susie's nearly full glass. "Let me top you up."

LILY WAS BUILDING A GUINNESS, tilting the glass beneath the beer tap and taking her time despite the Saturday night melee. Noise was a physical wall bombarding her eardrums, the bar a battlefield of bodies. Outside, October ravaged the coast, the wind coming off the North Sea like an open blast-freezer. But in this cramped oasis of beer, darts and slot machines, it was as hot as Venus and sweat trickled between her breasts like blood from a nicked vein.

The manager, Niall, caught her eye and gave her a nod to take her break. She gave him a smile, watched the light in his eyes turn hungry.

He fancied her, but she was not going there. Getting it on with the boss was icky. On cue, Rafael Domenici strolled up to the bar, lounging across it with the assurance of the bold and the beautiful, waiting for her to serve him.

In your dreams, pal.

She ignored him, gave the regular his pint and change, and headed through the flap at the end of the bar. She pushed through the mass of sweaty bodies to the backroom, heavy Latino eyes on her back, tracking her progress.

No doubt about it, Rafael Domenici was a good-looking guy and she wasn't immune to hotties, but she'd rather get it on with a goat than get involved with some skirt-lifting womanizer who couldn't say no to a bit of pussy even if it had teeth.

Anyway, she had other worries.

She poured herself some coffee, checked her watch, wondering if her mom was in bed yet. Should she call and check, or would that just upset her? Lily chewed her lipstick before sipping the syrupy brew. You'd think after so many years the grief would get better, but her mother just couldn't let go. She wanted someone to blame. She wanted someone to punish. And she could never accept that Chrissie might have been responsible for her own death.

The last twelve years had been hell, especially after her father died. Lily pushed her dyed-blond hair out of her eyes and stared into space. He'd been gone three years now, but she still missed him.

A warm blast of air ripped through the room as the door opened behind her. She didn't bother turning. "I'll be right out, Niall."

"It is not Niall." Rafael Domenici's accent was deep and rich.

"Well, trust me, Niall will be pissed if he catches you in here so go away." She tipped the dregs of coffee into the drain and rinsed the mug before drying it and putting it back on the shelf.

"Lily, I think we, how you say? Get off to a bad foot?"

Amused, she turned and quirked an eyebrow. "Ya think?"

Muscles bunched beneath a T-shirt as he scrubbed a big hand through his mop of hair. She tried not to notice.

"It is *jeitinho brasileiro*. The Brazilian way." He shrugged one shoulder and took a hesitant step forward. "You and I, we work together for the next three years, *sim?* I made a mistake. I no treat you with respect. *Sinto muito*." His pale blue eyes looked earnest against his gorgeous tanned face. "I am sorry."

Lily couldn't hide her surprise. "If this is another angle to try and get into my knickers, forget it."

He blew his hair out of his eyes in frustration. "I no

want to get in knickers." The word *knickers* sounded odd coming from his lips.

Lily cocked a leather-clad hip and challenged him with a look.

"Ah, *sim*, you very beautiful." He backed up a full step, his forehead glistening with sweat. His laugh had an unflattering edge. "I am weak. I no say no."

Lily snorted and whirled away. She was glad she made him sweat even if she wasn't interested.

"But…" He reached out and touched her arm, the skin-on-skin contact making her jolt. "I am sorry I treat you bad. We can be friends, *sim?*"

She tilted her head to look into his eyes and realized he wasn't pissing around. He was serious. Her neck ached from looking up because he was a big guy. She kept forgetting because her mouth and pride were both bigger.

But some days she got tired of fighting.

"Are you going to stop flirting with our supervisor?" The only thing that mattered to Lily, apart from her family, was getting her Ph.D. She didn't know why it was so important to her, she only knew it was. "Dr. Cooper isn't interested and you're stirring up a really bad atmosphere at work."

He let go of her arm and bowed slightly. "*Sim*. I promise I no *flirt* with you or Dr. Cooper." He stood tall, puffed out his perfect chest. "But your jealousy will never come between me and Mabel."

A laugh burst out of nowhere. Who'd have thought he'd have a sense of humor? "Okay, but if you act like a jerk again I'll have to hurt you." She grinned and realized she didn't laugh much anymore. One day when she wasn't looking, life had turned grim. She held out her hand. "Deal."

He took her hand, his palm smooth and hot against hers. "*Valeu*, Lily."

A stray flutter of attraction caught her by surprise and stopped her breath. Niall barged through the door and stared at their joined hands before Lily jerked free.

"Who the hell are you?" Niall asked.

"Niall, this is Rafael. I work with him in the Gatty." She ignored the anger in her boss's stance. Jealousy didn't win any points with her.

"Nice to meet you, Rafael. Now bog off." Niall held the door wide and pointed his thumb in the direction of the bar.

Rafael nodded formally, staring at her as if he had something else to say. His eyes flicked to Niall, whose irritation was starting to show in the set of his jaw and lowering of his brow.

"*Boa noite*, Lily. I see you Monday." He nodded to Niall as he passed, but Niall ignored him and released the door to swing shut on Rafael's heels.

"You're not seeing that wanker, are you?" Niall asked.

"You have got to be kidding." Lily rolled her eyes. "We share the same supervisor." She glanced at the telephone, wondering if her mom had remembered to turn off the burners after her nightly cocoa. But Niall was watching her and she didn't want anyone to suspect there were problems at home. "Okay, slave driver, I'll get back to work."

"You've still got five minutes." Niall stepped closer, his voice softened to warm toffee.

Maybe one day she'd put him out of his misery, but right now she wasn't in the mood. She patted his cheek on the way out. "Don't worry about me, sweetheart. You just rest your old bones."

She thought she heard his growl behind her back and grinned. Men were easy to control. It was women who gave her hives.

"GIMME SHELTER" PLAYED on the stereo, stirring up memories of when Dougie, Gray and Nick had shared a damp, poky flat as undergrads. Of drunken parties and the unrelenting hope of having sex at a time when all that mattered was getting inside a girl without knocking her up or catching HIV. Then Nick met Chrissie and everything changed.

Dougie laughed at something Leanne said. Some story about how the first time she'd got on a horse she'd gone straight over the other side. Nick watched Dougie squeeze his wife's hand, one of those intimate little gestures between couples that excluded everyone else.

Nick smiled grimly. Love was rare and precious. Needed to be nurtured and not taken for granted. No one deserved happiness more than Dougie. He'd give his left nut to protect the guy. Without Dougie, he would never have survived Chrissie's death. Dougie had looked after him, dried him out and eventually kicked his ass into shape. Got him focused on doing something useful with his life, rather than pickling his internal organs. Even so, Nick didn't know which of them was more surprised when he'd joined the police force.

Susie shot him a glance from under her lashes. She'd been talking to Gray since he'd arrived, totally at ease with the other man and hiding from Nick.

That was okay. He let her think she was safe for now. He glanced at the clock on the wall. It was getting late and excitement buzzed along his spine, tingling just beneath the surface of his skin.

Tonight he was finally going after what he wanted.

"Where's the Thruxton, Nick?" Gray had a tanked-up gleam in his eye.

"Nick's got a kick-ass motorbike," Leanne whispered to Susie.

"A Triumph. A total babe-magnet." Gray grinned, oblivious to a chocolate smear on his chin. If it had been Susie wearing chocolate, Nick would have helped her out, but Gray was on his own.

"I want a ride on that bike," Leanne murmured quietly in Susie's direction.

Dougie scowled. "Over my dead body."

"I want to borrow it." Gray slid Nick a hopeful glance.

"Over my dead body," said Nick and everyone laughed. Gray never drove a vehicle without putting a ding in it.

"Anyway—" Nick's chair creaked as he stretched out his legs "—I put it in storage this morning."

Autumn in Scotland was not the place to be riding a motorcycle unless you wanted iced testicles. He'd taken Lily for a ride yesterday because she'd pestered him all summer and he hadn't been able to put it off any longer. But one good thing about visiting Emily had been finding out all about the Heathcotes' new neighbor, Susie Cooper.

This morning he'd run a background check on Susie Q and she'd come up cleaner than bleach. She was so perfect he should be getting a rash.

"How come you weren't at the wedding?" Susie addressed him for the first time since she'd asked him about Lily in the kitchen. Credit to her for rooting out the facts and not wanting to get involved with a man she thought was screwing one of her students. Although the thought of shagging Lily made him gag.

"Something came up." Testifying in court against an arms dealer who'd legged it to Paraguay a day before the Serious and Organized Crime Command could make its move. Extradition was a bitch.

And it still burned that he'd let down his best friend and missed the wedding.

"Nick could tell you, but then he'd have to kill you." Gray smirked.

"Oh, that is *so* interesting," piped up Patricia on his right.

Patricia was pretty with shoulder-length brown hair. Cute, if you liked short, curvy women. Any other night he might have seen where that flirtation led, but not tonight. Not with Dr. Susie Cooper sitting less than six feet away, looking as bright as a newly minted five-penny piece. The fact he got hard just watching her was a complication he had to deal with.

"Nick's the only man I know who hates the sound of his own voice." Leanne smiled.

"Hey!" Dougie protested.

"It's a sexy voice." Susie grinned at Leanne, but the others missed it.

She'd had too much to drink because Leanne kept topping up her glass when she wasn't looking.

Patricia ran a fingertip down the stem of her glass. "So what deep, dark secrets are you hiding, Detective?"

CHAPTER FOUR

NICK BRUSHED THE QUESTION OFF. Probably said something funny because everyone at the table laughed, everyone except Susie. She flinched and hid her face in her wine at the words "deep, dark secrets." No one did that. Women were always fascinated by undercover work. God knew why. But Susie kept her head down, not moving, fading into the background with perfect camouflage—the way he had done a million times in the seedier side of London's underworld.

What deep, dark secrets could the daughter of a United States senator harbor? And how could he use them?

Nick finished his coffee, mesmerized as Susie teased the last remaining bit of chocolate mousse out of the bottom of her bowl. He'd stopped drinking hours ago. Watching Susie lose her starched politeness after a few glasses of wine had opened his mind up to a whole host of other possibilities better conducted without being trashed.

Susie finally pushed her bowl away and Leanne stood to clear the dishes, but Nick climbed to his feet.

"Sit yourself down, Mrs. MacDonald. You cooked, we'll clear." He kicked Gray's boot, which jerked the man up and out of his seat in one quick motion. Dougie stood as well, though Nick knew he wanted to sneak a cigarette more than he wanted to help wash dishes.

When Nick collected Susie's plate his fingers

brushed the back of her hand. Her eyes flew to his, irises flashing, nostrils flaring with instant awareness.

"Hello." He smiled. She looked away, her cheeks flushed and rosy. He should be ashamed of himself for playing with her, but he wasn't. In the kitchen he dropped scraps into the bin while Gray started on the pans.

"You need a dog," Nick shouted to Dougie who'd scuttled outside for a fag.

"I think Patricia fancies you," he told Gray and the man's head swiveled so fast Nick winced.

"Me?" Gray's ruddy cheeks and unkempt hair hid a deceptively brilliant mind. After his M.Sc., Gray had started his own computer programming company designing military communication software. He could buy half the town, but still dressed like a student and was chronically allergic to opening his wallet.

"Aye. Why not? You're a good-looking bloke." Nick planted the seed and shut up. Hitting your mid-thirties as a single man made you rethink your options when it came to relationships. Most people got less picky.

Not Nick, though. He hadn't been tempted by a woman in years and then along came Susie Cooper. Just his luck.

"This isn't like that time you set me up with the psycho-chick from the philosophy department, is it?" Gray asked.

"You went out with her for two months." Nick loaded the dishwasher, kept his eyes averted because those memories might be funny, but they could still sting. "Maybe if you splashed around some of your cash, your girlfriends wouldn't climb into other men's beds."

Nick's bed to be precise.

Gray stopped scrubbing and they exchanged a cringe. "She was a bloody nutter."

Nick laughed. "You were better off without her."

Gray grunted but rinsed the pans in record time. His chirpy whistle told Nick he was off to build on tonight's potential love conquest. Dougie came back inside just as Susie tripped through the kitchen doorway and picked up the telephone. Her feet pointed toward him even as she twisted around to speak to Dougie.

Yep. This was just his luck. Mutual attraction with the one woman he couldn't have. Nick rubbed the back of his neck as blood diverted from his brain.

"I'm calling a cab," she said with a frown. "I think I drank too much wine."

There was a hint of vulnerability in her voice and from what he'd seen, Susie Cooper didn't like to be out of control. That made tonight the perfect opportunity, maybe the only opportunity, to get what he wanted.

The familiar feeling of guilt settled into his gut.

"I'll drive you home in your car if you like, and get a taxi back to town," he offered.

"Good idea." Dougie wrapped his arm around Susie's shoulder with a salacious grin designed to make Nick jealous.

Susie shook her head and Mickey Mouse's ears jiggled. "I don't want to put you out."

"You're not putting me out. I live to serve, remember?" Nick willed her to look at him, to hold his gaze for more than a ricochet glance. He held his breath as her chin finally came up and her head tilted. Her eyes turned a darker blue. But in the depths, where her soul gathered, she was wary of him the way women were instinctively wary of dangerous men.

Smart girl.

"Susie, I'm getting a cab home anyway, at least this way you'll have your car at home. It's no trouble. I've got a Sunday league soccer game in the morning." He glanced at Dougie, who was also playing in their team, and made a big show of checking his watch—as if he didn't stay up 'til dawn on a regular basis. "And it's late."

Sex would be good.

That thought had been lurking in the shadows all evening. At least God had a sense of humor.

"Grab your stuff, Susie Q. I'll give you a ride home." And with a narrow-eyed look at his smirking friend, he went to give Leanne the biggest thank-you kiss in the history of dinner parties.

STASHING HER PURSE at her feet, Susie sank into the black leather upholstery and regretted buying such a small car.

Her head was spinning from too much wine and something far more primitive. She recognized the signs. She was attracted to the looks, the body, the attitude— her last boyfriend had been the same and he'd completely screwed her over.

Broken hearts.

That's what she and Dela had been recovering from when they'd taken off to the Fraser coast. She blinked as memories overwhelmed her. *Water teeming with fish in a sea so blue it dazzled like a billion sapphires. The hull of a scuttled ship coming into focus. Turning to smile at Dela, to share the wonder, only to see her friend kicking for the surface—too fast, too fast, too fast!*

She wrenched her eyes open. Dela was dead and Susie had gotten the bends trying to save her.

Nick eased his length into the driver's seat, the heat

from his thighs radiating across the thin whisper of space. She cracked a window trying to hide the fact that her hands were shaking. Nick turned the ignition key and they got blasted by Sheryl Crow's "If It Makes You Happy."

He lowered the volume.

"I should just stay the night." She looked longingly at Leanne's front door and suddenly the breath was squeezed from her chest as her seatbelt cut into her sternum. The car jerked to a halt.

"Susie…" Nick turned and stared at her with those dark eyes, the engine running with a noisy purr. Her mouth went dry as her heart forced blood through suddenly fiery veins. "I'm a police officer. I promise to get you home in one piece and completely untouched unless you want it otherwise." His voice was melted butter, rich and ultimately bad for her health.

"Promise?"

She had no intention of acting on the attraction pulsing neon-bright between them, but she knew she needed to get away from Nick Archer before the effects of alcohol outcompeted good old-fashioned common sense.

His fingers flexed around the tiny steering wheel. "If that's what you want."

"That is exactly what I want."

One side of his mouth bent into a crooked smile that didn't exactly look trustworthy, but he put the car in gear, headed along the narrow lane that led toward the main road. RAF Leuchars glittered in the distance, reflecting off the River Eden, which glistened like tar in the moonless, starless night.

"So." He shot her a quick look. "You like Sheryl Crow?"

Susie appreciated his effort at civilized conversation

even if she didn't think they were going to get very far. "And you like the Rolling Stones."

"My dad played them when I was a little kid." Nick shut up, as if he'd already said too much.

Mr. Loquacious.

"Where's your dad now?" Susie gripped her seatbelt, a little nervous about the way they whizzed around a particularly curvaceous bend.

"Your guess is as good as mine."

"I'm sorry." She always seemed to say the wrong thing to him. He put her on edge and she went from sophisticated university professor to gauche single female in an instant.

Susie tried again. "For some reason I like angry, cynical female singer-songwriters."

"All-men-are-bastards-who'll-do-anything-for-a-quick-shag-and-then-dump-you-for-your-best-friend sort of stuff?" Nick's expression was serious. "I can't see a woman like you taking crap like that."

"Ah, but you don't know anything about a woman like me." She kept the bitterness off her tongue. Nick wasn't one of her failed past relationships and she intended to keep it that way.

He took a sharp left-hand bend and her thigh brushed his, setting off fireworks in all the wrong places. Striving to put out those flames, she hit on the one topic he really didn't want to discuss. "I am sorry about your wife."

Susie actually felt the mental door slam tight. Even the air turned icy and she boosted the heat just to have something to do with her hands.

He surprised her when he replied. "Everyone said we were crazy getting married so young. I guess they were right, weren't they?" The cold words belied the look of guarded pain that flickered in his eyes.

She didn't know what to say so she said nothing.

St. Andrews was a blur. They went through the Westport and along South Street, heading past the Gatty on the way out of town. Mist rolled off the waves like a cloak hugging the bay.

"How do you know where I live?" she asked suddenly. She hadn't told him.

"Lily pointed it out yesterday." He shot her a weird glance. "You actually thought me and Lily were seeing each other?"

Susie bit the inside of her cheek. "It seemed logical." She shifted in her seat. "Lily told me she had a hot date, then ran outside and flung herself at you." She glowered defiantly at her distorted reflection in the glass.

"Everything is a hot date to Lily." He grinned, obviously at ease talking about Lily Heathcote as opposed to her dead sister. "She's a good kid." He gave a shudder. "And I'm old enough to be her father."

Susie flinched.

"We went to visit her mother." His sideways smile was full of self-mockery but sexy all the same.

Dammit. She had a hunch everything about Nick Archer looked sexy, with or without imbibing a bottle of Merlot.

"Emily told me all about you, Dr. Cooper."

Lily's mother had befriended her over the past month, but Emily's smiles never quite reached her eyes. The skin of her face crinkled, her lips angled upward, but the light inside never seemed to brighten. Now Susie understood why—the loss of a child. She gripped the seat, the combination of wine and speed making her head spin.

"Are you all right?" Nick asked, turning down the bumpy lane toward her home. Susie nodded as she blew out a steadying breath.

They turned into her drive and a security light flooded the gravel yard, revealing the beautiful old stone cottage flanked by patches of heather and herbs.

Home. *Thank God.*

Grabbing her purse, she shoved open the door before they'd stopped. Dormant wheat fields stretched behind the cottage, which bordered a golf course. Emily and Lily's cottage topped a low rise three hundred yards away, tall hedges giving both houses seclusion and privacy.

Nick stood beside the car door, one foot on the sill, hands on the roof, looking delicious. His eyes darkened as they met hers. "Still want me to call a taxi?"

The air between them crackled with possibility, but Susie nodded. She wasn't some easy lay for a stranger. She needed to believe she was worth more than that.

"Can I at least walk you to your door?"

Susie looked over to the French doors twenty yards away up three uneven stone slabs. Nick's request was a baited trap, but he wasn't that irresistible. She nodded.

Fog billowed along the lilac hedge that marked her property, enfolding them in a soft mystical silence. He fell into step beside her and handed her the key fob. She moved ahead up the steps, brushing an old lavender bush that released its fragrance through the night air. Fumbling, she dropped her keys and Nick bent to retrieve them before she had the chance.

"Nice place," he commented. "Secluded. Wouldn't have to worry about upsetting the neighbors with loud music or screaming sex."

Her skin sizzled and every sense felt electrified as if

someone had plugged her in and flipped a switch. Her eyes widened, her chest tightened. This was dangerous. She was too aware of him, too interested in the idea of screaming sex, and too damn drunk to run as fast as she should.

And he knew it.

She pressed back against her door, her shoulder blades drawn up tight together. Nick slipped the key into the lock and took a step forward, bringing him close enough to touch if she so much as took a breath. So she didn't. The lock clicked and he took a step back with a grave expression on his face.

"I'd kiss you goodnight if you didn't look so scared," he said softly.

"I'm not scared."

"Good." His eyes sparkled as he lowered his mouth to hers.

Mistake! Her mind screamed but it was too late. The breath whooshed out of her as he pressed the gentlest kiss to her lips—as fine a sensation as the stroke of a feather across sensitive skin. And the world stopped. Then every sense climbed to high alert as he took a half step closer, the bulk of his shoulders blocking the wind, and heat coming off his body like rays from the sun. He smelled spicy and male, the leather of his jacket creaking as he shifted his stance. He took her by surprise as he slipped one hand beneath her coat, resting it possessively on her hipbone. Startled, she opened her eyes.

But he kissed her again, this time less gently. Sliding his hand to the base of her spine, the burning impression of each finger pressing through the cotton of her T-shirt, brushing bare skin. His lips were teasing and coaxing, not what she expected from a man who screamed danger. Her palms braced against the muscles in his chest, but they weren't exactly beating him off. He eased her toward him, enticed a trembling response from her body, but all of a sudden he jerked away and stuck his hand in his pocket.

"Bloody hell." He pulled out a cell phone, adjusting it to read the display in the poor light. Swearing, he looked at her with an apology in his eyes. And regret. Because she was a sure thing. "I've got to go."

"You're on call?" Susie couldn't believe the disappointment in her voice. *Go! Please go.*

His smile was a slash of white. "Criminals always know when I have a night off." His eyes slid to her car. "Can I borrow your Mini?" He gripped the back of his neck, looking up at her from under heavy brows. "I'll get it back to you before morning."

"Take it." Susie wouldn't be accused of getting in the way of law and order, plus it would get him away from her faster. Next time she saw him she'd be sober and prepared. "I'm not planning on going anywhere tomorrow so there's no rush to drop it off."

She opened the front door, pulled the keys out of the lock and twisted off the ignition key from her octopus key fob.

"Here." She threw it to him, not surprised when he snatched it out of the air without even moving his gaze. His intensity was unsettling.

"Susie...I'm sorry."

She dashed inside and closed the door. Locked it. He could have her car, no problem. But he couldn't have her. She wanted a relationship, a future, a family. Nick Archer was a lousy bet for anything except orgasms and heartbreak, and not even the orgasms were guaranteed.

TRACY SHRUGGED INTO HER FLEECE and hitched her canvas bag over one shoulder, pulling her hair free of the strap. The lab was empty tonight. The night-watchman had done his first set of rounds and gone on to the next building with a terse reminder to turn off the lights when she left. She pulled a face. He gave her the creeps with his beady little eyes and smelly flat-cap.

Her footsteps echoed as she walked the quiet corridors. After turning off the lights, it was dark and eerie, totally different to daytime, when the bright Scottish sunshine poured through the skylights and windows. A tremor shivered along her spine and she stopped and glanced around. There was no one there except deep, abiding emptiness.

Tracy crossed the foyer and stared into the darkness outside. She wasn't scared. She could look after herself. Being raised in foster homes for cash taught you self preservation faster than most kids learned their ABCs. She flicked her hair out of her face and raised her chin. She was used to being alone, but tonight the isolation welled with an overwhelming sense of sorrow. Another Saturday night going back to a sterile apartment in Albany Park shared with five other girls, none of whom she particularly liked. Going home alone. Again.

For some reason her feelings about sexual freedom had disintegrated into self-disgust. Everyone else had someone to share their lives with. Her they just screwed. Maybe the dissatisfaction was because of what she'd done after she'd left the Gatty last night?

She'd bumped into him on her way out of the building and he'd invited her back to his place. To begin with it had been exciting, but afterward she'd felt dirty. Very dirty.

She slammed the lock-release button on the wall,

pushed through the glass doors and ran outside, taking a deep breath of fresh air. Maybe she wasn't as sexually liberated as she'd imagined. She huddled deeper into her jacket. The haar, that ghostly east coast mist that plagued the region, had rolled in off the bay enshrouding the buildings, muting the landscape.

She'd never role-played before.

He'd told her next time she could choose the roles, but she wasn't sure she wanted to be that defenseless again and she wasn't sure she believed him. He wasn't the submissive type.

She rubbed her wrists.

He'd been rough. And then he'd made her beg. And it had hurt and she'd begged anyway until he'd done everything he'd wanted and she'd come so hard she'd nearly had a heart attack.

The heat of humiliation crept up her neck. Hugging her arms tight across her chest she glanced around the car park and started walking. She didn't hear anything except the sea, but she gripped her keys like a weapon, just in case.

What she needed was a real boyfriend, one who walked her home before spending the entire night cozied up in her bed.

Merciless wind blasted her face and she tucked her nose into the raised collar of her coat, stepping onto the path that ran along the seafront. There was a streetlight farther along the path, an amber beacon. She walked faster toward it.

Crack!

Tracy jolted into the air, dropping her keys. She grabbed her chest where her heart banged against her ribs. *What the hell was that? Shit!* Then she started laughing. It was just a branch slapping the windows of the Gatty, shadows lashing in the mist.

Shaking her head, Tracy bent to pick up her keys. A shoe scuffed the pavement behind her an instant before white-hot pain exploded in her skull. The sound of crunching bone shocked her even as her knees gave out and she fell to the ground.

Icy dew soaked her clothes. Instinct kept her moving, despite her injuries, despite the sharp tang of blood in her mouth. She rolled. Over the grass, then out of control down the short slope toward the beach. The lip of the seawall jarred her to a stop, the pain in her head excruciating, as if someone had bashed her brains with a red-hot poker.

"Please. Help."

She tried to scream, but her voice came out like a kitten drowning. A foot gave her a shove and for a moment she hovered, weightless, before she smashed into cold sand below. Grit got in her mouth. She spat it out.

She couldn't stop shaking. Terror froze all thought except survival, but she couldn't make her muscles work. Each beat of her heart pumped blood from her body, but she refused to die. She would not die before she'd got what she wanted out of this damned life. A scream of fury and frustration roared through her mind, but her vocal cords didn't work. She couldn't get enough breath.

She twisted onto her belly and began to crawl even though it *hurt*. Sand was smooth and cool between her fingers. She dragged herself forward, sweat pouring off her forehead, arms shaking with exertion. Then running shoes appeared before her and she stopped, raising her head to look at her attacker. It didn't make any sense.

Her life was cursed. "Why? Why me?"

"Because nobody cares about you."

That awful truth punched Tracy as hard as any blow. She was going to die and nobody would care. The hammer came toward her—death in slow motion—and she could do nothing but watch.

CHAPTER FIVE

NICK SAT IN THE CAR, his gut churning like a combine. He'd done worse things in his time, scarier things, but they hadn't made him feel this wretched. He put his fingers on his lips feeling the murmur of betrayal that had crossed his mouth. He'd wanted to keep kissing Susie Cooper until dawn broke.

Instead he'd stolen her wallet.

He flipped open the turquoise suede. Ignored the ID card with Susie's smiling face staring up at him from the clear plastic window. He pulled out a slim electronic keycard that opened the front door of the Gatty Marine Lab. Lily had one identical. Dropping the wallet to the passenger seat, he started the engine and noticed a light was still burning in Emily Heathcote's cottage.

Did she have trouble sleeping at night, too?

He tossed the keycard onto the dash and started driving. Tried to ignore the fact his fingers itched in a way they hadn't itched in a long time. He didn't like the knowledge he'd had to force himself to let go of Susie Cooper once he'd finally got his hands on her. He'd been tempted to go for goal and abandon his scheme for another night, but it had already waited twelve long years.

Father Mike—the man who'd raised him after he escaped his mother's hellhole—always told him he had too much pride. As a teen he had been dumb enough to think that was a compliment. But that's what they said, right? Pride before a fall? And he had fallen long and hard, and was still struggling to get back on his knees.

Chrissie had shaped his life from the day he'd first met her, but what had he known about marriage? *Nothing.* Not a goddamned thing. And when he discovered she'd slept with Sizemore, he'd kicked her out.

His first mistake.

He drove to his flat in town to gear up. His dog, Rocket, whimpered and threw himself into a whole-body wag as Nick pushed open the door.

"Sorry, boy." Nick rubbed his thick fur and tossed him a biscuit from the tin on the kitchen counter. "You can't come."

Nick grabbed what he needed, tucked it into the back pocket of his jeans along with a small flashlight. He debated over the knife he habitually carried. Having it would increase the potential for charges if he was caught, but he had no intention of getting caught. He had lived in the real world for too long to play nice. He played big boy rules for big boy games. He pulled on a black sweater and a black watch cap to cover his hair and ears, swapped oxfords for trainers, the dog licking his face as he bent to tie the laces.

"Oh no, you don't, you wee bugger." He gave Rocket one last pat, touched a hand to Susie's wallet and checked the time. One-fifteen.

He drove to Albany Park and slid into the crowded car park behind blocks of student housing. A couple of students were heading home for the night. He hung tight for a moment, watching them go inside their box-like little flats. Then he got out and pulled his toque low, the wool itching his forehead, reminding him of other times he'd done this sort of thing and all the reasons he'd quit.

The haar smothered this stretch of coast like a clingy lover. Mist kissed his face, the vapor from his lungs mixing with the atmosphere like dry ice. He couldn't see anyone on the path, but kept his head bent, checking for lights inside the Gatty building. Nothing.

Good.

He turned the corner, noted there weren't any cars in the car park, nor lights in the newer structure that rose up behind the original nineteenth-century building. Excitement made his blood pound in his ears and his mouth felt parched. The night-watchman was due back in a couple of hours, but Nick would be in and out in twenty minutes tops.

He'd given the force most of his adult life, three years so deep undercover there were days even he'd forgotten he was a police officer. And now he was risking everything, his career, his reputation, his honor, all to prove Jake Sizemore's guilt.

His fingertips felt numb inside latex gloves as he swiped Susie's card through the electronic slot at the door. He waited for the buzzer to click and quickly entered the Gatty.

If anyone checked, the computer log would show Susie Cooper worked late. With a little luck nobody would ever know or care she hadn't been there at all.

Susie was the perfect patsy. He didn't allow his thoughts to stray to her soft scent or the feel of her lips. He had no intention of adding to her reasons to hate men, although he was pretty sure if she knew he'd stolen her wallet, he'd be top of her shit list.

Putting thoughts of Susie aside, he moved along the dark corridors which hummed with electricity from unseen machines. If he was caught, Dr. Susie Cooper would protest with enough honest indignation to convince even the most hardnosed cop she was not involved; whereas Lily, whose card he had contemplated borrowing on more than one occasion, would have 'fessed up and sent her career down the crapper.

And he'd already done enough damage to the Heathcote family.

He headed up a flight of stairs, risked his flashlight in the stairwell. Inched the door open carefully, wincing as its hinges squealed. He slid through the gap, along the corridor to the open-plan office that housed the secretaries' desks. Skirted hulking masses of photocopiers and file cabinets and found Jake Sizemore's office door.

It was locked.

Nick took the lock pick kit from his back pocket, held the torch close and blocked the light with his body. It took three seconds to open the lock and Nick crossed into Jake's private sanctum.

If there was any proof Jake had dumped Chrissie into water teeming with great whites, it would likely be in this room. Nick started with Jake's desk, careful not to disrupt the order in which things were placed as he rifled through file folders. There was a copy of *A King's Treasure Lost* by Howard J. Murray on the desk. Nick eyed it speculatively and moved on.

Mountains of paperwork produced nothing, but there was a half box of condoms in the bottom drawer. Nick wondered what Mrs. Sizemore thought of that, given Jake had had his gonads snipped nine years ago.

"Dirty bastard." The words rolled around Nick's teeth, more habit than malice. He looked at the walls, stood with his flashlight pointed at the pictures, his body blocking the light from the windows as much as he could. His heart pounded as he found a picture of Chrissie and Jake, both of them standing on the prow of a sailing boat, smiling at whoever was taking the photograph.

He touched his finger to the curve of her cheek, swallowed the knot of anguish that welled up inside him and choked his throat. Chrissie's hair was jet black, plastered flat against her skull as if she'd been diving. Her dark eyes sparkled, lips bowed in a cheery smile that still affected him like a bullet to the heart.

She'd betrayed him.

Then she'd died.

Nick turned away, frustration winding its way through his muscles and squeezing his gut. There had to be *something*. But what? A confession? A bloodstained knife? He walked over to the filing cabinets, pulled open the top drawer, staring at the internal report the university had compiled after Chrissie's death. A tedious piece of bullshit exonerating Professor Sizemore and laying the blame squarely on Chrissie's bloodless shoulders. She'd taken a boat on her own. Gone diving in dangerous waters without a buddy and paid with her life.

Which was bollocks because Chrissie was the most safety-conscious person he'd ever known. She was a queen bitch Divemaster and would never have taken off alone. And that left one alternative. Murder.

But there was no evidence.

He rifled through the rest of the drawers, hope draining with each heartbeat. Suddenly blue lights flashed outside the large plate glass windows that looked over the bay.

Busted.

The door locked behind him, Nick raced down the stairs through to the old part of the building where Chrissie had had a cubbyhole office in the good old days. After passing the electron-microscopy suite, he lit out of the rear fire exit, hopped over the fence and was in Susie Cooper's Mini warming the engine when his cell phone buzzed for real.

What the...?

Pulling off his toque, he answered dispatch, trying not to sound out of breath. "D.I. Archer."

"Sir, I know you're not on call, but we've got a report from East Sands of a dead body."

Jesus.

While he'd been searching Sizemore's office, someone outside had tripped over a corpse. It was probably a floater, grim even without being a reminder of Chrissie's death.

"I'll be there in five minutes." He rang off, cold sweat drying on his forehead that he wiped away with an even colder hand. *That had been close and for what?* Perhaps there was no way of getting justice for his wife's murder, at least no way that was legal.

He speed-dialed Ewan, who answered with a muffled, "Ugh?"

"We've got a dead body, East Sands. I don't have details."

Nick heard Ewan rubbing the sleep from his eyes, grumbling and groaning. "I'll call Amy's sister to come over. Should be there in twenty minutes. God, I hope it isn't a kid."

Nick shuddered. He hadn't thought of that. "I'll call forensics."

Nick rang off. He reversed the Mini, phone in one hand as he called the Forensic Pathology Team in Dundee, then drove to the main entrance of the Gatty Marine Lab and pulled up on the embankment overlooking the beach. A uniform on nightshift was tying off the area with police tape.

The haar had lifted with the receding tide and hovered like some malevolent beast, observing the proceedings from a prudent distance. Two girls, students probably, sat on a park bench farther along the footpath.

"What you got, Lewis?" Nick asked the square-faced policewoman. Her expression was serious. P.C. Julie Lewis was slow to smile, but smart and dedicated, with no pretensions.

"Those two found a body." She indicated the girls, who sat crying. "I think we're looking at a murder, sir." At his raised brow, she added, "Pretty hard to smash in your own skull."

Nick's stomach clenched. Murder?

He looked along the footpath, dread digging claws into his stomach and trying to find purchase. He knew homicide. He'd done four years' homicide after he'd finished his undercover stint, but St. Andrews hadn't seen a murder in years.

Had this poor bugger been bleeding to death when he had broken into the Gatty? Had he tracked the vic's blood into the building? Into Susie's car? Could he have saved a life if he'd been paying more attention to the present, rather than wasting his time trying to avenge the past?

Nick looked up at the overcast sky and thought for one split second he heard Chrissie's laugh. He was going to hell for a little B&E. Or maybe for wanting a woman in a way he hadn't in more than a decade.

The wind blasted his cheeks, icy and raw. Twin flashlights beamed into his eyes and he was instantly blind.

"Get those things out of my face," he yelled.

"Sorry, sir." Two synchronous replies.

Nick smelled blood in the air, sharp and cuprous. His intestines flip-flopped as he took another step down the grassy slope. P.C. Eric Mosel and Sergeant Hammy Soothill ran their beams over the body of a young woman.

Christ. "ID?"

Both men shook their heads.

"We tried not to disturb the locus." P.C. Mosel, or Mouse as he was known in the station, was normally a bit of a twat, niggling away at the division between CID and uniform coppers—the filth and the woodentops as they were called. But not tonight. Tonight he was all business. "I thought she might still be alive."

The back of her skull was smashed like a broken eggshell, pale bone gleaming amongst gore. The flashlights picked out blood matting her hair, streaking her neck, staining the sand beneath her body a rusty brown. It was bloody obvious she was dead, but they'd still need a doctor for verification. A body could be trailed from one end of the beach to the other, but police officers still needed a doctor to confirm death. Rules and regulations of the God-almighty handbook.

Sobs reached him, but all Nick could do was stand and stare. This woman was his first homicide victim since leaving the crime-ridden streets of London. He hadn't expected to feel quite so appalled, but St. Andrews was the one pure spot in a life of brutality and it had just been violated.

He nodded toward the wailing girls. "They report it?"

"Yes, sir." Sergeant Hammy Soothill waved his flashlight as if looking for footprints, but the sand was too dry. There wouldn't be any tracks down there worth saving. "The one lassie slipped and fell in the blood."

The distaste on Hammy's face was echoed by Nick's stomach. There was none of the usual black humor that accompanied sudden death and no one prodded the corpse with a ubiquitous black boot.

They were all somber as they got on with the job, maybe because no matter how many cases they'd had in other places, this was the first of its kind in St. Andrews.

"Get the photographer down here when the doctor's finished. See if we can get hold of floodlights for the forensics team. Mouse, we'll need a scale drawing, and Hammy, I want you to oversee every piece of evidence and make sure it is catalogued like the Crown Jewels." He glanced at his watch. His boss would want to be notified, and the Procurator Fiscal.

His gaze lingered on the young woman's body. Her skirt was hiked up around her thighs, suggesting a possible sexual assault, arms outstretched over her head as if she'd tried to crawl away.

All that blood…

She'd taken time to die.

Why her? How had she attracted a killer's attention? Or was she simply in the wrong place at the wrong time? Cursing, he walked on the tarmac, trying not to step in blood. But it was everywhere, glistening thickly in the dim light. Had he missed it earlier, or had the girl been attacked when he was inside the Gatty?

"Hey!" He turned and yelled to P.C. Lewis and pointed along the path he'd just walked. "Get this area roped off too. There's blood everywhere."

The sobs grew louder and Nick resisted rolling his eyes at his witnesses. The fine line of irritation was about to trip his temper. Lucky for him doing the job was as automatic as breathing, and muscle memory had him jerking out a notebook and stabbing a pen in its center. He thought he'd escaped this crap. This was St. Andrews, not Stoke Newington. He'd thought he was finished with death and destruction.

"I'm Detective Inspector Nick Archer. Can you ladies tell me what happened?"

A short, chubby brunette had her arm thrown protectively over the blonde's shoulders. Both wore Gor-Tex rain jackets, blue jeans and trainers that were covered in a dark sticky substance that was probably blood. The brunette had a big handbag on the bench at her side, a flashlight beside it.

"We were just walking hame." The broad Glaswegian twang cut through him.

The whining pitch of her voice set his teeth on edge, but he nodded. "What's your name?"

"Tina Bell." The girl met his gaze briefly. "People call me Tinker."

'Course they did.

Her gaze shifted to her friend, whose head wobbled when Tina shook her gently by the shoulders. The blonde looked up, her pupils optical saucers, telling him exactly why the brunette was being so damn protective. At least one of them was surfing the cosmos and it wasn't him. When the blonde didn't say anything, Tinkerbell plowed on. "And this here is Cynthia Parkinson. Cyn." She shook her friend again and the girl's head bobbed.

Nick wrote it in his notebook along with their address, then he verified their ID. "Mind if I take a look at your cell phone?"

Tinkerbell dug deep into her coat pocket.

"Thanks." He flipped through the call history and checked the time of her last call. One twenty-three, to 999, the emergencies services. When he'd been busy in the office above their heads, rifling through Sizemore's desk. A visceral heat swept through him and opened his pores.

Had the girl on the beach still been alive?

"Mind if I take a look in your handbags?" Nick asked, ignoring his own emotions and doing the job. Not that these two were likely killers, but he couldn't afford to ignore the obvious.

Tinkerbell was smart, he could see the understanding in her eyes. "Go ahead, but we didn't kill her."

It was too much to ask to find a blood-soaked blunt instrument in the recesses of a canvas tote, but killers were generally careless and often unintelligent, and regularly hung out at their crime scenes. There were no other spectators, and no media to control yet, which was a blessing.

"Did you see anyone? Hear anything?" He passed the bags back and Tina shook her head.

Cynthia chose that moment to quit crying, her blond curls damp around pinched features. "I slipped. And when I put my hand on the path it got covered in something sticky and then Tina got out her torch and we realized there was blood everywhere. We thought maybe some animal had been run over and we wanted to try and help it. But then...then we saw the body..." She started wiping her palm across her knee in a repetitive gesture that made Nick queasy.

A sliver of sympathy worked its way free.

Finding a body would haunt them for a long time. No need to point out doing drugs was stupid. They'd either figure it out or they'd become another statistic.

The sobs started again and Nick looked up, relieved as a rumpled, sleepy-looking Ewan rushed to his side.

"We need an official statement." Nick raised his brows in query, but Tinkerbell, who looked more like a prop forward than a fairy, was gathering her stuff before hauling the other girl to her feet. "If you go with this detective—" he pointed to Ewan "—he'll take care of you."

Ewan smiled like a benevolent uncle.

"Anything else you think of…" Nick was already backing away, leaving Ewan to deal with the technicalities of the two young women and their awful needy emotions.

"I know we weren't very nice to her, but I didn't want to see her dead." Cynthia's knees buckled. Tinkerbell hung on determinedly before giving up and slumping onto the bench in defeat. Nick's eyes latched onto Tinkerbell's.

"You *knew* her?" He stopped backing away. "How did you recognize her? Did you touch the body?"

Tinkerbell's eyes flooded with tears, which she tried to wipe away. "She shared a flat with us." She held his gaze, angled her chin toward Albany Park. "We didn't touch her, but I recognize her jacket and hair." She sniffed. "Her name is Tracy Good. She was doing a Ph.D. at the Gatty."

A bolt of excitement seared his nerves and made every sense flare to life.

"With who?" Nick's voice was harsher than he intended, and the girl's eyes widened under the sodium vapor.

"I don't remember his name." The whiny pitch was back. "But he's the head of department."

"Sizemore? Professor Jake Sizemore?"

Tinkerbell nodded, her lip trembling.

Exhilaration dragged shame in its wake. A young woman was dead and he was still obsessed with revenge.

He met Ewan's gaze over the girls' heads and his colleague mouthed exactly what he was thinking. "Fuck."

CHAPTER SIX

A HANGOVER RAGED QUIETLY behind Susie's eyes as she sat at Emily Heathcote's kitchen table pretending not to suffer. The old woman's hands shook under the weight of the teapot but she didn't spill a drop. Susie had been about to go for a walk along the beach to clear her head when she found Emily on her doorstep. Her neighbor had insisted she come over for tea and biscuits.

"Milk and sugar?" Emily's accent was English rather than Scottish, easier to understand than the local dialect.

"Just milk, please." Susie clasped her hands tight in her lap like a little girl visiting royalty. "Have you lived in Scotland long?"

"It seems like we've lived here forever." Emily's eyes lost focus. "Peter and I moved up from Essex when Christina started as an undergraduate. We came for a visit and fell in love with the place." She poured milk from a small jug painted with blue flowers made at a local pottery in Crail. "It saved money on rent by her living at home." Memories clung to her smile. "And then she met Nick and they were so happy. It seemed like a fairytale romance."

That had ended in tragedy.

Added guilt weighed like lead across her shoulders. Christina Heathcote had died long ago, but kissing Nick last night felt like adultery.

"It must have been awful when you lost her." Susie

lowered her head and stared into her lap. She could relate to that loss even though her own child wasn't dead.

"Peter helped, but then he died." Emily stirred sugar into her tea, the spoon circling faster and faster. "For the longest time I didn't know what to do..." She blinked away what looked like heartbreak. "Anyway, enough of that."

She got up, her skirt swishing against her nylons, and fetched a cookie jar back to the table. She frowned when she opened the lid and pulled out a set of keys. "How did these get here?"

"Oh I do stuff like that all the time," Susie reassured the older woman. "Last weekend I left a book in the refrigerator and didn't find it until I went hunting for a snack."

Emily eyed her steadily with one eyebrow raised. "I'm sure you are just saying that to make me feel better, but I do find old age and battiness rather liberating." She smiled and spread cookies on a plate. With a nod, she indicated for Susie to take one. "I hope Lily is working hard for you."

"She's a good student." Susie bit into a cookie, the taste of home-baking melting on her tongue and reminding her of her grandmother's kitchen, where she'd spent some of the best days of her life.

"I wish she'd give up that job in that awful pub." Emily shook her head, fragile silver hair falling from where she'd pinned it to the top of her head. "She didn't get home till 2 a.m. last night."

Susie wiped crumbs from her lips. "It's good she tries to help out financially."

Emily shot her a sly look. "I bet you never worked to get through college."

"My mother forbade me." A trace of bitterness leaked out and Susie pressed her lips together. If her mother ran for president she needed to learn to guard even the tiniest of secrets.

"Mothers like to protect their babies." Emily twisted her wedding band then looked away. "If we can."

Emily's grief was palpable and tore at Susie's heart. At least her own child was alive and well.

"Would you like to see a photograph of Christina?" Emily's skin looked ashen, but her eyes were sharp, cataloguing Susie's reaction to what Susie suspected was a rare honor. Did she want to see a picture of the woman Nick Archer had loved and lost?

Heck no.

"Of course." Susie nodded and smiled, trapped by someone else's motherly love.

Emily stood, polyester swishing, slippers padding across worn linoleum, and went through the door into the back of the house. Susie didn't know if she was supposed to follow or wait in the kitchen. She stood uncertainly, blew out one cheek into a ball.

"Through here," Emily coaxed in a soft voice.

Hesitant, Susie walked through a homey living room with overstuffed couches, a battalion of knickknacks and a fat black cat asleep on a chair. She followed the light of an open doorway distorted by the old woman's shadow.

"Lily's asleep." Emily pointed to another door and placed her fingers to her lips, waving Susie into a small pink-walled bedroom with a twin bed pushed against the wall. Emily closed the door behind Susie, which spooked her for no reason at all.

The walls were covered in framed photographs. Baby portraits, school shots, university graduation with

Christina in a cap and gown. Every dimension of development catalogued and captured in a parental shrine.

Snow White was the first thing that crossed Susie's mind. The girl looked like some Hollywood version of Snow White. Midnight hair, blue eyes, ruby lips. Nothing like Lily. Except who knew what Lily looked like under all that paint?

"They were very much in love." Emily pointed to a picture of Christina and Nick on their wedding day.

Susie avoided looking at it and instead picked up a framed photo off the dresser. "Christina was a diver?"

Emily's hands twitched nervously. There was a group of people in the shot, Nick looking impossibly young and lanky, his arm draped possessively across Christina's shoulder. They looked tired but satisfied, the way it felt after the perfect dive.

Hot panic shot along Susie's nerves, and beads of sweat popped out along her brow.

Dela rocketing to the surface. Susie racing after her. The sound of her own breath booming in her ears as she inflated Dela's lungs with her own.

Susie swayed slightly, blindsided by the rush of emotion cruising her veins.

"All marine biologists are divers, aren't they?" Emily was oblivious to Susie's reaction. Instead she took the photo from Susie's fingers and returned it to the exact same spot on the dresser.

"Not always." Lightheaded, Susie held on to the edge of the drawers and hoped she didn't faint. Her heart skipped erratically and her mouth felt like ashes. She'd thought she was over the trauma of her friend's death, but obviously she was mistaken.

Suddenly the door burst open and there stood Nick. His eyes flicked from her to the photos on the wall and eventually landed on Emily. If Susie hadn't been propping herself up, she'd have just fallen over from the appalled expression on his face.

"I knocked, but there was no answer." He looked exhausted, the lines around his eyes cut deeper, as if he'd been up all night. She wondered what case had caused that level of weariness but decided she didn't want to know.

"You don't have to knock, Nicholas." Emily shuffled past Susie and embraced her son-in-law. "I was just showing Susie a photograph of Christina."

Great. Now it sounded as though she'd inquired after the dead girl. Nick didn't look at her and Susie grimaced, the throbbing pain of her hangover intensifying so that she closed her eyes. *Damn.*

"What's going on?" Lily came out of her bedroom in charcoal flannel pj's that swamped her tiny stature. She squinted up at Nick. "I thought you had footy this morning? I was going to come and watch." Her blond hair stuck out and the remnants of last night's makeup smudged her eyes. Susie would have been mortified to wake up and find her Ph.D. supervisor, her brother-in-law and her mother chatting over pictures of her dead sister, especially when one of them was a cop. But then Susie didn't look half as cute as Lily did when she woke up. She was more the rabid squirrel variety.

Lily didn't seem to care one way or the other.

I should have stayed home in bed. But then it would have been her in her pj's when Nick returned the car. Although maybe he hadn't even gone to her house? He'd probably dropped off her car, left the keys in the ignition and come up here, hoping to avoid her. Mortification grew and she could feel fire pouring into her cheeks.

"I had to ditch the game. Something came up." Nick ruffled Lily's hair in a careless gesture and directed her toward the kitchen with an arm over her shoulders. Emily followed and Susie trailed behind. He avoided looking at her, obviously embarrassed about last night. She raised her chin. He wasn't the only one.

"Tea. Good." Lily grabbed a mug and poured herself a cup from the still warm teapot.

"Nick, let me get you something." Emily took a china cup and started pouring tea, treating him like the prodigal son.

He held up his hand. "This isn't a social call." His green eyes bored into Susie's with an emotion she couldn't decipher. "There's been a murder and I need to ask Dr. Cooper some questions."

"Oh my God! Where? When? Was it someone we knew?" Lily's eyes blinked rapid-fire.

"I can't tell you, yet." Nick stuffed his hands in his pockets and frowned at her. "What time did you get off work last night?"

Lily wrinkled her nose attractively at his refusal to answer her questions. "I got a taxi back around quarter to two." Her jaw dropped and she grabbed his arm. "I saw police cars by the Gatty when we drove past, was it someone from the lab?" As Lily's voice rose so did the tension stretching Susie's nerves.

Nick stood silent for a moment, then let out a quiet breath. "This can't go any further. We need to notify next of kin, but one of Jake Sizemore's students was murdered outside the Gatty last night."

Emily collapsed into the chair beside the table. "That dreadful man has done it again!"

"No way. Was it Hannah? Mikey? Or Tracy? Oh my God, say it wasn't Hannah. I've got to call her." Tears streamed down Lily's cheeks and Nick put his hands on her shoulders and shook her gently.

"You can't call anyone until I've spoken to the family. Show some respect."

Susie sagged against the kitchen countertop, unable to control the lightheaded sensation that swirled around her head. She'd met all of Jake's students and each one had been young, vigorous and full of life.

Not anymore.

Life could be snatched in a moment. She'd already learned that lesson the hard way this year.

"I saw Tracy in at work yesterday. I know she often works late." Numb to the bone, Susie started to shiver because somehow she knew it was Tracy who'd died.

Something flickered in Nick's eyes. "Yes, it was Tracy Good who was killed last night."

Lily sobbed and covered her face with her hands.

Emily looked up from the kitchen table and wagged a finger at Lily. "That's the girl you told me was sleeping with that monster."

"Mother!" Lily dragged her fingers down her face. "How can you say that when she's dead?"

Nick frowned at Lily, who glared at her mother. "Is it true?" he asked.

"Of course it's true. Isn't it obvious?" Emily's voice turned to a screech and Susie's hand reached for the doorknob.

Nick held up his hand for silence, pointed a finger at Susie. "Stay. I need to talk to you."

She froze.

He turned back to Emily. "I don't like the bastard any more than you do, but it doesn't mean he killed this girl." The conviction in his voice sounded as if he meant it, but the gleam in his eye told a different story.

Emily pursed her lips. But her heavy breathing crackled through the air. "I expect there won't be any evidence. The police are so useless they wouldn't find the murderer even if he was bent over the body covered in blood!"

Nick went still as silence boomed around the kitchen.

"Thanks for the vote of confidence, Em." His eyes glittered like chips of ice. "I'm going to forget you said that."

"Fine," Emily muttered, wringing her hands together. "Forget it, the same way you *forgot* that man killed your wife. And now it looks like he's done it again."

"Tracy didn't have a family." Lily's lips were alabaster pale as her eyes shot between her mother and Nick. "Tracy hasn't got any relatives, or legal guardians. She was raised in a foster home."

"Well at least there's no one to mourn her." Emily threw a contemptuous look at her son-in-law.

"I need to verify the information before her name is released to the media." Nick put his hand on Lily's shoulder, ignored his mother-in-law. "Not one word of this leaks until I say so, got it? No phone calls, texts or emails to your friends, understand?"

Lily wiped her reddened eyes and nodded. "Why do you need to talk to Dr. Cooper?"

"Police business." His expression was void of emotion.

"You don't think *she* did it, do you?" Emily's eyes bulged as if Susie had suddenly morphed into a murder suspect.

Susie sent her a strained smile.

"Susie is one of the few people I know didn't do it."

Her cheeks heated as Lily sent her a speculative glance. Susie twisted the doorknob and opened the door.

"We were at a dinner party with mutual friends," she explained before she escaped. She took in a huge breath of fresh air, watched the Bellrock lighthouse flash far out to sea. Poor Tracy Good.

Nick came up behind her and caught her elbow. "Come on, Susie Q. I've got some questions for you. Let's go somewhere private where we can talk." He touched her shoulder, the slight pressure spreading awareness and anticipation along her spine.

They started down the single track road toward her cottage.

"You shouldn't have kissed me last night." Susie didn't want him to think something was going to happen between them.

"Why not?" He looked exhausted, but his voice held humor.

She didn't appreciate his amusement. "Because I was drunk."

Nick bumped up one shoulder and kicked a stone along the dirt. "I wasn't."

Susie caught his gaze and his eyes, though tired, shone with mischief. "Come on, Susie. We both know it was going to happen sooner or later, you being drunk just fast-forwarded all the boring bits."

"*Boring bits?*" Fury blasted away her hangover. "You mean like actually getting to know me?"

He had the grace to look shamefaced. "That's not what I meant."

Susie batted cow parsley out of the way.

He caught her hand and she tried to wrench it from his grasp, but he held fast.

"That isn't what I meant and you know it."

His eyes were the color of green grass after rain with lashes turned golden by the sun. His gaze dropped to her lips and she knew he was going to kiss her, only this time she wouldn't have any excuse when she kissed him back. The marram grass started rustling and a dog flew out of an overgrown beach trail and landed in a spray of sand at Nick's feet.

"I wondered where you'd got to." Nick let go of her hand and the spell was broken. He picked up a grungy, wet tennis ball and launched it over the sand dunes back onto the beach.

"That's *your* dog?" Susie watched the mutt explode along the path.

"Yep. Rocket. A highly trained police K9." He checked his watch as if he had somewhere to go and, to her relief, began walking again. "The Gatty log shows someone used your keycard to enter the lab at 1:20 a.m. last night."

The statement was so left field it took a moment for Susie to register the words. "But I was in bed."

"I know you were and I know you didn't have anything to do with the murder." His voice was deep, soothing, but couldn't dispel the whisper of fear that sprouted inside her. "But I need to know how someone got hold of your keycard and whether or not it is related to the murder."

"I don't know." Gooseflesh broke out on her arms and she tried to rub it away. "I left the lab at around four yesterday afternoon. I haven't been in since."

"Do you want to borrow my jacket?" Nick's eyes assessed her in a way that had her crossing her arms.

Nice choice. Nipples on high alert or wearing his jacket like a high school crush.

"No, thanks."

His smile told her he knew what she was thinking and that irritated her, too.

"You had the keycard when you left work yesterday afternoon?" He reverted to cop mode, shortening his stride to match hers.

She bit her lip, trying to remember. "I don't know," she admitted. "You only need it to get into the lab, not to leave."

"Do you keep it on you at the lab?"

Susie didn't like his questions, his inference her card was tied to a murder. She shook her head, which reignited her headache. *Ouch.* She put her hand to her brow. "The card stays in my wallet, which stays in my purse in my office." She shot him a look. "And no, I don't lock my office when I'm at work." Never had, anywhere she worked.

Nick's sand-encrusted dog crashed through the undergrowth again and lay panting at Nick's feet.

Probably like a lot of women.

"Could someone have sneaked into your office yesterday and taken the card?"

"I suppose so." Jeez, what a thought. "Or maybe I dropped it when I was in the parking lot." Neither sounded good. Either a thief, or possibly a murderer, had been in her office yesterday, or she'd been dumb enough to drop a keycard to a secure building where anyone could find it.

Great way to start a new job, Susie.

She was shivering badly now. Nausea roiled in her stomach. She hated making mistakes, and, heaven knew, she'd made some doozies in her time. Her mother had a thing about perfection and Susie had inherited the expectation gene but not the follow-through.

A seagull cried above their heads, riding the blast off the sea like a surf god, twisting in the wind with tiny adjustments of his feathers. Shading her eyes, she watched its flight, wishing she could just take off and escape Nick Archer.

"I need you to check your wallet and handbag, see if anything else is missing." Nick's gaze also followed the gull.

"I went to the shops on the way to Leanne's house, so I know I had my wallet then... I'm sure none of my bank cards are missing." She tried to remember. "But I'll check."

"I need to verify all the information." He tilted his head and softened his lips into a smile that should have made him look less dangerous, but his eyes glittered with such startling intelligence she wasn't fooled.

Nothing about Nick Archer was quite what it seemed. If he hadn't been a cop, he'd have made a damn good criminal.

CHAPTER SEVEN

NICK WISHED HE'D NEVER met Susie Cooper.

She stood beside him, her teeth chattering while he followed this phony line of inquiry. But if he didn't ask the questions, someone else would and he didn't want to become a suspect in a murder he hadn't committed or get thrown off the case. Not for a lousy walk-through that had got him no closer to solving Chrissie's murder than he had been twelve years ago.

Other officers were canvassing Albany Park for information on the victim and any possible witnesses last night. He wanted to make sure the woodentops stayed as far away from Susie Cooper as possible.

He'd burned the keycard that morning, along with his running shoes. Watched them melt into a mass of congealed plastic. Then he'd dumped the trash in a skip, careful not to leave even a fingerprint. Call him paranoid, but something about this case felt rotten.

He hadn't gotten any sleep and now he was so tired he could just curl up on the side of the road and close his eyes. Blinking, he used the cold outline of Susie's body to keep him awake.

Ding dong.

Being distracted by his dick in the middle of a murder inquiry wasn't a good idea either. Nick took off his jacket and draped it over her shoulders and wished he'd left her out of this. Everything about her turned him on. Her body, her accent, even the way she folded her arms in that defensive pose that plumped her breasts and made his blood head south. He didn't want to want her. The woman was uptight, prissy and vulnerable. Not even close to his type. But he did want her in the worst possible way.

She sent him a polite smile, which he returned just as civilly, and they continued toward her cottage as if they were strolling through some Jane Austin flick.

He needed to get back to the station. Ewan was due to pick him up in five minutes. This investigation would wreak havoc on his colleague's carefully balanced family life. Christ knew it was already a disaster zone.

Rocket dropped the ball at his feet and Nick kicked it along the gravel path, the dog skidding in its wake. Amy McKnight's life was Nick's worst nightmare, her body wasting around an astute mind, *knowing* she was a burden, *knowing* she was never going to get better. And not being able to do a damn thing about it.

Christ. He'd have topped himself years ago.

He rubbed a hand over his face. *Come on, Archer.* Do the job. Concentrate on the one thing you can do and catch Tracy Good's killer.

"Did you know her? Tracy?" he asked Susie.

She shook her head. "I'd seen her around, but never spoke to her." She scrunched up her nose. "I can't believe she was murdered. I mean, St. Andrews seems so safe compared to the U.S."

"It is safe." This was his town and he intended to keep it safe. "Just watch your back."

"Me?" Her voice came out as a squeak.

"Tracy Good didn't have much going on in her life except work. And despite the popular idea of faceless strangers popping up out of the ether, the majority of people are killed by someone they know." He let the facts sink in.

"So you think someone in the Gatty murdered her?" Her bottom lip wobbled as she drew in a shallow breath. He didn't like the effect her lips had on his professionalism, or maybe it was the guilt eating away at his insides for wanting her the same way he'd wanted Chrissie.

Look how well that had turned out...

Defying the urge to put an arm around her shoulders, he shoved his hands into his pockets.

"Someone from the Gatty or someone from Albany Park probably killed her." Either way, both were too close to Susie and Lily for comfort. He wasn't sure when Susie's safety had become a concern for him, but he'd involved her in this mess and he'd be damned if he'd let her get hurt.

They were almost at her door when he spotted Ewan trundling along the lane in his white Ford Escort. Susie huddled deeper into his coat as she climbed the steps and entered her cottage.

Shame ate at him. The fact she hadn't locked the door when she'd gone out this morning had saved him from his second breaking-and-entering spree in twenty-four hours. He'd put her wallet back before heading up to Emily's house.

"I'll find my wallet and purse." She hooked a tendril of hair behind her ear. He left the door open, letting the cool breeze into the room as Rocket lay panting on the stoop.

The décor was plain white with hardwood floors and pale cream furniture. It was nice, neat. A big colorful Scottish landscape dominated the wall above the fireplace, but apart from that it was hard to tell anything regarding the cottage's owner. Was Susie's personality more like the splashes of color on the landscape or the cold white on the walls?

It was too late to find out.

Susie brought her jacket to the kitchen doorway, rifling through its pockets.

"It's here." She fished out her wallet and flipped through the contents. "Cash, credit cards, everything except the keycard. I must have dropped it." Worry put lines on her face that weren't there before.

Nick paced the hallway that divided the kitchen and living room. He spotted an office full of boxes, computers, air cylinders, a nice regulator/octopus rig and a drysuit hanging on the wall.

"You're a diver?" His background check had thrown that up, but he'd forgotten.

"I used to be." Her expression closed up and she turned away. "There was an accident, I got bent and I don't dive anymore."

He wanted to ask what had happened, but there was a knock on the door and Ewan poked his head in.

"Sorry to intrude, but the door was open." He nodded to Susie who smiled back at him. "I'm Detective Sergeant Ewan McKnight and you must be Dr. Cooper."

It didn't matter who Ewan was talking to, criminals, church ministers or delinquents, he treated them all with the same quiet respect that made him a favorite on the force and drew confessions out of the innocent as well as the guilty.

Nick watched Susie immediately relax, and jealousy seeped inside his mind. It didn't help that Ewan would be a good-looking guy if he dropped thirty pounds.

Jealous of Ewan? How the mighty had sunk. But Ewan was a better person than Nick would ever be.

"As we suspected, Ewan, Dr. Cooper's keycard is

missing." *Christ*. He rolled his eyes at himself. He sounded like a total wanker.

"Do you think it's related?" Ewan gave Nick a funny look, clearly wondering what was going on.

Nick shrugged. Ewan's gaze narrowed on him like the focusing of a laser and Nick turned away. "I doubt it, but we can't rule anything out at this point."

Susie hovered anxiously but he didn't have time to provide reassurance or comfort. He had work to do, including an autopsy to attend. *Dammit*. He'd figured he was done with pathologists when he'd moved from the Met's Homicide Unit. It was a pity the sick bastard who'd murdered Tracy Good hadn't read Nick's plan for a cushier life.

"I haven't traced next of kin." Ewan was unashamedly snooping around Susie's house, craning his head to peek into the kitchen. "Nice place you've got here, Dr. Cooper, if you don't mind me saying." He smiled politely. "My wife always wanted to live near the beach."

Nick's stomach clenched.

"Would you like something to drink, Sergeant?" Susie asked.

Nick turned away. She hadn't offered *him* a drink, but then it wasn't a drink he was after and they both knew it.

Ewan slanted Nick a glance, knowing him better than anyone. "We're out of time, and I think the boss is ready to go. Thanks anyway, Dr. Cooper." His wedding ring glinted as he shook Susie's hand.

"Call me Susie." She had a sweet smile that squeezed Nick's throat like a hand-fitted noose.

"Ah, Susie Q." Ewan grinned at her.

"Detective Inspector Archer called me that." A frown tugged the skin between her brows.

She hadn't called him Nick yet.

"It's a song," Ewan explained.

"Oh."

She obviously had no clue and Nick was happy to keep it that way.

"I love the way—" Ewan, the bastard, began to sing off-key but loud.

"Let's go." Nick shoved his colleague toward the door and stood in front of Susie, wanting to say something significant but coming up blank. This was goodbye. They were done. He put his hand on her shoulder and watched trepidation enter her blue-gray eyes. He slipped his fingers beneath the warm leather of his jacket and slid it from her shoulders. She looked confused for a moment and then an embarrassed flush rose up the column of her throat.

She'd forgotten she was wearing his coat.

Her scent mingled with his, the soft leather heated by beautiful woman and pure Scottish sunshine.

"Be careful, okay?" he told her.

Her eyes narrowed with an argumentative glint. "I can't treat everyone I work with as a potential murderer."

"No. But I can. Especially Professor Jake Sizemore."

Irritation darkened her eyes. "He's my boss." There was a mutinous tilt to her chin, which pissed him off.

"Two women who worked for Sizemore are dead. Even if you have to work with him, don't do anything stupid like be alone with him." He pulled his business card from his pocket, took her hand and pressed it into her resistive palm. "Call me if you need me."

Walking away, Nick wished murder hadn't found him in this safe haven. He turned on the stoop and Susie bumped into him, blinking in the bright sunlight. Trees swayed and hedges rustled in the breeze coming off the North Sea.

Nick pressed a tender kiss to her lips, taking them both by surprise. It was so brief his body complained as he strode away. He climbed into the passenger seat beside Ewan, not looking as Rocket hung his head out the back window, drooling. Nick knew exactly how he felt.

"You Can't Always Get What You Want" played on Ewan's stereo, but his colleague didn't comment. What just happened was monumental and they both knew it. Neither spoke until they were back at the station.

SUSIE WENT OVER TO LEANNE'S after lunch. It was that or drive herself nuts reliving the events of the morning. Her insides already felt like yarn in the claws of a kitten.

"Susie! Come on in." Leanne grinned and threw a hug around her shoulders. "I still can't believe you live close enough to drop by."

"I'm not interrupting, am I?" Susie looked for Dougie but couldn't see him.

Leanne waved her inside. "Don't be silly. The only time you might be interrupting, we wouldn't be answering the door." Her snort was the other side of dirty and Susie laughed. "Dougie's gone to pick up Nick's dog, who's coming to stay with us for a few days."

"How come?"

"Nick asked us to watch him while this murder investigation is in full swing. Isn't it terrible? Did you know the girl?" Leanne's hair stood on end, making her look as cute as Betty Boop. "There hasn't been a murder in St. Andrews for over a decade." Her mouth worked so fast it was hard to keep up.

Susie got gooseflesh just thinking about the murder. She grabbed Leanne's hand. "Someone used my keycard to get into the Gatty last night and it might have been the killer."

"Holy shit! How'd they get it?"

"I don't know." Susie slumped into a chair at the kitchen table and rested her forehead in her fingers. "I must have dropped it." She felt violated, and as stupid as a cement block.

"Hey, don't beat yourself up." Leanne smoothed a hand over her shoulders and then went to fill the coffeemaker. "Mistakes happen."

That was for damn sure. "That rat you sent me home with last night kissed me."

Scoop in hand, Leanne twisted to face her, eyes gleeful. "Was it fabulous? I bet he's an amazing kisser." Dimples flashed. "And don't tell Dougie I said that."

"I don't want to talk about it." Susie groaned then started laughing. "I don't want anything to do with him."

"Why not?" Leanne looked baffled.

"Because I finally figured out what I was doing wrong with all my past relationships."

"You were dating losers because subconsciously that's what you figured you deserved."

Susie looked up across the bright kitchen space and shook her head. "I hate you, you know that, don't you?"

Leanne snorted. "I'm a psychologist. You think I didn't work this out years ago?"

"And what? You couldn't fill me in?"

Leanne came over and sat beside her at the table. She took Susie's hands, which had somehow become twisted together like pretzels, and prized them apart.

"Sometimes we have to work it out for ourselves. You told me you'd done years of therapy after the rape…"

Susie flinched and shifted in her chair. "It wasn't rape."

"You were fifteen."

"It still wasn't rape. I led him on."

The memories were distinct. Her tinkling laugh and flirtatious suggestion to take a walk by the lake. His eyes unable to look away from the skimpy skirt she'd worn to tempt him, because her breasts were non-existent. She looked down. They were still non-existent.

Leanne squeezed her fingers a little too hard. "He was forty-two," she stated quietly. "Old enough to know a kid like you was off-limits."

Susie closed her eyes against the light of reason in her friend's eyes because Susie knew the truth. She'd been there, she'd led him on and everything that happened had been her fault. And now it was impossible to make it up to Clayton because he was dead.

"I thought I loved him," she admitted. A laugh came out like a sob. "I thought if I gave him what I'd heard men wanted, he'd love me back."

"For the love of God, he was *forty-two years old*, Susie!" Leanne planted her hand on her hip and raised her voice. "Would you seduce a teenager?"

"Of course not," said Susie.

"You're only in your thirties, yet you know it would be taking advantage and downright wrong to have sex with an underage kid, right?"

Susie nodded but she could never fully shrug off the responsibility, because everything had gotten so screwed up after that day.

"He knew what he was doing with a child whose parents were too busy to notice." Leanne stroked her hair. "You never dealt with it because your mother let the bastard get off."

"You can't blame her for that." Susie wiped her eyes, pulling away. She hadn't come to rehash the past. "I told her if she reported it I'd kill myself."

The memory wasn't funny, but right now it made Susie laugh.

"Oh, the drama of being a teen." Leanne rolled her eyes and Susie knew her friend understood.

"Stupid, huh?"

"Dumb as a rock," Leanne agreed. "But she could have reported him without your name being made public, she knew that."

Susie shuddered, remembering her despair during that awful time. Her brother had discovered them in the boatshed and he'd beaten the crap out of Clayton. Weeks later, when she'd realized she was pregnant, humiliation had morphed into a defiance that had gone nowhere and spiraled into depression.

"Your mother used what happened to gain political power." The passion in Leanne's voice undid Susie, and even though she tried to hold them inside, tears fell on their joined hands. "She squeezed every bit of political blood she could out of your pain. I know she's your mom, but I wouldn't vote for her if she were running against Paris Hilton."

Leanne and Darcy Cooper had despised each other on sight. And it felt good to have someone standing so firmly on Susie's side, even if Leanne didn't know the whole story.

"I'm over it. Really I am. And that's precisely why I'm *not* getting involved with Nick Archer." Susie pulled a tissue from her purse and wiped the tears from her cheeks. "I'm looking for something serious, something like you and Dougie share."

"Nick is a good man," Leanne said quietly.

"Pah—"

"But he was a fabulous kisser, wasn't he?" Leanne's eyes sparkled. "And I spoke to Patricia on the phone this morning and it seemed you weren't the only one who got a goodnight kiss. Although I think Patty got the extended version." Her eyebrows bobbled and Susie laughed.

"Aren't you the little matchmaker?" Susie stood to pour the coffee.

Leanne went over and pulled a bottle of whisky out of the cabinet. "This is Dougie's best stuff." She held up a Bowmore single malt. "Don't tell him we put it in the coffee."

There was a pause as they stared at each other, sadness tightening the edges of Leanne's eyes. "I'm not pregnant. I took a test," she explained. "I must have bought out the entire drugstore over the last six months."

"I'm sorry." Susie didn't know what else to say. "I didn't know you guys were trying for a baby."

"I didn't want to say anything, I was afraid of jinxing it. But now I think there might be something wrong with me." The petite brunette caught her lip in her teeth. She looked tired and pale. "My old sins catching up with me."

Susie boosted her smile. "Now who's holding on to adolescent drama?"

Leanne smiled but her eyes remained far away.

"Have you talked to a doctor?" Susie threw a spoonful of sugar into each mug before carrying them over to the table, where Leanne added a shot of whisky.

"Not yet, but it's been six months." Anxiety tugged at the corners of Leanne's lips.

"Six months isn't that long to try for a baby."

"But some people get pregnant the first time they have sex. It is so unfair."

Susie's hands shook. Her best friend, the super-smart psychologist, didn't even notice.

"Just give it time." Susie was surprised at the strength in her voice. The control. She'd never told anyone she'd given up her baby, signed him away without even holding him. The secret was like a vacuum sucking up her self-worth, and she didn't know if she'd ever get it back. "Have you tried taking your temperature and pinpointing the exact day of ovulation?"

"No, we've just been going at it like rabbits." She sat up straighter in her chair, stretched her arms above her head. "Tell me about the temperature thing."

"Well, I only know this because I worked with a woman in Brisbane who'd been trying for years." Susie sipped her coffee and sighed at the fabulous aroma. "Eventually she started tracking her temperature, found out exactly when she ovulated and jumped her husband frequently over the next twenty-four hours."

It sounded so easy. All you needed was a man who wanted to make babies.

"Oh God. I can see it now." Leanne's eyes lit up. "Phoning Dougie in the middle of a lecture to come home and *take me—*" she dropped her voice to a husky whisper "*—right now.*"

Gales of laughter drowned out the arrival of Dougie and Nick's big hairy dog, who did a brisk lap of the downstairs before dropping his muzzle into Susie's crotch.

"Rocket." Dougie shook his head solemnly. "Men have been murdered for less."

He whistled and the dog raced back to him, wagging his tail. Dougie took one look at their faces and jammed his brows together at the sight of his whisky bottle. "I dinnae ken what you've been gossiping about and I don't want to."

"But you will," Leanne promised, holding his gaze. "You most definitely will."

CHAPTER EIGHT

THE FIRST MURDER in St. Andrews in over a decade was being given high priority by Fife Constabulary and the local press. Thankfully there were no royalty in the town to turn a dog and pony show into a three-ringed circus. It was Sunday, but the pathologist and his assistant were both in the sterile tiled basement that housed the mortuary.

It wasn't like in the States where each corpse had a drawer to themselves. In Scotland bodies were stacked a dozen to a fridge.

Nick stared at the pale cadaver on the steel-top table. The stench of formaldehyde and bleach never quite disguised the odor of human decomposition. But it wasn't the smell he detested, though that punched you in the gut at the door and clung to your clothes and skin until you scrubbed it off. It wasn't the body parts displayed like offal in a butcher's shop. It wasn't the coarse, ugly incision, stark against smooth alabaster skin.

What Nick hated most was the knowledge that one day the body being dissected on the slab might be his. His heart gave an extra hard squeeze in protest.

Dying didn't bother him, but having some saw-wielding mortuary technician peel off his face sent a quiver of fear into his bowels. And he hated being scared. It reminded him of that terrified little kid who'd held a knife to his mother's throat all those years ago.

"There's sign of sexual activity, but difficult to say

if it was forced." Cutter glanced up from washing his hands in the old Belfast sink.

"Any semen or trace?" Nick asked.

Intelligent black eyes gleamed as Cutter nodded, drying his hands on paper towels. "I sent it to Forensics, priority." His beak of a nose jutted out from a face that was almost hairless. "Cause of death is blunt force trauma to the back of the head."

No shit, Sherlock.

Runrig belted out "Loch Lomond" on a radio perched high on a bench behind him. With help from the mortuary assistant, a girl with hair as straight as a plumb line, Cutter rolled Tracy Good onto her side and pointed to two gashes on the girl's skull.

Nick raised his eyes to the pathologist. "Hammer?"

Cutter nodded. "Possibly." His bony shoulders stabbed through his lab coat in a shrug. "Probably. I've included scale photos of the lacerations with the report."

Where was the murder weapon? Where were Tracy Good's belongings? Was this a simple case of robbery gone wrong, or something more sinister?

His boss, Superintendent Pamela Richardson, had promised him every resource as long as he nailed the killer. He and the supe had gone through Police College together, but while he'd been mired in the filth of London's organized crime, she'd been fast-tracking up the ranks at record speed. Didn't mean she was a bad copper, but she was one hell of a politician. She generally left him alone to get on with the job, but that would change if he didn't get a result. It might change if she knew who his chief suspect was.

"Her palms and knees were abraded and her clothes were covered in grass stains." Cutter laid Tracy Good back onto the table.

"From the blood splatter I'd say she was probably hit first from behind as she walked along the footpath." He demonstrated on his assistant who fell as directed. "She dropped to her hands and knees and rolled down the embankment and fell onto the beach. The killer followed, stood over her from the front and hit her again." Cutter stood before his assistant and raised his hand. "The second wound is the mirror image of the first and the second blow killed her."

The assistant stayed on the floor for a moment looking like a dead body extra on *CSI*. Then she got up and brushed off her white coat.

"It took time for her to die. At least ten minutes."

Nick closed his eyes. *Was she dying when I walked past?*

"Time of death?" His voice was croaky, but he coughed it out.

"Between midnight and one. Probably closer to one given the lack of rigor."

Shit. Nick stared at his boots. There was enough margin for error that she could have been breathing her last gasp as he passed by. Not that he could have saved her, but the idea of her dying alone bothered him. Chrissie had been alone in the water, floating around in the ocean feeding the fish. And now another of her supervisor's students had turned up dead.

"No evidence of postmortem injuries or sexual assault, although she did have ligature marks on her wrists—as if she'd been tied up—but the marks were around twenty-four hours old."

Nick went over and looked at her wrists, raised his brows. "She was seen in at work that day."

Cutter adjusted his cuffs. "Maybe she just liked being tied up during sex."

The assistant turned away and Nick didn't want to know why Cutter's cheeks turned ruddy.

"The tox screen came back negative for drugs and alcohol. No signs of a struggle or defense wounds." Cutter pursed his lips as he stared at what was left of Tracy Good.

It sounded like a surprise attack from behind.

Nick remembered the thick haar that had boiled over the edge of the sea last night, reducing visibility to only a few feet. The weapon suggested premeditation. The swift, brutal nature of the crime suggested organization.

Was Tracy's death planned? Or did someone just take advantage of a girl walking home alone late at night?

Christ, what if Susie had been working late?

He shut out that thought, kept his mind off Susie Cooper. He had no intention of seeing her again. It was time to back away from that particular explosive device. He stuffed his hands in his pockets. Preliminary police interviews suggested Tracy was a studious loner who'd recently developed an appetite for sex. Nick would bet every penny in the bank he knew who'd caused that particular conversion.

"There's no family." Which he personally thought was a blessing.

Cutter's gaze was penetrating and black. "I expect the university will take care of funeral arrangements."

They'd offered to do the same for Chrissie, even though they'd blamed her for her own death. Rage flowed through his blood and made his heart pound.

Nick bared his teeth and pointed a finger. "Do not release this body until I say so, no matter what the university says."

He stalked over to the wooden bench near the door, picked up the report Cutter had laid out. Nick took a moment to level his anger. Anger would not catch Tracy's killer. He cleared his throat. "I appreciate you doing this on your day off."

"I did it for her," Cutter said patiently. His assistant stood by his side, her glance measuring Nick.

Cutter was right, this wasn't about him or his long-dead wife. Nick let his eyes rest on the victim. Death had stolen her dignity, her beauty and her future. All he could give her back was justice.

Except justice was a fickle bitch.

Nick nodded to the pathologist and left. This time was different. Homicide was his business and Tracy Good had been murdered on his patch.

IT FELT FUNDAMENTALLY WRONG to be at work on Monday morning when a student had been murdered just thirty-six hours earlier, but Susie didn't know what else to do.

A couple of reporters were camped out on the beach like crows scenting carrion. She'd averted her eyes as she'd passed the crime-scene tape fluttering in the wind. A bored-looking uniformed cop patrolled the area. She'd taken the poor guy a cup of coffee before the lab's chief technician had interrogated her over the lost keycard. He'd eventually given her a new card, albeit reluctantly, and with such a skeptical expression on his face she figured it was her last.

Support staff ruled the world. Everyone with half a brain knew that.

She sipped her morning coffee and flinched when Jake Sizemore sat beside her, Nick Archer's warning fresh in her mind. Jake shifted in the seat, his impeccable appearance reduced to wrinkles and creases as if he'd slept in his clothes.

She put down her coffee and looked at her watch.

Her lecture wasn't until the afternoon, but it had been moved to the Bute Medical Building out of respect for the dead girl. Tracy's work spaces had been sealed off, and most of the staff and students were sitting around in a sort of stunned stupor.

There wasn't much work being done, except for Lily and Rafael, who'd spent the morning cleaning out the CT room. For some reason Rafael appeared to have cooled his hormones and had started treating Susie like a proper boss. Maybe Lily had had something to do with it, or maybe Tracy's death had given the young man a long overdue kick in the butt. It didn't matter why, as long as they could establish a platonic working relationship and she didn't have to worry about being alone with the guy.

Susie wanted to ask Jake questions about purchasing equipment for the CT room, but now didn't seem to be the time to bring it up.

"I need to organize a memorial service." Jake's eyes were fixed on nothing.

Sunlight poured through the break room, dappling the octopus motif on the floor and turning the man's skin to paste.

A swell of pity took Susie by surprise. "If I can do anything to help…" she offered her boss.

Jake nodded absently. "The police are on their way to interview everyone who knew Tracy." His tone was gruff and his hands shook as he raised a University of Texas mug to his lips.

Nick thought Jake was dangerous, but right now he just looked pathetic and old.

Susie was just about to stand when she heard the door open behind her and felt a draft of cold air wash through the foyer. Everyone swiveled to look.

It was the cops. She knew from the tightening of people's expressions and the subtle tingle of awareness spreading along her spine. A moment later Nick Archer rounded the chairs and stood directly in front of her. His lips took on a sneering twist as he looked from Jake to her, pissed she wasn't obeying his instructions, although Jake had sat next to her, dammit.

"Susie." Nick's green eyes glittered.

Jake's eyes flicked over her as if suddenly repelled, and she pressed her hands between her knees. Nick's colleague stood behind him and sent her an encouraging smile. Automatically she smiled back, feeling like a kid caught smoking behind the gym, trapped between a parent and the principal.

"You two know each other?" Jake asked.

"Not really—" Susie began.

"Not yet." Nick cut in. Marking territory to a man he believed killed his first wife.

Well gee, thanks. The warmth in her cheeks could have heated the city, but Nick's attention had already moved on. How very male.

"How've you been, Jake?" Nick's blond hair shone like a halo in the morning light.

"I can't believe *you're* in charge of this case. I'm going to put in a complaint."

One side of Nick's mouth turned up in a smile. "If you want to impede the investigation into Tracy Good's murder and waste police time, be my guest, but the only person to gain from that is Tracy's killer."

There was a collective gasp and Jake looked around the room with a flare of horror. "No. No, I don't want that. She was a lovely girl. I want to catch her murderer as much as you do."

"Right then, let's go up to your office and have a

chat. Unless you'd rather come to the station?" Nick's voice was polite, but it grated like dry chalk across slate.

Jake staggered to his feet, using Susie's shoulder for support. Nick's eyes narrowed, but Susie doubted whether Jake even realized he'd touched her. The guy was running on fumes.

"P.C. Lewis and P.C. Mosel will start interviewing everyone else in here, if that's all right? And take volunteer DNA samples from the blokes?"

Jake lost all color. He either had something to hide or a raging fear of cotton swabs. Doubt rippled along her spine, and apprehension made her shiver. What if Nick was right about Jake? What if he was a killer?

"We need to interview everyone who works here." Nick put a hand on his hip and Susie caught a glimpse of ridged stomach muscles as his shirt gaped. He glanced down and noted the direction of her gaze, and her cheeks flamed so hot she could have third-degree burns.

"Don't go anywhere, Dr. Cooper." Nick's eyes darkened. "We need to talk."

Nick recognized the route from his Saturday night break-in. Without speaking they tromped up the stairs and along the corridors, Sizemore's hoarse breathing the only human sound. They passed two doors with police tape stretched across them.

Crime scene techs had done their thing yesterday, found a billion fingerprints and enough biological trace to generate life on Mars. Nick wanted to look the rooms over, to get a feel for Tracy Good's life, but right now he wanted to have a go at Sizemore.

Nick glanced over his shoulder and Ewan quirked an eyebrow in silent accord. Guilt rolled off the professor in waves of sweat, and excitement lifted the fine hairs on Nick's nape.

He could imagine the prison doors slamming shut on this bastard. Smell the fetid air of a cell. Twelve years of waiting had led to this one perfect moment, and he intended to make sure the takedown was noisy and painful. They walked to the end of the corridor, through the brightly lit open-plan office. Three women stopped chatting as Nick entered, six eyes focused on him as if he was the Antichrist.

"Candace, can you get the detectives some coffee, please?" Jake strode to his door, finally remembering he had a pair.

Pushing Jake's buttons was something Nick had waited for a long time to do and he wasn't missing an opportunity to make the bastard bleed. Deliberately he stopped at Candace's desk and gave her a slow smile.

He took his time looking. She was long, lean and toned, with shoulder-length curly brown hair and red lipstick that gave a man all sorts of ideas. No wedding ring. Just the type of woman he normally went for. He waited in vain for some faint stirring of attraction.

"I take mine black, Candace. Please." He glanced at the other women in the office. One with short blue spiky hair and everything pierced, the other with a school teacher's gray bob. He didn't recognize either of them from when Chrissie had worked here.

"Can I get milk and two sugars, please," Ewan interrupted loudly.

Nick turned high-wattage charm on Candace. "I bet nothing much gets past you, does it, Candace?"

Her smile grew sly. "Not so much as a pimple, Detective."

"How about I take you to lunch so you can help me out with some of my routine inquiries?"

"Routine?" Candace gave a husky laugh. "There is nothing routine about me, darling." Without breaking eye contact she reached a hand to take something from someone who stood behind Ewan. Nick recognized Susie's fingers as she handed over a file.

Damn.

He leaned around Ewan and watched Susie stalk out of the office. He hated the way he reacted to Susie. He sent Candace a grin that didn't begin to reveal what he was feeling and sauntered into Jake's office. Chatting up Candace was working the case and if sex was on offer—well frickin' terrific. Get rid of the boner he'd been carrying for Susie without messing up either of their lives.

He looked out Jake's office window. Nice view in daylight. Slowly he walked the walls and stopped in front of the photograph of Chrissie and Jake on the sailing boat in South Africa.

"Nice shot." Nick didn't let his emotions slip. "Who took it?"

Jake sat behind his desk, gripping a sheaf of papers with both hands. "My daughter, Callie. She was eleven."

Eleven when Chrissie died.

Jake's other kids were a bit older. Had they known their father was cheating on their mother?

Nick leaned against a window. Jake's hands shook. Ewan took his cue and cleared his throat as Candace sashayed through the door. The woman moved like single-malt sex.

"Here's your coffee." She smiled at everyone in turn, touched the tip of her tongue to her bottom lip as she passed Nick his cup.

And it did nothing except scare the shit out of him. *Bloody hell*. He took the coffee and placed it on the window ledge. He was taking Candace to lunch because admin assistants knew everything, and it was sure to get under Jake's skin faster than a ravenous sheep tick. But he wanted to *want* her. And all he could think about was kissing a prissy blonde who acted as if she had a poker up her ass.

Ewan made sympathetic noises as he stirred sugar into his coffee. "This must be terribly distressing for you, Professor Sizemore."

This from a man who'd tended the bullet-riddled bodies of a gym full of five-year-olds following the Dunblane massacre. It didn't get any more distressing than that—unless you counted watching the woman you love die an agonizingly slow death. Respect for his fellow officer grew in direct contrast to his contempt for Sizemore.

Nick swallowed his own ego. This wasn't about him, or even Chrissie. It was about a girl named Tracy Good who had nobody else to care about her. Well, she was his now; another face to add to the gallery of dead people in his head.

"I can't believe this has happened. I can't believe Tracy is dead." Sizemore stared at his desk, his skin so pale Nick saw the network of blood vessels running beneath the surface.

He flicked a glance to Ewan to tell him to carry on.

"I'm sorry for your grief, sir, but you know we have a job to do. We need to catch Tracy's killer before he or she harms anyone else."

"The lab was her life." Jake shook his head, bit the knuckle on his index finger. "She'd never hurt anyone."

"Were you screwing her?" Nick asked.

Jake's shoulders straightened and his hands came down. "If those are the sorts of questions you want to ask, I'll call my lawyer."

Evasion. Interesting. Often it was what people didn't say, and how they didn't say it, that revealed the answers Nick was looking for.

"Come on, Jake, a guy like you? And a no-strings hottie like Tracy? It wasn't like she was married, now, was it?"

"I'm warning you—" Jake started to stand. Nick smiled and memories arced between them.

Sizemore standing over Chrissie's grave. Tears running down his cheeks, mixing with rain.

"Nick..." Dougie's warning. Too late.

Sizemore slipping on wet grass and Nick on him, pounding, pounding.

"You killed her. You fucking killed her!"

"I didn't mean for this to happen. I loved her." Sizemore straining away. His eyes rolling back in his head as Nick hit him again.

"Professor," Ewan broke in, scowling at Nick who jerked away from the memories. "We have to ask these questions. We need to know. Were you having a sexual relationship with Tracy Good?"

Sizemore's eyes flicked high right. "Depends what you call a sexual relationship," he hedged, cupping his hand over his mouth.

"The Clinton defense?" Nick put his hands on his hips knowing the man was lying. "You can do better than that."

"Can you tell me what Tracy was working on and if anyone might want to hurt her, or if she was involved with anyone else you know of?" Ewan switched directions.

Jake's head went down as he scrubbed his hands through his hair. "I don't think she was seeing anyone. I mean, she was a pretty sheltered young woman."

Until you got your hands on her, you rat-bastard.

"She was running tissue samples to estimate if sea pollution accumulated in the tissue of dogfish." Jake looked up at Ewan, making an attempt at sincerity. "She had no family, no social life, and I don't know anyone who'd want to hurt her."

"Do you mind if we take a sample of your DNA for elimination purposes?" Ewan pulled a tube out of his pocket and held out a sterile cotton bud. Jake paled but took the applicator, scraped the inside of his cheek and handed the sample back to Ewan.

"What time did you leave the Gatty on Saturday night?" Ewan wrote notes.

Jake shifted in his seat, leaned back, then forward again. "Five, maybe six o'clock in the evening. I don't remember exactly."

"And where were you between Saturday 11:00 p.m. and 1:00 a.m. Sunday morning?" Ewan's pen hovered expectantly above the paper.

Jake pinched the bridge of his nose, squeezing hard as if his eyeballs were trying to escape. "I was home in bed with my wife."

"We'll need to verify that with Mrs. Sizemore, sir."

Jake nodded, his face clenched against some unspeakable emotion.

"If you are lying about your relationship with Tracy, you know we'll find out, don't you?"

Jake's eyes darted to his bottom drawer and Nick remembered the condoms hidden there. It confirmed the sexual relationship in his mind—not that he could prove it. But Sizemore could no more keep his pants zipped than he could hop around the room on his dick.

"Did you kill her, Jake?" Nick leaned over the man's desk and got in his face. "Did she piss you off? Threaten you? Did you bash her brains out because she wouldn't go down on you anymore?"

"Is that how she died?" His voice shook.

"Did you kill her?" Nick used every bit of self-restraint not to slam the man up against the glass.

"No! No. I didn't kill Tracy!" Jake's voice was loud and shrill and he started sobbing, hiding his face against the desk as he bawled like a baby.

Nick didn't like what the signals were telling him so he turned away and stared at the beach where Tracy had been bludgeoned to death. Nothing remained—no shallow indent, no rust-colored stain, no drag trail where she'd pulled herself through the sand trying to escape her assailant. Rain and tide had washed it all away. The man behind him might be genuinely grieving but it didn't mean he hadn't been the one wielding the hammer. Nick wouldn't get anything out of him now, the guy was a wreck, and though it gave him some satisfaction to see Sizemore blubber, it wasn't quite the high he'd anticipated.

Nick turned and left the office, telling Candace he'd pick her up at twelve-thirty. He and Ewan went through the labs where Tracy worked but saw nothing of note except enough chemicals to poison half of Scotland. He left Ewan interviewing Dr. Imelda Chalmers, a gorgeous faculty member who could have doubled as a catwalk model.

No doubt about it, the Gatty was full of smart, beautiful women. Nick walked around to Susie's office, his tread heavy on the oven-baked tiles. He knocked on

Susie's door and tried the handle, surprised when he thudded up against solid oak. *Damn*. He glared at the wood, stuffed his hands in his pockets.

"Dr. Cooper has a lecture in the Bute this afternoon." The young Latino Nick had seen in the pub on Friday night came out of the aquarium behind him.

"What's your name?" Nick asked. Anger stirred inside him, shortening his patience and locking his teeth. He was pissed and ready for a fight.

"Rafael Domenici."

It was said with enough inbred arrogance that Nick knew the guy's parents were loaded and influential.

"You been interviewed regarding the murder of Tracy Good yet, Mr. Domenici?" Nick allowed his irritation to shine through his voice and the younger man grew still.

"No." Pale blue eyes narrowed but held steady.

Nick took a step closer. "Did you try it on with Tracy the same way you try it on with anybody in a skirt?"

The guy laughed, knocking Nick off his stride.

"Funny, Detective. I hear the same about you." Rafael Domenici's mouth was stretched into a smile, but Nick recognized a hardness in the depths of those young eyes.

His hands grew hot, drawing into fists. The guy hadn't answered the question and had deflected him so effectively Nick would have given him points if he hadn't wanted to smack the bastard.

But Nick wasn't so prejudiced as to develop tunnel vision about a crime. "Where were you Saturday night, sunshine?" He watched carefully for tells and lies.

"He was with me."

Nick turned and raised his brows. Lily stood in the doorway of an office, a highly decorated lab coat hang-

ing to her knees, green lace-up Dr. Martens filling the
gap from hem to floor. Her dyed-blond hair stood up
from her head, making her a foot taller than her five
foot nothing. Under the black liner and painted lips she
looked tired, but there were enough traces of her dead
sister in her features to squeeze his chest.

"You're kidding?" And now he sounded more like
an older brother than a detective.

Lily shrugged. "He was at the bar. We got talking."

Nick turned back to Rafael Domenici, letting the
young man read the threat in his eyes, biting down on
the words he wanted to say. Then he walked, leaving
Rafael and Lily alone in the corridor.

"What is his problem?" Rafael's face showed his confusion. "Why you lie?"

Lily shot him a look. "Do you *want* to be deported?"
She shrugged and tried to punch in the code to the
aquarium, but he blocked her way.

"Look." She twisted a silver hoop through one earlobe. "Nick's my brother-in-law and I may have said
some things that weren't exactly flattering about you
before Tracy was killed." Rafael's face revealed shock
at her words and she hastened to reassure him. "But I
know you're not a killer."

"How? How you know?" His brows pinched together
in a look of bewilderment.

"Because you're too busy screwing to think about
murder."

He closed his eyes and squeezed her shoulders in an
exchange that could have passed for friendship. "*Obrigado*, Lily."

CHAPTER NINE

IT WASN'T JEALOUSY. It wasn't hurt. It was white-hot rage that reverberated with every footstep as Susie pounded the path toward the harbor. She wasn't jealous of Candace, a divorcée who, according to gossip, had hit forty with the force of a psychotic Linda Hamilton taking on the Terminators. She was not going to be jealous of a woman who wore enough makeup to stucco a small ranch house and enough lipstick to paint every fire truck in Scotland.

Dammit.

Gulls screamed in the wind like storm harbingers and Susie hugged her wool blazer tight around her waist. She passed a middle-aged woman walking a toy-poodle and a younger woman whose hair whipped around her in a frazzled cloud as she pushed a screaming baby in a stroller. The baby's face was scrunched up with indignant fury.

Susie knew how he felt. She'd like to yell at Nick Archer—not that she'd ever let fly like that in public, she was too *polite.* Even the thought tasted sour on her tongue. She was sick of *polite.*

With a resigned sigh, the mother lifted the toddler out of the stroller, hugging him to her shoulder where he quieted.

A familiar pang shot through Susie and she looked away.

That could have been her if Clayton had stood by

her...but he hadn't. She'd called him to tell him she was pregnant, naïvely expecting him to ride to her rescue. A week later he married his childhood sweetheart and Susie had sunk into a depression that had lasted for more than a year. Long enough to give away the only thing that mattered.

Her fingers gripped the edge of her jacket. She'd been weak and foolish. Maybe she didn't deserve a second chance. The bony tops of her knuckles chafed in the icy breeze.

Compared to what had happened when she was a teenager, Nick Archer was an amoeba. She clanked over the metal bridge spanning the narrowest section of the harbor. Marched up stone steps, past the foundations of the Church of St. Mary on the Rock. On a whim, she cut through the entrance in the huge stone wall surrounding the ancient cathedral.

Who needed men anyway?

The grass was vivid green despite the cool temperature and, though it was way past morning, dew clung to the slender blades and soaked through the suede of her shoes. She huddled in her jacket, drew her hair back behind her ears, grateful to be out of the wind in this sheltered enclave.

And it was quiet, she realized, looking around. No tourists. The students mostly in lectures this time of day, or using the shock of the murder as an excuse to skip class and recover over coffee. This was pretty much what she was doing, Susie conceded, as well as avoiding a particularly lecherous police officer.

It felt strange to skip off in the middle of a work day, though her friend Dela would have approved. Dela was always dragging her out of the office and off on adventures, if only to man-watch on the beach. At least Dela had known how to live before she'd died.

Being a workaholic was a hard vice to break, which made her desire for a family seem ill-conceived. Men might be able to combine families with scientific careers, but women? Susie could count on one hand the number of successful women scientists who were in relationships and raising children. Gravel crunched beneath her soles as she wandered along the path. She stopped and took a breath, forcing some of the anger out of her system.

Walking these grounds, where Scottish queens had walked, sent a quiver through her blood that hummed from her toes to the tips of her ears. The sense of history was palpable. When the U.S. was being founded in 1776 on that warm Fourth of July, this cathedral had already been laid to ruins for more than two centuries. That put her life in perspective.

The tall square tower of St. Rule, the guy who'd supposedly brought the bones of St. Andrew to the town, stood solid and sure against time and man. On impulse Susie bought a token from the visitor center and climbed the narrow spiral staircase to the top, coming out into a strong northeasterly gale. She grabbed the lichen-encrusted wall and looked over the edge. Her stomach lurched.

Gravestones dotted the grass.

It gave her a little quiver to think of all those dead people down there. The emerald grass and vermillion pan-tiled roofs were the only splashes of color on an otherwise dreary day. The foundations of the cathedral ruins formed a pale cross in the grass, the spears of the East Gable pointing defiantly to the heavens. St.

Andrews might be a sleepy little town, but in medieval Scotland it had been a fulcrum of power.

Awareness swept into her core. Turning, she looked at the East Sands toward the Gatty Marine Lab and then farther along the coast toward her cottage, and it struck her...this place felt like home. The huge aching chasm that had been inside her for half a lifetime had stopped growing. Scotland felt like home in a way the Sunshine State or the Sunshine Coast never had. This was where she belonged and she knew it.

She was home, and no goddamned womanizing cop was driving her away.

Glancing at her watch, she realized she still had two hours before she gave her lecture. It wasn't that she didn't have work to do, but for once in her over-time-tabled life she didn't want to do it. She wanted to blow it off. She needed lunch, but had no appetite, so she climbed back down the stairs and started reading gravestones as she strolled toward the university library.

Newer markers mixed with old. A smaller stone caught her eye. Plain white marble. A four-month-old baby girl called Alice. She'd died March 4, 1968. Tears formed on Susie's lashes even though she blinked them away. She moved on to the next marker and her feet fused to the ground with shock. The marker was shaped like an open book, the page on the right-hand side empty and expectant like the Grim Reaper himself.

The left side was inscribed Christina Emily Archer (nee Heathcote). Beloved daughter and wife. Born January 7 1974. Died October 10 1998. "The stars are not wanted now: put out every one. Pack up the moon and dismantle the sun."

She knew the rest of the poem. "Pour away the ocean

and sweep up the wood. For nothing now can ever come to any good."

W. H. Auden.

Winter pansies bloomed purple and white in small clay pots. Blood thudded through her ears with a dull roar that seemed to slow time to a standstill. She was staring at Nick Archer's grave and he wasn't even dead yet.

Susie hadn't returned. He'd checked. Twice.

Nick phoned Candace from the car park. He was late for their lunch date and didn't think Candace was the sort of woman who appreciated being kept waiting. He'd spent a frustrating morning interviewing Gatty staff but finding nothing he didn't already know. Tracy was a hardworking student who'd recently got in touch with her inner siren.

"Gatty Marine Lab, Professor Sizemore's office."

"Ready for lunch, Candace?"

"Hmm. I'm not sure I'm hungry anymore."

"Well I'm ravenous." His voice was gruff, more from shame than desire. He'd conned drug lords and skin-heads, but lying didn't come as easily as it used to. "I really need to ask you some questions about Tracy."

"Okay, I'll be right down."

Whatever else, he'd gotten the impression Candace was damn good at her job. Thirty seconds later she was out the door striding across the tarmac in knife-edge stiletto boots.

They went to a new bistro, Table for Two, facing the Tron in the heart of Market Street. Nick ordered steak as Candace danced a finger around the rim of her wine-glass.

"How well did you know Tracy?" Nick slanted her a glance as her knee brushed his. Candace shrugged slender shoulders, making her breasts bounce and sending up a whiff of flowery perfume in his direction. She was beautiful, and Nick wished he could react to that beauty with more than his intellect. Her skirt had ridden up far enough to give him an expansive view of smooth creamy thigh and...*nothing*. Absolutely nothing.

"I didn't know her as well as some of the other students." She picked at a bread roll, crumbs scattering across her plate as she flashed him an embarrassed look. "I tend to mother some of them, I suppose. Try to keep them from blowing the simple things like turning up at a reasonable hour, turning in reports on time, that sort of thing."

She frowned, staring off into space. "Tracy didn't need that." She took a swallow of white wine. Licked her lips. "She was a model student."

She shot him a hooded look that suggested she might reveal something useful and Nick leaned closer.

"I suppose she came off a bit cold really. I think she wanted to make friends, but she didn't know how."

The food arrived, the smell of it stirring his empty stomach and reminding him he'd forgotten to eat breakfast. Again.

"She used sex to make friends," Nick ventured. He had a bite of steak and nearly groaned it was so good.

"I'm not the moral judge or jury." She looked him squarely in the eye, her blue gaze open and honest. "I like sex and I'm not shy about making moves on men, but..." She broke off and stabbed her fork into her pasta, dissatisfaction twisting her lips and stiffening her shoulders.

"But she was screwing the boss and it made things awkward at work?" Nick finished for her.

"Tracy had sex with at least three students in the

department that *I* know of." Candace swallowed a mouthful of spaghetti and used the time to organize her thoughts. "Jake isn't really a bad man," she said finally.

"Did you ever do him?" Nick asked with a sly half grin. Her eyes bugged so wide Nick thought she was choking.

"God, no!" She sputtered and knocked back a healthy measure of wine. "My ex ran off with his secretary." She shook her head and the look she gave Nick summed up everything she thought about men in general. "I don't shag married men and I don't have sex with the boss."

"He ever ask you?" Nick asked.

"What do you think?" Her smile was bright and slow, her eyes sliding over his body, which remained stubbornly indifferent.

"A woman who looks as good as you do? Damn right he did." Nick pasted on a smile, irritated because on the surface lies came so easily, and yet underneath he was drowning. He took a long swallow of water, closed his eyes. Susie's stiff-backed image floated into his mind, and memories of the sweet kiss they'd shared flickered along his nerves.

She was better off without him.

His fist squeezed in his lap. This was bullshit. He didn't want to be here, he didn't want to hurt Susie—or Candace for that matter, who seemed like a nice woman. Christ, Candace had already told him almost everything he needed to know. Sitting straighter in his chair, he took out his notebook. "I'll need the names of Tracy Good's lovers."

She told him the names and he wrote everything in

his illegible handwriting, jolting as she slipped a warm hand onto his thigh.

"So…?" Candace smiled. "You're not married and you're not my boss." She was attractive and available and definitely a no-strings encounter. "My place is just around the corner…"

And there on cue was Susie Cooper ambling out the Mercat Wynd and crossing the cobbles of Market Street.

Sweat beaded his brow. God, he wanted to have sex and his body finally reacted, but it wasn't to Candace. Fan-bloody-tastic. Slowly he took Candace's hand from his thigh and gave her fingers a quick press before letting go.

"I'm flattered." He really was. He managed a practiced smile that was much cooler than she deserved, and stood and gathered his jacket off the back of his chair. "Unfortunately, I have got to get back to the station."

"Later then?" Confusion brought high color to her cheeks, but then her eyes filled with understanding.

"I'll be in touch." The words tasted bitter on his tongue because he meant about the investigation, but it sounded like a brush off. Avoiding eye contact, he left enough money on the table to cover the bill and headed out into the sunshine.

Susie ducked into Bonkers, a gift shop on the corner of Market and Church Street that had been a favorite haunt of Chrissie's. Nick hadn't been inside in years. Even the smell fueled memories of Chrissie trying to turn their small rented flat into a home.

Nick watched Susie through the huge plate-glass windows that were stuffed with carved puffins and oversized ceramic plates painted with cats. Susie frowned, clearly undecided whether to buy a red cat plate or a blue cat plate.

She was pretty, biting her lip and trying to decide about something so inane.

Abruptly she looked up and caught him staring. She froze, looking angry before pulling her bag higher up her shoulder and marching out of the shop to stand directly in front of him, checking her watch. He was curious as to what was going to come out of her mouth.

"Sorry I couldn't wait for you to finish your interviews, Detective, but I had work to do."

Cold, polite, brittle.

Ah.

"So I see." Nick jerked his chin at the sparkling interior of Bonkers and let his irritation show. "Shopping. Much more important than a murder investigation."

"If you want to criticize my work ethic why don't you come by the lab at 10 p.m. some night, or maybe on the weekend, when I'm usually in?" Her perfect eyebrows arched and her smile drove spikes into his chest. The exterior might be cool, but fire burned within. She turned and walked away up Church Street, brushing him off as if he was begging for change.

He caught up with her. "I need to ask you some questions about Tracy Good."

She swept a hand through her hair, spun on her heel and stared at him, incredulous.

"No. No, you don't." Her face froze into severe lines, pinched lips, shadowed eyes. "You're playing with me and I don't like it."

It was the hurt in her voice that nailed him. She began hurrying away, but he wasn't ready to let go yet so he fell into step beside her.

"Come on, Susie Q." Hadn't he just refused wild monkey sex with a woman who looked as if she was an Olympic athlete at the sport? Exasperated, he touched her arm, deepened his voice to raw honey. "You like it just fine."

She shook him off with a furious jerk of her hand.

"Stop calling me that ridiculous name. Stop touching me and stop following me!" Fury vibrated through her voice like electricity through a live wire. "My life is none of your business. Last time I saw you, you were hitting on another delusional female you'd just met. Do I look *stupid?*"

People veered around them on the pavement. Susie lowered her voice. "Pretending I don't know what you are? Empty? Unfeeling? Knowing you don't love me, that you'll *never* love anyone but your dead wife?"

Astonishment paralyzed every muscle in his body. Temper bobbed to the surfaced but he couldn't grab hold of it. She shoved past him and he let her go. He swallowed and blinked away moisture that the wind had stirred up in his eyes.

CHAPTER TEN

THE PRESS, IN ADDITION TO Nick Archer, had destroyed her day.

Back in the Gatty Susie punched in the key-code to the aquarium, the sweet rancid smell of overripe seaweed besieging her senses. Moist air clung to her skin, and the noise of rushing water and fizzing air stones finally drowned out the shrill demand of the telephone, which hadn't stopped ringing all afternoon.

For a moment she leaned against a mustard-yellow tank. Something darted away inside, the vibrations zinging along the bones in her arm. She went upstairs where she had two octopi she needed to feed before she went home.

She unlocked the padlocks and opened the lids. Three hundred and seventy million years of boneless evolution made octopods the Houdinis of the animal world. She fed them fresh shrimp, one at a time, and let their gentle caresses soothe her shattered calm.

Susie checked the temperature of the water. Forty-six degrees Fahrenheit, eight degrees Celsius. Too chilly for cephalopod sex, which was why she needed a CT room.

The female octopus watched from a huge clay pot, shells and stones arranged over the entrance of her den like a garden. A smaller male sat in the opposite tank, his eyes on the female, wary but fascinated.

Unlike most animals, except humans, octopods had face-to-face sex. It had nothing to do with anthropomorphic love. But cannibalism was rife once the female got the sac of sperm she needed from the male.

Maybe that's what Susie needed? A sperm donor. A baby without the hassle of a man. It sounded too good to be true. Susie frowned thoughtfully.

Her mother would freak.

Susie locked the tanks, made her way back to her office. Surely it couldn't be that hard to find a nice guy to settle down with? Except…you never knew how long you had. Tracy Good had her life stolen by violence, Dela by an arterial gas embolism. Life was precious and there were no guarantees. Maybe it was time for plan B?

NICK PULLED UP IN FRONT of Jake and Judy Sizemore's detached Victorian on the outskirts of Anstruther. The door and window trims were painted British Racing green, matching the cast-iron railing that topped a low stone wall out front. The knocker was a big brass affair and Nick pounded the crap out of it.

Susie Cooper could go to hell.

He'd left Ewan going through witness statements at the station while a couple of uniforms finished canvassing Albany Park residents and checking Tracy's phone and email records. Nick had pulled her bank statements earlier and there was nothing of interest except a student bursary which was hardly enough to feed a sparrow. His boss was getting antsy.

He knocked again, shifted his weight from one foot to the other when he heard a noise from inside the house. Excitement heightened his senses. He was so damn close. The door opened and revealed a young woman, barefoot, in yoga pants and a sports bra.

"Is your mother in?" Nick frowned at what must be

Jake's youngest daughter. This was the kid who'd taken the picture of Chrissie that hung on Jake's office wall. She had streaked mousey brown hair, a pretty oval face and huge eyes that were slightly disconcerting.

"Hang on, I'll see."

A second woman with an American accent shouted from another room. "Who is it, Callie?"

"Tell your mother Detective Inspector Nick Archer wants a few minutes of her time, aye?"

The girl raised her eyebrows, indefinable emotion moving through her blue eyes. She knew who he was. She turned back inside, hugging the door and not letting him in. "Mom, it's the police."

A woman strode down the hallway, drying her hands on a dishtowel as she scowled at Nick. "You." Her stance was rigid, her gray hair frazzled and pulled back into a thick ponytail.

He tipped his head, kept his eyes fastened on hers. "Mrs. Sizemore."

"You weren't so quick when the garden shed was vandalized last week, were you? Didn't see any cops on the doorstep then, did we?" Her eyes were hard blue, her body shaking with what he had to assume was fury.

"Can I come in?" He raised his eyebrows and kept his tone neutral. Murder was hardly in the same league as trashing the garden shed. Judy Sizemore looked at her daughter and some silent communication passed between them. Callie opened the door and stood back.

He wondered what she remembered about Chrissie's death. Did she know her father screwed everything he could get a hold of?

Judy opened a door on her left and gestured for him to go ahead of her. It was a formal sitting room, full of old Victorian furniture that looked as if no one ever used it. Judy whispered something to Callie and closed the door on her daughter.

"Must be weird growing up with a kid who has a different accent to you." Nick studied Judy's unfriendly eyes and her closed-off body language, trying to put her at ease.

She put a hand on her hip, her practical wristwatch and wedding band her only adornments.

"She was born in the States but doesn't remember it. Should I tell her not to be like the other kids so they can tease her because she isn't from here and doesn't fit in?" The words were charged with bitterness. She hugged her waist, leaned back against the panel door. "I don't fight what I can't change."

Nick looked in her eyes and recognized truth. She wasn't just referring to her daughter's accent. He wandered around the room, picked up a glass perfume bottle shaped like a dolphin. "Did you hear another of your husband's students is dead?"

"You make it sound like they're stacking up, Detective, and how that must please you."

He turned and looked at her, always surprised by the lack of value some people placed on human life. There were gangland bosses who were more empathetic.

"Two young women are *dead*, Mrs. Sizemore. Nothing could please me less." He resumed his pacing and stared at a glass cabinet full of knickknacks. Why did some people feel the need to hoard stuff from the past when all it did was bury him alive?

He turned and noted her battle-ready stance. "Where were you between 8 and 9 p.m. on Saturday night?"

Her eyebrows knit. "Eight and nine? I thought…"

Nick smiled and her expression turned to loathing.

"I guess you've spoken to your husband then. Got

your alibis sorted?" He walked around the room and ran his finger across the mantelpiece of the fireplace, leaving a light streak through the dust.

"Look, Jake went to work, but when he got home we stayed in. Ate dinner, watched TV and went to bed." She shifted to a defensive pose. "He didn't go anywhere that night."

And even if he'd murdered a dozen students, she'd stand by her man. Why? "Do you and your husband still have sex, Mrs. Sizemore?"

Her nostrils flared. "That is none of your damned business."

"Did you know Chrissie was pregnant with Jake's child when she died?"

A flash of hurt crossed her face before she hid her reaction. "Says you."

He nodded. "That's right." And it still felt like a knife in his heart.

He'd give anything to go back and change things, to make his marriage work, but there was no way to turn back time or undo death. The hope of justice was all he had now. He went to the door, knowing he'd get nothing from Judy. "I think you must be a hell of a wife to support a man who can't keep his dick out of other women."

A thousand emotions battled on her face. "And you must be a hell of a husband to chase an imaginary killer for a wife who didn't even want him."

Nick smiled, let the bitterness swell inside his mouth. "I *was* a hell of a husband. But you know what? Chrissie's death isn't part of this investigation, but Tracy Good's sex life is."

He let the words sink in. Let them inflict pain. He pulled out papers from his jacket, handed Judy a copy.

"We have a warrant to search the premises for anything resembling a murder weapon."

The sound of the door knocker thudded through the house.

Blood leached from Judy's skin as her hands grasped the air. "You son of a bitch."

Nick laughed. "You got that right." Then he let the other officers in the door.

SUSIE GLANCED UNEASILY at the clouds racing across the inky sky. Struggling to open the main Gatty door, she used her knee to balance a box of papers. She just wanted to get home. The effort of acting normal all day had left her exhausted. The only good thing that had happened today was she'd been invited to write a review article for the *Journal of Shellfish Research.*

"I get that for you, Dr. Cooper." Rafael Domenici pushed on the door above her head and scooped the box off her knee.

"Thanks." She eyed him with caution.

His expression was one of polite deference. No lustfulness. No puppy dog eyes. No limpid stares. She sighed. One less problem to deal with in an over-complicated life.

"Call me Susie. Dr. Cooper makes me feel about a hundred years old." Once they were outside she held out her arms for the box, but Rafael shook his head.

"I carry to your car." He wore only a T-shirt despite the frigid wind. "I wish to talk to you, *sim?*"

Apprehension shimmered over Susie's flesh and gave her goose bumps. A murder had been committed here just a few nights ago, and what did she really know about Rafael Domenici? Only that he was young, good-looking and shifted his demeanor with octopus-like dexterity.

"I want to apologize for my behavior when I arrived." Rafael used perfect English, suggesting he'd been practicing the words.

They started walking. Susie was relieved she'd parked on the embankment overlooking the beach, next to a campervan that was aglow with light as a middle-aged couple prepared supper.

Rafael shot her a hesitant look when she remained quiet. "I come from a powerful family in Brazil, *sim?* Not as powerful as yours perhaps, but..." When he shrugged, young muscles bunched. "I no try very hard to get what I want."

"Especially women." Her lips quirked because he actually blushed.

"*Sim.*" He nodded slowly as they walked toward her car. "Especially women."

The incessant beat of waves pulsed through the night. "But I no want to get a doctorate like that." A fervent light entered his eyes. "I want to earn it."

Susie recognized that look, the desire to be judged on merit rather than on your family's fortune. Maybe she understood Rafael Domenici better than she'd thought.

"I'll make you earn it, Rafael," she promised.

He smiled, looking a bit embarrassed. "*Obrigado,* Dr. Cooper." He shifted the box to the other arm and held out his hand. "Susie."

Susie shook his hand, satisfied they could work together now they'd got sex and politics out of the way. She inserted the key into the trunk of her car, frowned because she must have left it open. Annoyed with herself, she lowered the tailgate and felt the moisture in her mouth evaporate. Rafael started to lower the box onto the black vinyl, but she flung her arm across his chest. "Stop!"

A rusty-looking hammer she'd never seen before and a canvas bag she recognized lay in the trunk of her car. The bag belonged to Tracy Good.

Forty-five minutes later Susie sat on a bench and watched Nick and a uniformed cop load her Mini onto a flatbed truck to be taken so it could be processed for evidence.

Why would a killer put that stuff in *her* trunk? She rarely used it, hadn't opened it in at least a week. The chill penetrated her clothes and her teeth chattered. She didn't resist when Rafael wrapped his arm around her in an effort to keep her warm.

His cigarette smoke ribboned through the night air, but for once it didn't bother her. The heavy box of papers lay at her feet, the breeze rolling the top sheet back and forth in time to the waves that churned on the beach.

Nick approached and Rafael removed his arm and climbed to his feet. He crushed his cigarette beneath his heel before picking it up and flicking it into a nearby trashcan.

"May I go?" Susie had hoped to never see Nick Archer again, and less than seven hours later, here he was.

"*You* can go." He pointed to Rafael, who looked more than willing to abandon her. "I need a word with Dr. Cooper."

When Rafael was out of sight, Nick took his spot on the bench and Susie was suddenly hyperaware of the space she occupied, the limits of her body redefined by his presence. Nick rubbed his hand over his face, squeezing his eyes shut as if his head hurt. Murder investigations must be hell.

"We have a problem, Dr. Cooper."

A girl had died so she swallowed any obvious retort. She'd had a lousy day, most of it due to him. She lifted an eyebrow, waiting for him to continue.

"I handled things badly, earlier." He leaned forward, propped his elbows on his knees and looked at her. His expression softened. "I took Candace to lunch to push Jake's buttons."

"Oh, please!" She snorted and rolled her eyes.

"And," he said, "to try and stop this thing that's growing between us."

"There is no *thing*." She raised her face to the sky. Hell, she might be hiding it, but it hurt. What the hell was so wrong with her anyway?

"I deliberately tried to drive you away."

"I get it. It worked. Believe me, if there was a thing, you killed it." Her breath came out in a cloud of vapor. She was frozen, tired and miserable. She deserved a break. Dela's death still haunted her dreams; she sure as hell didn't need more grief.

"Because I like you."

So what? Was she supposed to be grateful? She glared at him, holding back emotions, keeping them closed down tight so they didn't escape and make things even worse than they already were.

"I don't want a relationship." Nick's voice was soft in the darkness. "And I don't want to hurt you."

He looked repentant because they both knew he would hurt her if she gave him half a chance. Rejection smarted inside her chest like a wasp stinging her heart. What was so awful about her that men contemplated leaving before they even began a relationship?

"It's not even an issue so forget it." Her throat ached with the effort to force out the blasé sentiment.

Something vulnerable flickered in his eyes, then it was gone and emotions she didn't want to recognize shone in those green depths. Desire, resentment, frustration. Secretly, she felt a measure of satisfaction knowing she affected him as strongly as he affected her.

"I was bloody furious with you this afternoon. Those things you said…" He looked out at the white-crested waves just visible in the darkness. "Maybe you were right. Maybe I am empty and unfeeling…" But his eyes told a different story.

Susie could feel herself weakening, could feel the hot anger that had sustained her since she'd seen him flirting with Candace cooling into something as insubstantial as ash.

Nick rubbed his fingers into his eye sockets. "Anyway, none of that matters anymore because now I'm worried some nutter has it in for you."

What? She opened her mouth to speak but nothing came out. No one had it in for her. She hadn't been here long enough to irritate anyone that badly.

Nick shoved his hands into the pockets of his leather jacket and leaned back against the bench. One side of his mouth kicked into a grimace. "Whoever killed Tracy Good left her possessions and what is most probably the murder weapon in your car." The worry lines around his eyes deepened. "That was a conscious decision."

Her fingernails bit into the wooden bench. "It was just coincidence. Nothing more."

"What if it wasn't?" Nick's eyes held a glint of stubbornness. "You can't stay on your own tonight, Susie. You might be in danger."

"Come on. That's crazy." She forced a laugh.

"A young woman was beaten to death right here on this path." He nodded to the tarmac just yards from where they sat. "So what's crazy is you carrying on like Alice in Wonderland just because it doesn't suit your schedule."

God, he was infuriating.

"Why don't you stay the night with Leanne?" His eyes were bloodshot, probably from exhaustion, but he still looked too damn good for her liking.

She took a deep breath, leaned over to pick up the box of papers.

Nick took it from her, holding her gaze. "I'd stay at your place, but I need to go over the evidence we found in your car."

"No way." She shook her head. "You and I are never going to happen, Archer."

"Hey, I never said anything about *you and I*, Susie Q. I'm just concerned about your safety." But the spark in his eye was sharper than friendship or duty.

She regretted saying anything at all. She was a challenge now. She should have kept her mouth shut.

"Anyway, we're both mature, unattached adults. What are you so afraid of?"

What was *she* so afraid of? She wasn't the one who'd led him on and used another woman to try and drive him away. But she was too tired for anything except truth.

"I'm not a one-night-stand kind of girl, Nick." She licked her dry lips. She didn't want him in her life and possibly leaving scratch marks. "I want to settle down, get married and raise babies."

He shifted the box and his smile sent a shiver from

her scalp to her toes. "Have you found the person you intend to marry and have babies with yet?"

She held his gaze. "Nope."

He caught her chin and brushed her bottom lip with his thumb, making her pulse jump. "Well, when you do, let me know and I'll back off."

"I want you to back off now."

He stepped closer. "Do you? Or are you just saying that because you're scared it'll be the best sex you've ever had?"

The dare in his eyes should have irritated her, but the gleam of excitement matched the one she hid. The lure of him was instinctive and irrational. He was pushy, dictatorial and annoying, and she wanted to deny the attraction, but she wasn't that good a liar.

Nick grinned and began to walk toward his car. "One of these days you're going to admit you're attracted—"

"When hell freezes over."

"Temperature is dropping. The devil's wearing thermals."

Susie couldn't help it, she laughed.

The car was jostled by gale-force winds sweeping across barren fields. Nick forced thoughts of sex out of his mind, exhaled a breath and pushed back in his seat, wondering who the murderer was.

Susie had agreed to stay over at Leanne's, but needed her *stuff*. It was a concession that he knew he was lucky to get.

Dealing with Susie Cooper distracted the crap out of him, which was not what he needed in the middle of a major investigation. But she was involved because he'd driven her car to the scene of a murder. Protecting people was part of the job. Death wasn't an abstract image for him. It was a grim, brutal reality. So it was natural to worry about Susie's safety, especially after the way he'd failed to protect Chrissie. But the fear plucking his nerves, making him sweat, felt strange and unfamiliar.

Why would the killer leave evidence in Susie's car and when had the bastard put it there? The same night of the murder—or later?

Jake Sizemore had an alibi for the night Tracy was killed, albeit a weak one. Nick couldn't touch the bastard until he could link the guy with either motive or opportunity. The murder weapon hadn't been found in Jake's house, nor any blood on Jake's clothes, shoes or in his car. They'd also searched the rooms of the three students named on Candace's list of Tracy's rumored lovers. Two had rock-solid alibis—they were OTC and had spent the weekend on exercise near Inverness. Ewan was chasing down the alibi of the third. Nick wasn't about to let prejudice blind him to the possibility there was another killer out there with some other reason to cave in Tracy Good's skull.

He had a request in to the Brazilian authorities regarding Rafael Domenici's background. He didn't trust the little prick. DNA was due back by the end of the week. It was a miracle to get it done that fast.

A fox dove across the road and Nick slammed on the brakes, narrowly missing its bushy tail. Susie grabbed the dashboard and gazed after the animal as it was swallowed by darkness. His pulse pounded. His palms felt slick.

"That was close." He blew out a breath. They exchanged a relieved glance, both glad not to have to deal with more blood or death. He turned down the lane to Susie's cottage and noticed every light in the Heathcotes' cottage was blazing.

"What's going on?"

Susie leaned forward in her seat. "I have no idea."

"Hold on." Nick floored the accelerator along the lane. Susie grabbed the handle above the door but didn't balk. He slid the car to a stop outside Emily's cottage and jumped out.

"Stay there." He pointed a finger at Susie who frowned at him as he ran to the front door. He should have saved his breath because she was right beside him a moment later.

"Emily! Lily!" He raised his voice so it boomed out over the fields. Nothing. He strode into the house, did a quick search, including the spare room that always gave him the creeps.

Coming back into the kitchen he noticed a saucepan on the stove that had boiled over, a burnt rusty stain on the side of the pan. The burner was off but a cremated smell of burnt milk saturated the air.

"Where are they?" Susie clutched her coat to her chest.

He strode outside and shouted again, caught the whisper of a reply before it was dragged away on the blustery wind. He grabbed a flashlight from the boot of his car and snagged Susie's hand because he didn't want to lose sight of her until he knew exactly what was going on. They set off through the marram grass.

A voice called out again.

Was that Lily?

The loose sand shifted under his boots, making it awkward to run. They burst out onto the beach and he caught Susie as she slid down the last steep dune. It was dark, the tide out, the moon hidden behind clouds that billowed and raced around the world.

"There!" Susie pointed to the right, toward the water,

and he could just make out two figures struggling in the surf.

Thrusting the flashlight into Susie's hands he took off at a run. Jesus Christ. As he got closer he realized it wasn't someone being bludgeoned to death. It was Lily trying to haul her mother out of the sea, but Emily was fighting her off.

He wished he couldn't hear what she was saying.

"Let go of me! She's out there. I have to get Christina. I have to save Christina!"

The water stabbed his skin like a thousand needles as he splashed into the surf. Grabbing Emily's hand he yanked her toward him, but she staggered to her knees, his grip slipping on her wet skin. Waves whipped around him.

"Em! Come on, get out of the water."

She gaped as if she'd never seen him before, then her eyes cleared and recognition flared.

"Nick. Nick! Thank God!" The desperation in her eyes nearly kicked out his knees. "You have to help me. Christina's in the water, but I can't find her. She's in the water! Can't you *hear* her?"

He exchanged a horrified glance with Lily, who was shivering violently, makeup tracking down her face like black tears.

"Chrissie's dead." Nick held his mother-in-law's unfocused gaze, felt a spasm of shame so keen it stole his breath. He had to get her out of here. "Come on. Let's get you home safe."

She struggled as he tugged on her hand, and looked toward the ocean with frustration. "But I can't find her! I can't *save* her!" She started crying then, ripping out Nick's heart.

"I couldn't either, Em. She's gone." Silently, he

cursed himself for not hanging on to his marriage when things got tough. For not fighting for the woman he loved.

He dragged Emily out of the water, engulfed her soaking wet body in a hard squeeze. Then he tore off his jacket and wrapped it around the old woman's shoulders. Each wracking sob told him Chrissie's death was as fresh today as it had been twelve years ago. She didn't deserve this. Jake Sizemore was a miserable bastard who deserved more than a few years in jail.

Susie gave her coat to Lily and encouraged her up the beach. It was freezing and Susie was shivering in just her cotton blouse. Nothing he could do about that until they got back to the cottage. At least she was dry.

Emily clung to his arms, making it hard to progress up the beach. She was too heavy to carry and too fragile to drag. His jeans were damp, his testicles chaffed, boots waterlogged. At least the wool jumper he was wearing wasn't completely drenched. Emily's silver hair was plastered to her face, her lips tinged blue. He stripped off his sweater, took the jacket from her shoulders and pulled the sweater over the thin nightdress the old woman was wearing. Then he draped the jacket around her again and propelled her up the beach. They had to get her out of those wet things before she caught hypothermia.

Susie urged Lily into the house, turned around to see if Nick had managed to get Emily along the path yet.

There. He was just coming.

Emily was a mess. Lily collapsed onto one of the kitchen chairs, shaking uncontrollably. Susie was freezing and she hadn't even gotten wet.

Remembering basic first aid, Susie went through the door into the main part of the house, tried a couple of doors before she found the bathroom. She knelt to put the stopper in the tub and blasted in the hot water, adjusting the taps so the temperature wasn't scalding. Steam swirled and her pounding heart reminded her of another time, another emergency. She squeezed her eyes shut, remembered sealing Dela's lips and blowing life into her friend's wounded lungs. She remembered how their bodies had rolled beneath the surface of the ocean with each frantic breath.

She blinked as Nick entered the room. His eyes were viridian in a chalk-white face. He put a hand on the small of her back as she bent over the tub, a small connection that fused her bones with unexpected warmth.

"Thanks." He nodded at the bath. "Lily is getting Emily undressed. I'm going to call the quack." And then he was gone.

Feet shuffled in behind her as Lily maneuvered her mother sideways beside the tub.

"Thanks, Dr. Cooper. I'll take it from here." Teeth chattering from cold, Lily looked uncomfortable for the first time in their acquaintance.

Susie tried to reassure her. "What happened to calling me Susie?"

A sad twitch touched Lily's lips. Her leather pants were ruined and she was huddled inside Susie's wool blazer. Emily leaned heavily on her daughter's shoulder, her expression slack.

"The most important thing is getting your mother better." The small bathroom didn't give them much space to maneuver. "You get out of those wet clothes," Susie told Lily. "I'll get your mom into the tub while you get dry. Then you can come back and be with her."

Lily hesitated, but Susie was already helping Emily out of her dressing gown. "Go on."

Susie got Emily into the tub without too much hassle, though the older woman's movements were stiff from cold. Once she was submerged in the warm water Emily closed her eyes. Susie pulled the shower curtain across so she had privacy if Nick barged in.

Suddenly Emily grabbed her hand in a strong grip. "Did you see her?"

Alarm shot through Susie, making her jolt. "Who?"

"Christina. I heard her, but I couldn't see her..." Tears welled up in the misty blue depths and spread over her weathered cheeks. "Mothers shouldn't lose their babies."

Emotion clutched Susie's throat. She gripped the old woman's hand so hard she felt the bones shift. "No, they shouldn't." She climbed to her feet and turned away. A mother's grief was a terrible burden to witness.

At the door she found Nick hovering with two hot drinks. She took a mug to Emily, placed it on the side of the tub. Nick waited in the hall and handed her the second mug. Coffee. She drank quickly, savoring the warmth that eased her throat and thawed her insides. Emily seemed to be suffering from some sort of dementia, whether brought on by sorrow or age, she didn't know.

"Here's your jacket, sorry it's wet." Lily came out of her bedroom and thrust a black wool sweater at Susie along with her damp coat. Handing the mug to Nick, she pulled the sweater over her head, welcoming the warmth. She hooked her jacket over one arm and took the mug back, Lily squeezing past them into the bathroom and closing the door.

Nick stared after Lily. There was a haunted light in his eyes that made Susie ache in sympathy.

"What do you think happened?" Susie whispered.

He shrugged. "The anniversary of Chrissie's death and this new murder...it must have driven her over the edge." He turned away and made his way to the kitchen.

Susie followed, noticing he wore dry jeans and a dry shirt. She frowned. "How d'you get dry?"

"I keep a spare set of clothes in the back of the car just in case." When he saw her face he laughed and tapped her on the nose. "For diving and work, not because I might get lucky. You have a dirty mind, Susie Cooper." His grin told her he was the one with the dirty mind. She was just duly suspicious.

She opened her mouth to defend herself, but with one hand low on her back, he drew her toward him and swept his tongue into her mouth, igniting some basic need. Even though she'd denied it, there was a pull deep inside her that wanted this. He tasted like coffee and passion as she kissed him back. The muscles of his chest were solid against her breasts, the sensation of dark and wicked seduction made her muscles tremble and her bones grow weak.

He lifted her up, and she hooked her legs around his hips, hot needy blood rushing through her veins and arousing her flesh. She couldn't get close enough even as she strained against him and he ground against her.

There was a knock on the door and they sprang apart like guilty teens. His eyes slitted in narrow assessment as a man entered the house.

"Dr. Cummings?" At the doctor's nod, Nick let her go. "Patient's in the bathroom. This way."

Susie's cheeks grew hot. She stood for a little while, flushed and disconcerted by the staggering sensations whirling through her mind. Burnt milk blackened the ceramic stovetop so she began clearing up the mess, leaving the pan to soak in a sink full of detergent.

Suddenly she felt ridiculous. Why was she waiting for Nick to come back? After she'd told him she wanted nothing to do with him and then virtually inhaled him the first time he touched her? She closed her eyes, amazed at her own weakness and stupidity.

Her home was a few hundred yards down the lane and she was invading the Heathcotes' privacy during a difficult time. There was no reason for her to stay. No murderer lay waiting under her bed. Whoever it was had used the opportunity of finding her trunk unlocked to get rid of the murder weapon.

Susie let herself out of the kitchen door, grabbed her box of papers from the back seat of Nick's car. Maybe Tracy Good's killer had wanted the police to find the evidence. If they didn't, they'd have dropped it off the end of the nearby pier.

So what was the problem? She'd done them a favor.

Checking her keys and cell phone, she hefted the box higher in her arms and started down the uneven gravel road. Had she really just kissed the heck out of Nick Archer? Despite all the warnings she'd given herself? She could not afford to get involved with that man. She would not spiral into a relationship with no future, not when she'd finally begun to understand exactly what it was she wanted out of life.

The wind had dropped and the clouds had cleared, revealing a moon that sailed overhead like a beacon guiding her home. The waves pulsed on the shore, but gently now, the frenetic energy dampened into a calm rhythmic tumble.

An owl hooted, sending a shiver across her skin. But as she reached the edge of her driveway the security lights came on, blinding her and reassuring her that nobody lurked in the shadows. She sighed. Maybe she should get a big hairy dog like Nick had, but she worked long hours and traveled a lot. And if she didn't have time for a dog, could she really fool herself that she had time for a child?

The adrenaline dump in her system had burned off and she felt exhausted by the events of the evening. Letting herself into the cottage, she locked the door behind her and placed the box of papers on the floor. Tomorrow a guy was coming to install an alarm that would be linked directly to a security firm. Because the cottage was so remote she'd intended to get one anyway. Knowing there was a killer in the area had just moved it up on her agenda.

Flicking on the light switch, she picked up her mail. Found nothing except bills and flyers. She threw them on the side table in the hall, picked up the box and walked through to the spare bedroom she'd set up as an office. Drysuits, octopus rigs, fins, cylinders, and dive computers took up half the space. She didn't know why she hadn't sold it all in Australia because there was no way she'd ever dive again, but maybe selling it would be an admission of failure and she wasn't ready to go there yet. She'd even had the air cylinders filled as soon as she'd arrived, out of habit, out of a cold desperate need to pretend she was the same person she'd been before Dela had died.

She dumped the papers on her desk, but decided tenthirty at night was too late to start writing a review article. There was no lecture tomorrow anyway, so she could work at home while waiting for the alarm guy to show up. Unsettled by the events of the night, she roamed from room to room, pretending not to check for would-be killers in the closets.

Emily hadn't seemed mentally unstable during their

earlier conversations. Maybe she was off her meds. Some days it seemed as if half the world used pills or alcohol to keep them sane.

Susie wandered into her kitchen, so spotless it glowed, which said more about her life than she wanted it to. Angry, she turned away. A chasm of loneliness yawned wide. She had a nice home and good friends, but there was no one to come home to at night, no one to run her a hot bath and no one to distract her from her troubles.

Why was it so hard to start a family when all it had taken when she was fifteen was thirty seconds humping against a wall? She pulled off her borrowed sweater and flung it on the bed, balled up her pants and threw them into the laundry basket with enough force to knock it over. She hated being needy. She didn't want to be lonely or pathetic. She pulled on plaid pants and a baggy gray T-shirt, punched the pillow before turning out the light. Tomorrow she intended to start the rest of her life, beginning with a little research in how to get pregnant without a man.

CHAPTER ELEVEN

SUSIE CAME INSTANTLY AWAKE, a soft knock on her bedroom door shooting her off the bed and making her heart pummel against her ribs. And there stood Nick, dark-eyed and grim-faced.

"What are you doing here?" she whispered.

"You disappeared. I was worried. I needed to check you got home safe." He dangled the spare key the Heathcotes kept in their kitchen.

"I'm fine." Self-conscious, she propped herself up on one elbow. "How's Emily?"

Nick lowered his hand, twirling the keys with clever fingers. She couldn't take her eyes off the dancing metal.

"Doc thinks she stopped taking her antidepressants and had an episode. She'll be okay once they get her meds sorted again. Have you got your stuff packed?" His tone was guarded as his eyes traveled the room.

Tired, Susie pushed her hair off her forehead. "Oh, I'm not going." She furrowed her fingers against her scalp. "It's nuts to think I'm in any danger."

"This isn't some joke." Nick's voice dropped. "This isn't about me being some paranoid nancy-boy or wannabe hero. Tracy Good had her head smashed in and whoever did it put the murder weapon in your car. You work in the same place as the dead girl and you often work alone. You are on his radar."

Susie gritted her teeth. She wanted to shout at him to

leave her the hell alone like she had earlier that afternoon, but she held it together, maintained the illusion of composure. "I'm not playing games, Nick. I want you to leave."

"Well, I can't do that until I know you have some sort of security in here!" His voice shook the ceiling. She narrowed her eyes. Repressed emotions were not Nick Archer's problem. He made no sound as he advanced toward her. "I know what you're scared of."

She wanted to laugh but his eyes were locked on hers and she couldn't force the air past her lips. "Go on then, oh great detective genius, let's hear it. What am I scared of?"

"You're scared of letting anyone see behind the cool, highly-educated Susie Cooper façade."

Bullshit.

He moved closer and her heart thumped hard as she gripped the plain white coverlet.

"What's the matter, Susie? Scared you're going to turn out to be just as flawed as the rest of us?"

Her focus sharpened, but she said nothing. Why should she care what he thought?

"What is it about the real Susie Cooper people won't respect or admire?" He stood over her and brushed the pad of his finger down her cheek. It felt like a teardrop.

She batted his hand away. "I thought you had work to do? Evidence to go through?" She was annoyed with him, annoyed with kissing the heck out of him earlier.

"It'll wait. I need sleep otherwise I'm going to fall over." Undeterred by her glare, he ran his hand around to the nape of her neck, freed her hair from where it was trapped beneath her shirt. "I doubt your secrets are as black as mine."

Oh God. How did he even know she *had* secrets?

How did he see her so clearly when people she'd known for years had never even guessed she was less than what she pretended to be? She met his gaze and knew what he wanted. Her to spill her guts. To tell him every dirty little confidence he thought she hid. Except it wasn't some minor indiscretion, it was a great big sordid screwup that had led her to abandon a baby.

And she might not have the right to claim the title of mother, but she wasn't going to barter her child's happiness to gain Nick's trust. If Darcy Cooper ran for president, Susie's son could be in danger, and she would never let that happen.

"I don't have any secrets, Nick, but if we're going to swap fairy stories, why don't you start?" She'd been raised around the best poker faces in the world, but he smiled as if he knew she was lying, and the room suddenly felt too small as he hunkered down in front of her, their knees brushing.

"I was raised by a priest." He caught the back of her head with one large palm, drew her close, his breath on her lips. "And my mother was a whore." And then he kissed her.

Dammit.

The feel of his body beneath her hands was amazing. Energy that had simmered and seethed since she'd first seen him ignited. He was everything she didn't want—dangerous, arrogant and sexy as hell. The taste of him weakened her resolve not to get involved, and his mouth fed the sensuality she'd never quite been able to destroy.

Men like Nick thrived on the chase. No way he'd stick around for a relationship or to raise rug rats. They'd have sex and he'd move on to the next willing victim. His fingers stroked her collarbone, her pulse jumping as his thumb grazed her skin. Anticipation was as strong as the desire he aroused. She wanted this. She hated herself, but she wanted him anyway.

Maybe she should just do it? Get him out of her life? A farewell fling before she settled down to a new life. *Why not? Why the heck not?*

She drew him to lie on the coverlet. His hand slid to her hipbone and hers crept around his neck, absorbing the lean hard muscle, enjoying the heat of his body. His eyes narrowed into thin slits that revealed only thoughts involving her naked.

And it thrilled her.

It meant nothing and yet it filled her with power. His teeth scraped the skin of her throat, shooting her pulse into high gear. His palm slid down her body, cupped her between the legs and she moaned. His weight, his scent, his clever hands crammed all the needy places inside her. He touched her through the cotton, used the material to caress her. Her thighs trembled and her head fell back as everything contracted to that single point of contact and her mind exploded and reverberated around the universe.

When she opened her eyes he was staring at her and all she could see was a desperate need and terrible loneliness.

Something changed. Some indefinable chemistry inflamed. He pulled her shirt over her head and before the cool air hit her skin his hands had her nerves dancing. They kissed harder, deeper, driving each other crazy.

This man knew his way around a woman's body and he wasn't afraid to use it. He caught her hand beneath her back, pulling her up and into him as he tasted her. The sparks and vibrations were too good to do anything but enjoy. She groaned when he released her, squirmed as he blew a warm breath over damp skin. It was impossible to lie still when all she wanted was to touch him the way he was touching her.

She grabbed his sweatshirt, pushed it over his head, did the same with his tee and admired his body as he sat back and tried to free the tangled mess. Lean six-pack abs contracted under her hand. His chest was sculpted and covered in a sparse sprinkling of golden hair. Her appreciation turned to unease. She wasn't even close to perfect. Her boobs were flat and her butt wasn't. Her soft contours contrasted sharply with the naked perfection of his.

Nick looked at her and smiled, an interested light entering those keen eyes. "What are you thinking?"

She looked away. "Nothing."

"Susie, Susie." He grinned and Susie had the disconcerting sensation he'd slept with so many women he was an expert on how they thought. "I'll take a wild guess, shall I?"

His eyes flashed with mischief. The man was incorrigible.

"You're worried about your body?" He traced a finger from the tip of her nose down the center of her torso, a welt of sensation running in its wake. She held her breath as his finger rested just south of her navel. Her whole existence centered on that hand, expectation controlling her body like a puppeteer controlled a marionette.

"You're thinking you're either too fat or too thin, and don't ask me which because..." his eyes slid to where his fingers slipped inside her "...you look bloody perfect to me."

She shook, she told herself it was from cold even though she burned. Quickly he stripped them both of their remaining clothes, sheathing himself with a condom before he moved over her, pushing her knees apart.

Oh God. She panicked. "I'm not ready."

She didn't think she would ever be ready for Nick Archer.

The expression on his face told her she was a liar. His hipbones collided with hers as she felt him, a hard ridge against her. She quivered, her fingers clawing at the bedspread when they really wanted to cling to him. She squeezed her eyes shut just as the wide tip of him kissed her opening. Her breath came in tiny pants, sweat building just beneath the surface of her skin as she held back from taking everything she wanted. He didn't move, but she could feel the racing of his pulse intimately against her hips.

Oh God, move, move. She wanted to plead. He was doing nothing to arouse her except skin-to-skin contact and drenching her in his scent. She bit her lip, knowing she was close to begging. But he held back, taking his weight on his elbows, until she opened her eyes and saw those green depths staring at her with laughing amusement.

"Ready yet?" He nudged against her and grinned.

She closed her eyes and shook her head, knowing she was never going to be ready for this man. She saw that now. Maybe she could make this the most boring sex he'd ever had so he wouldn't want a repeat performance. So his eyes would stop following her whenever they were together and he'd stop touching her with those intimate little gestures. And maybe then she'd stop wanting him.

His hand slid between them, his fingertips brushing soft petals of skin and making desire ping through her senses. She gritted her teeth to keep from arching into his palm, her traitorous nipples bunching tighter like little red flags of lust.

"Do you have a problem with sex, Dr. Cooper?" he asked, his lips bussing a hot path along her carotid artery, his shaft pulsing thick and heavy against her thigh. "Or is it just with me?"

Oh God, did she have a problem with sex. She wanted to squirm and take him in one big thrust. So much for self-control. She blinked.

"What do you mean?" she asked, innocently.

"I mean, Dr. Cooper..." He nibbled one earlobe, making her stretch beneath him, her legs opening wider as he sank against her. His caresses felt better than anything had in a long time. "...I'll respect you even if you enjoy it."

Chagrin stole through her as she admitted, "I figured if we had dull sex you wouldn't hang around."

He leaned back on his elbows, the movement sliding just the tip of him inside her. He closed his eyes, every feature strained as he hissed out a breath.

"Oh boy." The sensation of him being almost there made her muscles contract and her fingers scrabble.

Sweat beaded his brow as they stared into each other's eyes. "I don't do long term, Susie. Don't make any sacrifices on my account."

Of course he didn't. She held his gaze for a moment longer, then shifted her thighs wider, determined to take what she wanted from this man the same way he was taking from her. He drove into her forcefully, proving she was more than ready for him, and she was lost.

Clinging together, they writhed, tangled, entwined. He grabbed her hands, pinning them above her head. His other hand slid beneath her, raising her hips off the mattress, and the effect was intense as he drove deeper. A waterfall of sensation bombarded her, each touch more enthralling and compelling than the last. They reeled, twisted, ended up on the floor with him beneath her, a million pinpricks of pleasure dancing all over her skin.

She stared down at him. Naked. Aroused. Invulnerable. Hers for one night... She sank onto him slowly, twisted her hips as she rode, his eyes burning as bright as atomic fission. His fingers took their turn clutching her hips, but she controlled the pace and set the rhythm. She felt her release build in a slow avalanche of wonder and kept riding until his eyes rolled back and he cried out.

The moon set, the stars faded, and cold settled in, but neither spoke. They slept.

"NICK, WHAT'S THE STATUS on the investigation?"

He jumped, then blinked at his boss who'd caught him thinking about sex and the satisfaction of being a well-used male, rather than evidence and motive and murder.

In her black-and-white uniform Superintendent Pamela Richardson looked soft and cuddly as a panda bear, but she had fangs the size of a butcher's blade. Her corkscrew curls were rigidly controlled by plaits and pins, not one hair out of place on her super-efficient head. The supe was as straight as gravity in a world of procedure and anal-retentive standard operating procedures and the God-almighty handbook. Nick, on the other hand, was more of a Celtic knot.

"Ma'am." Nick nodded. He'd known her for twelve years now. They weren't exactly friends, more like collaboratories, but he respected her and he didn't respect many of the brass.

"Cut to it, Nick. I want to know what's going on." She perched on the edge of Ewan's desk.

"Forensics are going over the stuff in Dr. Cooper's car. D.S. McKnight is there right now—" he checked his watch "—to see what they've come up with." He was lying. Ewan was working from home because Amy's care-worker had the flu and he hadn't been able to get a replacement yet. But no way was Nick dropping his pal in the shit.

The supe watched him with cool hazel eyes and a fixed smile. Nothing much got past her.

"Any viable suspects other than Jake Sizemore?" she asked.

He didn't trust her modulated tone. She knew Nick's history with Sizemore because twelve years ago he hadn't yet learned to keep his trap shut. Nick didn't need a lecture on impartiality from anyone and it wasn't as if they had unlimited manpower. He was doing the best he could.

"DNA from the semen samples should give us IDs in a couple of days, providing we have a match from the volunteer samples we got from the Gatty. We've conducted preliminary interviews with the guys we know Tracy was shagging and executed search warrants for their places of residence. But we still have no evidence and no motive except rumors she was playing around with a married man."

He blew out a frustrated breath. As far as he could tell Tracy Good had had no enemies and no friends. He picked up a pen and tapped it on a sheet of paper he'd been writing notes on. His boss straightened some files on Ewan's desk. She wasn't housekeeping. She was stalling.

"What about the lecturer who found the murder weapon in her car?"

"*Her* I can rule out." His smile was as thin as a blade. Nobody touched Susie, not even his boss. "She was with me on Saturday night."

Nick held the supe's gaze and let her think they were up to fun and games even then. "I borrowed her car to drive to the murder scene." And please God don't let the murder weapon and Tracy's bag have been put in the boot when he was doing his B&E, because it was bad enough they were going to find traces of the dead woman's blood in the driver's footwell.

The look the supe gave him was both disapproving and sympathetic. The former he ignored, the latter pissed him off. Pam had been married to the same bloke for twenty years and she thought all single men were dogs when it came to getting some action. She was mostly right. But he hadn't felt this good after sex in years and that scared the hell out of him.

"I can't let you take the lead on this anymore, Nick."

His head snapped up. *"What?"*

She stood, moved to the small sash-window that overlooked North Street. "You're too involved."

"You have got to be shitting me." But her expression was serious. "So what? You're going to give it to Ewan?" Who was a damn fine copper but treading a thin line while trying to cope with his wife's illness. Her eyes flickered. "Oh, no. You are *not* calling in someone from outside." He launched himself out of his chair, disgust burning through him as he paced the few square yards of his office. "It took *how* many years to get detectives into this nick and as soon as we have our first real case, you call for outside assistance?"

Her lips thinned, but she wouldn't meet his gaze.

"You do that and the next time there's a budget cut—which is every fucking fiscal quarter—me and Ewan will both get transferred to Cupar or Glenrothes and you'll be left swinging in the breeze, begging for CID help every time some drug dealer turns up in town or some student gets robbed."

"You are not impartial." Her jaw clenched and unclenched. "You *hate* Jake Sizemore, and I don't blame you." Those hazel eyes locked on him. "This is a perfect chance to get revenge."

"Jesus, Pam—" his heart pounded and his shirt stuck to his back "—I'm a better cop than that. I'm the most experienced homicide detective north of the border."

She smiled, but it was like the cracking of an ice sheet. "We all know you have the greatest homicide expertise in this constabulary, D.I. Archer, and we also know you can take your pick of assignments. But your judgment is clouded and it could affect the prosecution's case in this murder inquiry."

"I've run this investigation by the book." He shoved a hand through his hair then held her stare. "If I'd wanted revenge that bastard would have disappeared years ago and no one would have had a fucking clue."

She inclined her head, but didn't relent.

Smiling because he was damned if he'd let his boss know just how much she'd got to him, he sat down and leaned back in his chair and turned back to his email. "Whatever you say, Pam. I'm sure I can find other stuff to keep me busy. I hear Tesco had a shoplifter yesterday, maybe I'll go watch the surveillance tapes. Stake out the joint."

She drew an audible breath, then stalked out, her footsteps pounding the hallway like jackboots.

How the hell had she managed to get the drop on him in the first place? Pissed, Nick lifted the handset to call the lab, but saw a file already downloading to his PC so he replaced the receiver and opened the attachment and let it run. Like hell he was handing over this case.

At first he couldn't hear anything so he turned up the speakers to full volume. A crackle. The sound of scrabbling, rustling material and deep breathing reverberated around the room.

"Let me get the condom." It was a raw whisper.

That was Jake Sizemore. Nick sat up straight in his swivel chair, eyes focused on the screen.

"Not yet."

Was that Tracy Good? There was the sound of a zip. A groan, a strangled "Is the door locked?" A giggle, a bang. "Oh Jesus. Oh God, yes."

The sounds of a man being blown were not hard to decipher. Thumps and bumps like furniture being knocked and the clatter of what sounded like a pencil falling to the floor.

"What do you want, Jake?" a female voice asked with a giggle. Nick leaned closer to the monitor as if that would improve his hearing. He heard the supe's footsteps backtracking down the corridor toward his office. He held back a smile as she poked her head through the door.

"Jesus, Jesus! Ow!" The sound of clothing rustling and sudden silence, except for harsh breathing. Then. "You have the most amazing tits." Sounds of sucking. Little female moans of pleasure.

"Tell me what you want, Jake," the woman purred.

Nick visualized her. Tracy, assuming it was Tracy, holding back on the main prize for the dirty old bastard.

Jake's voice cracked and he sounded as if he was gripping tight to something or someone. "I want *you*, Tracy. I want to have you every way I know and then I want to fuck you all over again."

Nick's stomach twisted. Had Jake used those same words on Chrissie? Had she panted and cried out like that when the bastard had mauled her? Betrayal tasted like bile and made his stomach heave.

"And what will you give me if I let you?"

Nick sat up straighter and swapped a look with Pamela whose eyes had narrowed to pinpricks of concentration. Had Tracy been blackmailing her boss?

The sounds of wet lips sucking flesh followed, but Nick knew Tracy still had her knees pinned together because she hadn't gotten what she wanted. Yet.

"Anything." Jake's voice was rougher, rising higher, breaking, desperate and out of control. "A job, references, a vacation, whatever the hell you want."

"A job first." The sound of material rustling was greeted by thick silence. There was another thud, like someone jumping up onto a table. Nick could visualize her long naked legs swinging, knees spread on the narrow worktop of her tiny office. Silence for a second. Another groan. Probably Sizemore popping a vein. Then Tracy again. "And the best fucking reference you've ever written."

There was a harsh gasp as flesh met flesh, Sizemore whispering dirty promises while Tracy made funny little sounds. Nick was trying hard not to think about Susie while listening to this. Hard for the animal inside not to get turned on by the sounds of sex even though the cop wondered if this act had led to Tracy Good's death.

Tracy started to scream as she came, the noise quickly muted as if Sizemore put his hand over her mouth. Nick hadn't tried to quiet Susie, whose scream still echoed around his head and whose scent still clung to his skin. But then they hadn't been committing adultery or moral turpitude.

More grunts. Then repetitive banging as if they didn't care about the noise anymore. Harsh breaths until finally the last one tore from Sizemore's throat like a snarl.

"I'll give you the best fucking reference in the world."

Then Sizemore started laughing; both of them giggled like children and the sound crawled up Nick's spine like a tarantula.

He turned his head to look at his boss, raised one brow in question.

"The dirty bastard." A look of disgust twisted the supe's features. "Fine. Bring him in, but one mistake, Nick…" She pointed a finger at him and he read his boss's expression as clearly as bloodred ink on starch paper. *Fuck this up and you're out.*

SUSIE WOKE TO THE RELENTLESS sound of the telephone ringing. She sat up, rubbed the grit from her eyes, holding the sheet across her breasts as she realized she was naked. Then she remembered exactly what was missing from this morning's equation.

She grabbed the phone. *Maybe it was Nick?* "Hello?"

"Susie, darling." Her mother's voice was shrill along thousands of miles of fiber optics. "I've been trying to get hold of you for *days*. Why didn't you return my calls? I know you're upset with me, but I've been worried."

Susie huffed out a breath and pulled a pillow behind her so she could rest against the headboard. It wasn't Nick calling to whisper good-morning and, yes, that had been the best sex ever.

"Sorry, Mom, I've been busy."

"Oh, please!" the senator scoffed. "You think I don't recognize that lame excuse? I use it every day."

Payback's a bitch.

Susie rubbed her forehead and squeezed her eyes shut. She was being uncharitable and despite everything that had happened in the past, she loved her mother.

"Really, Mom, I have been busy, and then there was a murder just outside the lab and last night my neighbor was taken ill."

"Murder?" Darcy's voice dropped to serious. "I thought Scotland was safe."

"It is." Susie could kick herself. Whatever their disagreements, no matter her age, her mother still took the overprotective view of parenting. "Some poor girl was killed on the beach in front of the marine lab. It was the first murder in this town for ten years, can you imagine if Washington were this safe?"

"I'm sending a bodyguard," said Darcy.

"Don't be ridiculous." There was no way Susie would tolerate being shadowed 24/7. "I'm not having some stranger making my life more complicated than it already is, the press is bad enough."

"This is something we need to discuss, Susie—"

"No. It isn't." No way her mother was getting her own way on this. Between Darcy and Nick she was being suffocated with good intent and look where that had gotten her. And suddenly her mother's meaning registered. "Even if you become president of the free world, I am *not* having a bodyguard." Dismay filled her as the implications of her mother's political ambition hit home like rubber bullets.

"You might not get a choice," Darcy told her. "The United States takes the security of its leaders very seriously."

What about Susie's son? Darcy's secret grandchild? Would he get a bodyguard? Susie dropped the sheet and jumped out of bed, needing to be dressed for this conversation. There was a knock on the front door as Susie dipped into her lingerie drawer.

She stilled, frowning. "Mom, I have to go, I'll call you later."

"You haven't got a man there have you?" The inflection edged toward sophisticated amusement that made Susie's teeth grind.

Ignoring her mother, she peeked out of her bedroom window and saw a short, chubby, mustached guy in a flat-cap, wielding a toolbox the size of her car. She wiggled into her underwear and snagged a pair of Levi's out of another drawer.

"Mom, it just so happens I do have a man here and for all I know he could be the father of all those grandchildren you want for your campaign ads." Bitterness surged inside her because her other child hadn't been good enough. "I'll call you later."

Susie hung up, tapped on the glass, hiding her nakedness behind the drapes. "I'll be right out," she called.

It was a guy from the alarm company. Nick had no reason to come back for an encore. He didn't do long term, she reminded herself. He didn't even do the morning after. She should be grateful he was just a one-night stand, but instead she was pissed. Men like Nick Archer might fulfill her sexual fantasies, but they'd never help heal her heart.

CHAPTER TWELVE

"I COULDN'T GET PARKED outside and I only put one of those parking vouchers on my car and I'm *not* paying a fine so this had better be quick." Sizemore's square chin jutted and his chest puffed out with belligerence as the desk-sergeant let him through to the back of the police station.

Nick flicked a glance at P.C. Lewis, who was back on dayshift. She picked up her cue. "If you give me your keys, Professor, I'll bring your car around to the back of the station." She gave Sizemore a quiet smile as if she were embarrassed on his behalf. "Just between us, sir, I think the parking system in this town sucks."

Jake's hostility dropped a notch as he absorbed the feminine charms of P.C. Lewis.

"Yeah, it does. Thanks." He handed over his keys. "It's a dark blue Toyota sedan parked outside Luvian's ice cream shop."

Lewis left without a word, but she'd already achieved what he wanted.

Sizemore's eyes latched onto Nick, who sat quietly in the corner keeping his mouth shut. He had professional training in interview and interrogation techniques, Scientific Content Analysis, nonverbal clues and neurolinguistics. He knew how to get results and he knew how to read liars. But the first hurdle was always to get a suspect talking, to develop a rapport. With Sizemore, Nick had more chance of catching rabies.

"And I don't want that SOB anywhere near me." Sizemore pointed in Nick's direction.

Nick kept his expression sullen, but he'd planned this to the last detail. Adrenaline raced through his veins and heightened his senses, but he forced his breathing to remain calm and steady. He didn't believe in coincidence. One supervisor, two dead girls. The odds were stacking up against Sizemore, and Nick intended to be the one brandishing the handcuffs when the fucker went down.

This was what he'd been working toward for twelve interminable years. This was why he'd joined the police force in the first place.

Ewan did his thing. "I'll be conducting the interview, sir. Not to worry." He flicked an ashamed-to-be-associated glance in Nick's direction. Nick had already put together a personal history folder on Jakey-boy. And an outline of questions he wanted asked. Ewan was a natural. Getting Sizemore a coffee, a biscuit, being courteous and kind. People trusted that bumbling demeanor, not realizing the copper behind it was as sharp as a diamond tack.

His boss entered the office.

"Nice to meet you, Professor." Her accent was soft as her cheeks. She held out her hand to shake Sizemore's as if he was a visiting dignitary, not a murder suspect.

They all wanted this bastard. Nick could almost scent the excitement of hunters seeking prey. Maybe they were overdoing it, but no, Sizemore was lapping it up, his shoulders relaxing, taking deeper breaths into his barrel chest.

"I'm afraid D.I. Archer has to sit in on the chat as he's the senior officer assigned to the case, but rest assured he knows his boundaries. We need to make sure everything is above board. You understand, of course?" The supe smiled so benignly, Nick half believed her himself.

Sizemore's eyes flashed in his direction, more confident. Assessing. Potentially cruel.

How cruel?

The supe tapped Sizemore's elbow in a consolatory move. "Be assured D.S. McKnight will be running the show."

She shook the guy's hand again before she left. Mother Teresa saving the world, a hard-nosed cop who hadn't got to the top by being a fairy godmother to criminals.

"Right then." Ewan took a deep breath. "Shall we go through?"

"Yes, let's get this over with." Sizemore was relaxed and in control now as he followed Ewan through the door. Nick gave them a moment to get settled, enough time for Sizemore to waive the right to a lawyer before they had their chat.

Nick walked through the booking office with its tall filing cabinets, barrage of forms and box-files all neatly sorted and stacked. The interview room was marked by a laminated A4 sheet of paper taped to the cherry veneer. Sizemore sat on the far side of the table. He'd removed his jacket and unbuttoned his shirt collar. Ewan was just sitting down after turning on the recording equipment.

"Let the record show D.I. Archer entered the room," Ewan clarified for the tape, a paragon of protocol.

Nick pulled a chair to the corner of the room, as close as he could get to the door. He looked up out of the barred windows with a bored expression on his face. If he had his way, Sizemore would see bars for a long time. He clamped down on the hate and concentrated on the job.

Ewan looked at his notes. "Professor Sizemore. Do you mind if I call you Jake?"

Jake eased back in his chair and shrugged his shoulders. "Sure."

"Jake, do you know why I've asked to talk to you today?"

"Frankly, I have no idea. I've already answered all your questions and I'm a very busy man."

"I understand, sir, and I appreciate you coming in." Ewan was even better than Nick had expected. "Who do *you* think may have committed this crime?"

Sizemore shifted in his chair, leaned forward and back, finally staring up and out the window at the diffused afternoon sunlight. "No idea."

"Tell me why you wouldn't have done something like this."

Sizemore's nostrils flared as he glared at Ewan. "I'm the goddamned head of department at one of the top universities in the world! I'm not capable of doing that to someone. I have a solid reputation, a wife and children." He blinked rapidly and glanced at Nick, who remained impassive.

So far Jake was showing all the signs of being a big, fat liar.

"How do you think the results of this investigation will come out for you?"

Sizemore sneered at Nick, his top lip curled. "If it were up to Detective Delusional over there I'd be beaten black and bloody, and locked up 'til I'm dead."

Nick repressed a smile. He could hope, right?

Ewan gave a disappointed little shake of his head and shot him a look. Nick raised an eyebrow, but remained silent. Three years undercover and four years homicide were paying off big time in this little room as he watched Sizemore sign his own confession. He was not going to screw up putting this bastard's ass in jail.

"Would you take a polygraph?" Ewan asked.

"About the murder?" Jake hedged.

Ewan pressed his lips together. "Yes, about the murder, what else would I be talking about?"

Sizemore's eyes slid away. Cleverly he hadn't answered the question. But Ewan moved on. Nick had coached him on the importance of getting Jake to relax, to get the guy to think he was in control, that he could walk away any time he wanted.

"Can you tell me what sort of girl Tracy Good was?"

Jake stared at the carpet, closed his eyes for a moment as if remembering. When he opened them they were clear and focused. "She was an excellent student." His eyes moved up and to the left. The neurolinguistic indication he was telling the truth, assuming the man was right handed.

Ewan must have read Nick's mind because he passed over a piece of paper and a pen. "Do you think you could write down a few key words to describe her for us?"

"What is this, some kind of remedial psychology test?" Jake picked up the pen with his right hand, staring suspiciously at Ewan and Nick.

Ewan chuckled. "Something like that. You don't have to write anything if you don't want to."

Sizemore jotted a few words and sat back, passed the paper back to Ewan who studied it carefully. Nick wondered what Jake had written, but for now it was irrelevant.

Ewan continued in his soothing voice, the soft Scottish burr calming even Nick's coiled tension. "Did you have a sexual relationship with Tracy Good?"

Jake's eyes flicked high right and he touched his nose. *Liar, liar pants on fire.* "How can you even think I'm capable of sleeping with a student? I was raised to be a God-fearing Christian."

So was Nick. He suppressed a grin that felt sharper than broken glass.

Jake hadn't answered that question either. He swept a hand through greasy-looking hair before he leaned back in his chair, brows lowered, lips tight.

"I need an answer for the tape, sir," Ewan repeated.

"I just gave you a goddamned answer! I swear on my mother's grave I never touched her!" His eyes flicked up and right and once more he touched his itchy nose, confirming what they already knew. Whatever lies came out of Jake Sizemore's mouth, he had been screwing Tracy Good.

Ewan picked up his notes. "She was a good-looking lassie. Gossip in the Gatty suggests she was a bit of a goer." Ewan gave him a subdued version of a male smirk. "Did she ever make advances on you?"

Sizemore shifted his weight from one buttock to the other. "Well, yes, actually she did, but I didn't want to speak ill of the dead."

Rage boomed inside Nick's head, sending pain through his skull.

"This is a murder investigation, Jake," Ewan reminded him. "We need the truth, no matter how potentially embarrassing."

"I didn't touch her." Sizemore's voice rose, his fingers rapidly kneading his trouser leg.

Ewan frowned and kept his voice moderate. "Then how do you explain this?" He opened up a laptop on the desk and clicked on a file. The sound of sex filled the air.

Sizemore's countenance remained indifferent until his voice came over the speakers, and then his mouth gaped.

"Tell me what you want, Jake."

"I want you, Tracy. I want to have you every way I know and then I want to fuck you all over again."

The blood drained from his face. He hadn't known about the tape. Maybe that's why he'd been happy to dispose of the murder weapon and Tracy's bag inside Susie's car.

"Was there an argument?" Ewan pulled out a photograph of the crime scene. Tracy's matted hair, dark crusted with crimson, her smashed skull against a backdrop of blood-soaked sand. "You lied about a sexual relationship. Did you kill her as well?"

Jake swallowed forcibly.

"Did you kill Tracy?" Nick echoed Ewan's question.

Jake's eyes swung toward him, wide, trapped.

"Did you kill Tracy Good?" Louder. Meaner. Nick wanted to force the confession from the bastard's lips.

"No! No, I didn't kill her. I did not kill Tracy!" And Jake's eyes flickered left, like an innocent.

No, no, no, no, no! Nick's breath constricted in his throat, his heart beating furiously as the pressure in his veins rose. He could feel Sizemore slipping away from the noose he'd crafted for his neck. He left the room as Ewan finished the interview.

Nick shoved out the door into the walled-off car park at the back of the station and his failures rose up inside him like a flood—and he was drowning. He leaned against the wall, the rough brick scraping his fingers. Desperate to catch a breath, he tried to slow the pounding of his heart and quiet the ugliness that surged through his blood. If he believed his own so-called expertise, Jake Sizemore was only guilty of adultery.

He booted the wall and a bone snapped. Then he did it again.

Half an hour later Nick stood on his balcony overlooking the harbor. Gulls marauded through the sky looking for easy prey. The sun glared fiercely off the water and made his eyes hurt.

"Did you ever think...maybe...she just died?" Ewan's voice was low. Somber. He was talking about Chrissie, of course, not Tracy.

Nick glanced at his colleague, noted the lines of strain around Ewan's mouth, and the gray hairs that outnumbered the brown. Jake had finally admitted to a sexual relationship with Tracy Good, but there was still no evidence he'd killed her. Nick wished he could just sink his blade into Jake's heart, twisting as he pushed the hilt home. It would be simpler. Quicker. The man was guilty, but Nick might never be able to prove it.

But twelve years ago when he'd joined the force, he'd sworn an oath to uphold the law. It wasn't just about personal vengeance; he'd needed to believe in something positive otherwise he'd have ended up as useless and depraved as his junky whore of a mother. He'd always wanted to bring down Sizemore in the most public and humiliating way possible. Showing him for the lying, cheating piece of shit he really was.

"It would be easier if I just let it go, wouldn't it?" But Chrissie hadn't just died. She'd been killed by a combination of Nick's pride and Sizemore's lust. Nick gripped the rail. "She was too safety conscious to go diving on her own, especially in shark-infested waters." The usual rage that accompanied thoughts of Chrissie's death felt as cold as the mortuary. "Someone got her out to sea, maybe drugged her, probably made her bleed and then tossed her into the water."

Had she tried to swim for it, knowing she was attracting the deadliest predators in the ocean? Or had she been unconscious and unaware, unable to help herself? The thought of her suffering made his intestines twist. "Would you let it go, if it was Amy?"

Ewan stared silently at the water for a long time before he shook his head. "So who's the prime suspect for Tracy Good now?" He sipped his coffee. "The wife?"

"We definitely need to talk to her," said Nick. Judy was a miserable human being, but he didn't figure her for a killer. He frowned. "Why would you stay with someone when you knew they were going to leave you for someone else?"

Neither spoke for a moment, then Ewan slanted him a guarded look. "Were you going to divorce Chrissie?"

Nick didn't want to answer that question. He'd been raised in an environment that considered divorce more grotesque than murder. If marriage to Chrissie had been a test of faith, he had failed in every possible way.

"Yes," he finally admitted. "I was going to divorce her." The infidelity still stung, mixed with the overriding sense of guilt that had shaped his life ever since she'd died. That they'd loved each other so passionately and she'd turned from him so easily. And that he'd let her.

An image of Susie popped into his mind.

He'd been with hundreds of women since Chrissie died. Why did Susie Cooper have to be the one he couldn't stop thinking about? He looked out to sea and knew he'd hurt her already and would do so again. But he could no more resist that temptation than he could walk on water.

Ewan slurped his coffee, reminding Nick there were all sorts of tragedy.

A seagull squawked overhead.

"Aw, shit!" Ewan rubbed at a patch of white guano dribbling down the front of his suit. "At least it's supposed to be lucky," he grumbled, searching for a tissue.

Nick let out a weary sigh. Not even the birds crapped on him.

SUSIE'S ALARM WAS STILL BEING installed and she hadn't heard a peep from Nick. Obviously potential killers only worked night shift. She kicked a pebble across the sand, huddled into her cable sweater, the hood drawn up over her head.

A redshank waded in the shallows, tugged backward as it yanked up a bivalve. Bivalves were distant relatives of her octopi, a fact that always amazed her. However, man was closely related to rats, which wasn't a stretch at all.

An unbidden image of Nick Archer flashed into her mind. He hadn't even said goodbye. She picked up an empty whelk shell and carried it along with her, rubbing the rough barnacles on the outside with her thumb. So. They'd had sex and now they were done.

Annoyed with herself for wanting more, she kicked a hole in the sand, spraying it in all directions, taking out her frustration on tiny grains that whipped back into her face on the wind.

"I think you killed it."

Susie whirled, gasping for breath as Lily stood and grinned at her. Lily's smile faded after a moment and she looked pale. For once she wasn't wearing makeup and her clothes were unremarkable blue jeans, sneakers and a Gor-Tex jacket zipped up to her nose. Black roots had begun to creep through the blond at her scalp.

Susie fiddled with the shell. "How's your mom today?"

Lily's lips wobbled as if on the verge of tears. She blinked them away, looking toward the slate roof of the cottage just visible above the yellow dune.

"She's good. Better, anyway," she qualified with a fleeting smile. "I fed her pills and left her sleeping." Lily walked a few paces closer to Susie and peered at the hole Susie had kicked in the sand.

"I need to work from home, until we get her medication sorted." Her expression grew earnest. "I'm no slacker, I'll come in to look after the animals and do experiments, but I have a laptop and can analyze data and read papers at home."

Susie hesitated, wondering how to phrase what she needed to say. "Lily, if your mother has Alzheimer's or another type of progressive dementia, there's going to come a point she'll need full-time care. It's gonna be hard for you to cope on your own, let alone do a Ph.D."

"It isn't Alzheimer's." Lily stuffed her hands in her pockets and dipped her face out of the wind. "The doctor thinks it was brought on by the stress of the anniversary of Christina's death last week." She looked up and Susie caught the worry edging her eyes. "Once she's back on her meds, which I'm going to administer from now on, she should be back to her old self."

"What was she like? Your sister?" Susie held her breath, having asked such a bold question. They started walking toward the rocks at the far end of the beach.

"I was ten when she died." A little crease marked the space between Lily's brows. "She was my big sister, you know? Wonderful. Vivacious. This bouncing ball of energy and enthusiasm who whirled in and out of our lives whenever she felt like it. As far as I was concerned the sun shone out of her backside."

Lily bent and picked up a piece of sea glass worn smooth by waves and sand. It was the color of Nick's eyes.

"But she changed, just before she went to South Africa. She moved back home, her and Nick had a huge fight and she spent most of her time in a foul mood or bawling her eyes out."

They'd been fighting?

Susie hadn't known.

Lily's mouth dragged down at the corners. "I think they were going to get divorced."

Susie knew her eyes bugged. She'd assumed Chrissie had been perfect, so it felt strange to realize the dead woman had had her faults and their marriage hadn't been ideal. Susie scooped up a razor-shell as an excuse not to respond. Because how could she say she was glad Christina hadn't been as flawless as she'd assumed?

"Dad was still alive then. I remember him shouting at Chrissie—which he never did—telling her to get her act together. I lay in bed, listening." Lily's face tightened into lines of anger. "She was having an affair with Jake-the-snake." She pulled a disgusted face that would have made Susie laugh if she hadn't been so shocked.

"Can you imagine him naked? Ugh." Lily leapt over a small stream that cut through the beach. She balanced nimbly on a piece of driftwood before hopping to the other side.

Susie got her feet wet. "Is that why Nick thinks Jake had something to do with her death?" It certainly explained the unsympathetic feelings toward her boss.

Lily shrugged. "I guess. I doubt Jake did it though, I mean the guy is a total lech. But a killer? Nah." She shook her head. "I think Chrissie did something stupid and died in an accident, but no one wants to listen to my opinions."

Susie didn't know what to think. She'd slept with Nick and worked for Jake, but Chrissie would never be anything to her but other people's perceptions.

"So, what's the problem?" Lily asked with a slanted look. "I solved the last one. Maybe I can help you with this one too?"

"How did you get Rafael to start behaving himself?" Curiosity got the better of Susie.

"It's a gift." Lily laughed, but it faded and she turned serious. "Actually that's not true. I don't know what happened. Friday night Rafael came to see me. He'd had a change of heart and apologized for acting like a twat. Since then he's been great, which is a pity because now he's not acting like a dickhead, I fancy the pants off him." She wriggled her brows. "But I sealed my fate by laying down the ground rules."

"A woman of honor?" Susie laughed.

Lily threw back the hood on her jacket. "I am indeed."

It felt good to be with Lily. Her openness was an outlet for Susie's own repressed emotions. Maybe she needed to act more like Lily. Let it all out. Secrets and all.

Maybe not.

They walked in silence before Lily stopped and stared as if she had something important to say. Instinctively Susie knew she didn't want to hear it.

"Nick loved Chrissie and she betrayed him." Lily's lips pinched hard together as if holding in an expletive.

"But he blames himself for her death and I don't know if he'll ever get over it." She reached out a surprisingly warm hand and squeezed Susie's hand. "Don't fall for him, okay? He'll hurt you, even though he doesn't mean to."

Susie forced a laugh and pulled her hand away. "I barely know the man." She blocked the image of his hair falling in his eyes, his face contorted in pleasure, the explosive heat of his skin. She looked up at puffy white cumulus drifting across the sky as if she had never seen clouds before. "Let me know if you need anything brought out from the Gatty."

Rejection slid over Lily's features and tugged at Susie's conscience, but Lily was her student not her buddy. Susie already felt like a damn fool where Nick Archer was concerned, no need to advertise the fact. She walked away and didn't see the hurt on Lily's face replaced by fury.

CHAPTER THIRTEEN

JUDY SIZEMORE SAT OPPOSITE Ewan in the interview room, her back as straight as a ladder-back chair, her lips rammed together, almost disappearing into her face. Ewan asked the same list of structured questions he'd asked her rat-bastard husband.

Her expression never changed and Nick couldn't tell from her answers whether she was innocent or guilty. The thing that bothered him about Judy as a suspect was, if she was really bothered by Jake's adultery, Fife would be littered with bodies. But there had been at least one other death…

Had Judy Sizemore killed Tracy Good in a fit of jealousy? Had Judy killed Chrissie for the same reason? Could he have been wrong all these years? His broken toe throbbed inside his boot and the pain helped ground him.

"Did you know Jake was having an affair with his student?" Ewan asked, his voice soft and compassionate.

She snorted. "Says who? Him?" Her eyebrows jerked in a derogatory fashion toward Nick, but he just watched her, trying to gauge what was really going on in that mind.

"We have indisputable evidence."

"I don't doubt there's someone more than willing to swear my husband had his tongue down some woman's throat, but that doesn't mean I have to believe it." Her eyes stabbed at Nick.

Something painful squeezed in his chest and he interrupted Ewan, who was about to ask another question. "Play the recording."

"Now?" Ewan squinted, brown eyes dubious, but Nick nodded and watched Judy's eyes flick between them. She was so uptight he couldn't read her body language. She was distancing herself from Jake and the victim by using impersonal pronouns—as if she'd never met Tracy, or Chrissie, as if she didn't care they were dead.

Well *he* damn well cared. Maybe the tape would help make it all a little more personal. Nick had cued it to a specific place.

Ewan pressed Play on the recording and Judy's expression shuttered, focusing inward, trying to block out the guttural grunts of sex.

"Jesus, Jesus! Ow! You have the most amazing tits."

"Tell me what you want, Jake."

Jake's voice cracking. "I want you, Tracy. I want to have you every way I know and then I want to fuck you all over again."

Judy's eyes locked on his, her pupils dilating until only a thin slice of blue remained.

How deeply did this betrayal cut into Judy Sizemore's heart?

"And what will you give me if I let you?" Tracy asked.

"Anything."

"Turn it off." Nick wanted Judy to wonder exactly what her husband had promised Tracy while they were screwing each other's brains out.

Ewan clicked the mouse, tightened his lips before

looking away from Nick's impassive gaze. Ewan Mc-
Knight was the conscience of their partnership and he
didn't approve of hurting people.

Unfortunately he was in the wrong profession.

"So, Judy, now you know that Jake *was* having a
sexual relationship with Tracy Good." Nick held her
gaze.

"It doesn't mean he killed the little slut!" Spittle spat
out like venom. Her eyes fixed on him with loathing.

As he stared back, the light in her eyes changed as
if finally she got it. He not only wanted her husband
behind bars, he had the power to put him there.

Ewan slid a photograph along the smooth surface of
the table. "Tracy Good was murdered."

Her eyes darted to the photograph and away again,
showing no outward reaction.

"Look at the photograph, Judy." Nick wanted to grab
her head and force her to look at the brutal image. Tracy
merited at least that much. "Do you think she deserved
that for shagging Jake? Especially when she wasn't the
one breaking marriage vows?"

Judy's hands squeezed into tense fists as she glanced
at the photo. "Women are always trying to tempt him."

"All you need to tempt your husband is a slot for his
dick."

Blinking rapidly, she chewed her knuckle and looked
away. Finally she was showing some real emotion.
"Stupid man." Tears flooded her eyes.

"Did he come home from shagging Tracy last Saturday night and climb into your bed?"

"No." Judy sobbed, her voice catching. "No, he
wasn't with me."

Nick felt a spurt of anticipation because maybe Sizemore had fooled him during the interview and maybe

he had committed murder. The guy had motive and opportunity. And body language wasn't infallible.

"But he didn't kill her." She raised her chin, met his eyes with a fierce glare. "He was at home, drunk as usual, asleep in the study. I killed her."

Shock shot through his body and he and Ewan exchanged a look. This was too easy.

She waited a beat and then gave him exactly what he'd been waiting for, for twelve long years. "I killed your miserable bitch of a wife too."

He stared into her triumphant face but felt nothing. No elation for finally catching Chrissie and Tracy's murderer, no shame from being wrong about Jake, no pain from his damaged toe. Just a big wad of nothing that might turn into agony if he let it.

Nick limped out of the room as Ewan finished up.

The supe came through the office door and patted his shoulder in congratulations. He shook her off, but she didn't seem to notice.

"Thank God that's over. I'll get in touch with the Procurator Fiscal and organize a press release." She'd been watching the monitors upstairs and had gotten exactly what she wanted. Another case cleared. Citizens of St. Andrews safe. Life back to normal in their cozy little town.

And wasn't that what he wanted?

Nick nodded but his tongue felt as if it was coated in lye. He couldn't utter a single word. He checked his watch, saw it was already after six and he hadn't phoned Susie. He ignored the other emotions that swirled around his head, concentrated on Susie. She'd been asleep when he'd left this morning and he'd wanted to wake her slowly and thoroughly. She'd looked so sweet

and soft. But the way he'd come apart in her arms last
night had scared the crap out of him and he'd run.

He picked up the phone in the booking room and
dialed Susie's number. He wasn't used to considering
other people, but he knew Susie deserved more than
wham bam, thank you ma'am.

The phone just rang. He let go of the cord, dropped
the receiver into its cradle. He'd call her later. Ewan
needed to get home to his sick wife. No way he could
wrap everything up, even though all Nick wanted to do
was crawl into Susie's bed and let the world carry on
spinning.

Finally.

Finally he'd found Chrissie's justice. Finally he'd
earned his release from that weighty vow and he
couldn't understand why he didn't feel like jumping
the moon. He turned to go back into the interview room
and tried to channel the man he used to be. Not the
abused kid or cuckold husband, but the coldhearted un-
derhearted detective who'd sacrificed emotion long ago,
in exchange for results.

A SCREECH PIERCED THE NIGHT and Susie shot off the
couch, woken from a deep sleep. It was dark, only the
light of the television flickering through the cottage.

"How do you turn this thing off?" Nick stood inside
her front door as if he had a right to be there and glared
at the control panel for the alarm.

The phone rang and Susie blinked, wondering if
she was dreaming. But she wasn't. She grabbed the
receiver and marched over to the doorway, punched a
six digit code into the box and pushed the reset button.
The alarm stopped squawking and her ears stopped
throbbing.

"Sorry," she spoke into the phone. "I forgot about the alarm and opened the door without thinking."

Idiot, she mouthed to Nick who pulled a face at her. Lines fanned deep around his eyes. Damn, he looked tired.

"Yes, I'm sure. Thanks." She hung up on the security firm and toed the front door wider for Nick to just turn around and leave. She glanced at her watch and tapped the dial. Ten o'clock. Too late for a date, just in time for a sleepover. "See ya."

He closed the door, locked it. "I don't think so." His eyes burned into hers.

Susie backed away, adrenaline making her take deep breaths, her mouth dry, her voice cracking. "I thought we were through."

"Through?" His eyes widened, dark energy rushing through their depths. He took a step toward her and she couldn't swallow. Raising a palm to cup her cheek, his eyes softened. "Susie, we haven't even started yet."

A moment later his mouth was on hers, cold lips contrasting with the heat of his tongue. And at first the kiss was gentle, but then he increased the pressure, his fingers working the belt of her robe.

Outrage bloomed only to be washed away by a rush of excitement. It swarmed inside her with frenzied heat. She kissed him back, tasting coffee and mint. He pinned her to a wall, hands bunching her robe, as he drew his unshaven jaw over the fragile curve of her breasts. Electricity sizzled along her skin leaving flash burns. Scorching power zipped through her nerves and destroyed rational thought. He stripped her and she leaned against the wall, disorientated, nightclothes at her feet. His bright green eyes held hers as he leaned closer, the roughness of his clothes brushing her naked skin. "We are definitely not done."

The television flickered like an electrical storm, coating the angles of Nick's face, part angel, part demon.

Susie swallowed. The safe reliable part of her nature wanted to push away from him and throw him out so she could move on to a better life. But the defective part of her brain was inexorably drawn to the wildness, the heat, the passion inside him. It matched an echo deep inside her she'd tried to smother for as long as she could remember. For most of her life, safe sex had had nothing to do with condoms.

He kissed her, slowly, gently, and the sudden change in tempo threw her off balance again. Her heart hammered against her ribs and she could feel it, feeding the inferno inside her as if she was possessed. His lips found her breast as he sank to his knees, fully clothed, the leather of his jacket creaking like a worn-out saddle as he eased forward. The grip on her hips sent primitive heat through her. Her hips started to rock but he held her still, his tongue stroking her ribs, her stomach and lower, just skirting along the edge of her soft curls. Sensation swelled inside her, but she stifled the sounds that wanted to escape. Held them back as a sign of weakness. She'd screamed so loud last night she was still mortified.

His arm pressed across her stomach, her back finding the cool smoothness of the wall, his tongue tracing a mesmerizing line across her skin. She knew what he was going to do, knew what to expect and still the feel of his soft hair brushing her thighs came as a shock. He eased her legs wider and dizziness whirled through her mind. A soft sound escaped the back of her throat as she dug her fingers into his hair and she felt him smile.

She began to shake, sensation banishing thought, replacing it with longing. Nick controlled her arousal with absolute concentration. Pleasuring her like a sex slave, driving her up with such determined focus, she couldn't contain the explosion.

His expression was one of warm male satisfaction and the glint in his eyes told her he wasn't finished. She trembled as he unbuckled his belt. But humiliation was still fresh in her mind all these years later.

"Don't lose me now, Susie." His eyes narrowed as the cold made her shiver.

She knew what he was saying, she wanted to let go, but the thought of being taken against a wall reminded her too much of the time she'd made the biggest mistake of her life.

"Can we go into the bedroom?" Her voice was small. The wildness Nick had released was slowly being pushed back into its nice little box.

He hesitated, his mouth twitching as if disappointed, but he shrugged, caught her up in his arms, strode into the bedroom and dropped her onto the bed. His eyes darkened as they traveled over her body. He was still fully dressed and she was completely naked.

She reared up and started pushing his jacket off his shoulders but Nick stopped her with a softly uttered, "Please."

He crawled up the length of her body, pulled out a condom and covered himself.

Susie clamped her lips shut, disconcerted at being so out of control, annoyed at how his zipper scraped her skin and his buttons pressed into her flesh. Then she felt him hot and heavy against her soft flesh, and she welcomed him. Greedy for more. Desperate for more. And then he filled her, big enough to be uncomfortable for those first few seconds, big enough to satisfy her perfectly.

Her fingers scored his neck, her teeth bit him, small punishment for reducing her to this quivering mass of lust. He cried out as he pulsed into her. And then she came again, betrayed by her own nature and her own Achilles' heel.

She pressed her face to his chest, unwilling to talk and terrified by what he might say. But he'd already fallen asleep, still inside her, still joined. Tears formed in her eyes because she just couldn't stop herself making the same mistakes over and over.

NICK WOKE AND DIDN'T KNOW where he was. There was a snuffle and then he recognized the unmistakable sound of a woman's tears. *Bloody hell.* He stuffed the pillow beneath his head, glared at the slit of light that crept inside the door. Chrissie had cried a lot before she'd left him and he'd never been able to say the right thing to make her stop. Maybe if he had, she wouldn't have died carrying another man's baby.

But this wasn't Chrissie, it was Susie, so he stayed where he was.

The iron band that had been wrapped around his heart for the last twelve years was finally eroding. He didn't feel good yet, but he didn't feel awful either.

Suddenly it was silent. Not even the distant crash of the sea invaded the darkness. He dragged his hand through his hair and closed his eyes. He'd been an animal. No wonder she was crying. She deserved more than him trying to nail her against a wall. And stealing her keycard. Bloody hell.

If only Susie Cooper worked anywhere in town except at the marine lab.

Glancing at the dull red glow of the clock-radio he debated with himself, then stripped. It was harder to throw out a naked man than one fully dressed and he wasn't done with Susie yet. He wanted to be. She was a complication he didn't need in his life. But somehow he could not bring himself to walk away.

He limped to the door. His toe still throbbed, which served him right for being stupid and kicking a brick wall. Susie was curled up on the couch, her face hidden in a cushion in the semi-darkness. God, he hated tears.

He sat on the couch and felt her freeze. He ignored the rigid tension of her body and pulled her onto his lap, cradling her against his chest. Her hair tickled his nose. She wore a long T-shirt and nothing else and he started to sweat. Damn, he hated being obsessed with sex after years of indifference.

"What's wrong?" he asked, even though he didn't want to know. Didn't need the grief. There were plenty of women in the world. Susie wasn't anything special.

She didn't answer, instead tried to pull away from him.

He held her tighter. "Did I hurt you?"

She laughed, but it sounded harsh. "I'd probably enjoy it if you did."

He frowned at the revulsion in her voice. Why was sex such a big deal?

"It isn't illegal. Plenty of people get off on it." He pushed her away a little so he could see her face, but her cheeks flamed with embarrassment even in the dim light and she wouldn't meet his eyes.

"I can't believe I acted like such a—"

"Susie," he interrupted, "we didn't do anything nasty. It was good honest sex." Honest as a heart attack. He tried to keep it light, kissing the top of her head. "I'm not complaining."

He should be apologizing for the way he'd treated her because there was something about Susie Cooper that made him want to be a better man. She fascinated him. Maybe it was her cool poise, now shattered, or her intelligent eyes now cloudy with self-reproach. He didn't get it. She was miserable after a bout of mind-blowing sex. So what made her tick? He needed to know.

"I take it you usually have sex in the dark, lying flat on your back with your eyes closed, visualizing the stars-and-stripes while reciting 'God Bless America'?"

She shoved his shoulders, but at least she laughed. "Maybe. Heck, I don't know." She wiped her eyes on her nightshirt, flashing bare thighs which did nothing to help his situation. "It's just I always choose men who never stay." Her eyes grew wide and stricken.

God, what was he supposed to do? What was he supposed to say? How could he convince her that this wasn't her fault? There was nothing wrong with *her*— she was a bloody miracle—he was the screw-up.

"It isn't your fault, Susie."

She struggled in his grip, but he jammed her against his chest and held on tight.

"The fact I don't do long term has nothing to do with you."

"But it's *me* here with you now. I'm the flesh and blood person you'll leave behind." Her fingers kneaded his chest. "Men like you—"

Men like him? "Don't lump me in with the other men in your life." He grabbed her fingers. "I'm sorry men are too stupid to see what a great person you are but there are things in my past…" He stopped, appalled when tears welled up in his eyes and his voice cracked.

Susie grew still and he could feel her eyes on him even though he looked away.

"I don't play happy families. I told you. I told you that from the start."

And she'd told him to stay away from her... Why hadn't he listened? Why hadn't he had the strength to just walk away?

"Is it because of your wife?" she ventured.

He closed his eyes. Felt a hole growing in his chest like an anesthetic kicking in. What difference did the past make anyway?

"Even with her..." It took a moment for him to squeeze the words past the memories blocking his throat. "We were having problems. Chrissie thought I was emotionally closed off." Inside, his bones felt brittle.

"She was having an affair," Susie said.

"Yes." God, it still hurt. He squeezed his eyes closed, reliving the moment Chrissie had confessed. "I threw her out."

Susie ran a soothing hand up and down his arm. "I would have thrown her out too."

His words felt like sandpaper in his throat. "But you don't understand. She knew I was holding back. She knew I had secrets that I wasn't telling her."

Susie swallowed and looked away. He knew she understood secrets. She had her own and that was okay. He'd made his life about discovering other people's secrets but never revealing his own.

He'd told his grandmother's priest about his abuse so he could stay with him rather than being dumped on Social Services, but he'd never told anyone else.

Not even Chrissie, especially not Chrissie.

He'd needed her to believe he was perfect. And because of his silence he'd driven her away and she'd been murdered.

"My granny died when I was eight and I went to live with my mother."

Susie was about to speak but he placed a finger on her lips.

"It was the first time I saw drugs. The first time I understood evil walked in the world."

Susie's mouth dropped open in shock, but she kept silent.

Falling in love with Chrissie had seemed like proof he'd gotten over his past, except he hadn't been able to share it with her. He'd been scared that being abused made him less of a man.

"I was in that hellhole for two months." Sixty days and several lifetimes.

"So I don't do long-term relationships because I was abused and raped and I'm screwed up." His past was violent and ugly. "But I like sex and I'm damned if I'm going to let those bastards steal anything else from me." There were tears in her eyes which he brushed away. "But I don't want you thinking you're not good enough, or that there's something wrong with *you* just because I won't stick around."

She ducked her head, her breath hot compared to the chill of his skin. "I don't know what to say. I'm sorry."

"Susie—" tilting her head, he kissed her gently, barely touching her lips "—you have nothing to be sorry for."

She didn't respond, just sat passive in his lap, this enigma of a woman who was so bloody smart and so bloody stupid. She was more fragile than he'd realized, vulnerable beneath the polished surface.

He didn't want a wife or kids. But the suffocating

weight of the strain of trying to catch Chrissie's killer had finally lifted, and perhaps it was time to deal with the guilt he felt over her death. And while he was dealing with that, maybe he could linger long enough to help Susie over her little problem. Claim a little redemption.

"It seems a little ironic that you're the one with esteem issues." His lips coaxed hers until the barest flutter of interest stirred in her breath. "But maybe I can help you with that."

His hands wandered up her thighs, cupped the soft weight of her bottom. Finally she kissed him back, her fingers gently stroking his skin.

Nick trembled and pretended to smile. It was as though he'd never had sex before, never sated himself, never experienced this raw intensity of emotion. He settled her over him with shaking fingers, intending to pull her down over him and smother the hunger, except...

"We need a condom." Breathing heavily, she pulled back, resting her head against his shoulder.

Shit. His mouth went dry. His hands turned to fists as he strained against the urge to bury himself inside her anyway. What would one time matter? She wanted a baby anyway, didn't she?

She could have easily taken what she wanted from him at that moment—he was powerless, mindless. But she was a better person than he was. He didn't want a child and she knew it.

He didn't know how to love a child.

She darted into the bedroom. He almost followed her into her comfort zone, but comfort zones had always proved dangerous to him. Undercover police officers often got a bullet in the brain when they got too comfortable.

He counted to ten, gritting his teeth until he heard her approach.

He smiled when he saw her. She looked amazing. Her hair tousled, her lips red from his kisses, and whatever crying did to her eyes didn't look bad in this light. She stopped and stared at him, gnawing her bottom lip. She didn't look like the cool, calm university professor anymore.

He didn't want to hurt her, but he couldn't let go.

Not yet.

"Come here." He held his hand out.

It took a moment before she moved toward him, dragging her feet as if reluctant, but it was herself she was fighting, not him, and he knew what he had to do. He moved to take the condom from her fingers, but she dropped it. As she bent to retrieve it, her shirt slid over her bottom and gave him a view that made his heart stop.

"Please God, stay right there." He put one hand on the small of her back, taking the condom and covering himself. She was bent over, her shirt hanging loose so he could see the line of her ribs and sweet curve of her breasts.

"*This* is supposed to instill self-esteem?" she muttered, but he heard excitement there, too, and desire.

"Trust me…" He maneuvered them closer to the couch, let her brace her hands against the cushions as he curled himself over her, cradling her.

"Trust me, Susie." He pulled her hair to one side and kissed her neck and she writhed as he held her tight against him. "Don't fight it. You can do whatever the hell you want to me. I don't care." He pushed the cotton shirt over her head. "Use me. Scream as loud as you like. Scratch me. Bite me. Anything. Just because we're screwing doesn't mean I don't respect you."

She went still as he knew she would at his crudity.

"Do you trust me?" he whispered, and then took the lobe of her ear between his teeth.

"I'm working on it," she admitted, groaning when he moved his hands lower. Then, "Yes…" and he finally slid inside her.

He smiled against her back, nudged her legs wider apart and changed the angle.

"I respect you, Susie." She exploded around him, and it took every ounce of control not to follow.

Why couldn't she see this sort of pleasure was something to be savored, not ashamed of?

He maneuvered her against the wall the way he'd wanted to earlier. Her eyes were wide and filled with some inner anxiety. What would it take to blast away that reticence, to destroy the barricades? What would an uninhibited Susie Cooper be like?

Nick intended to find out.

He held her gaze. Waited for her to acknowledge and agree to his silent request. She gifted him a pure, simple smile. Then he lifted her up and eased inside, squeezing his eyes shut against the pleasure. His hands dug into her hips and sweat beaded on his brow from the effort of holding back.

"Take whatever you want from me." He wanted to bind her to him. He needed something significant from her and that scared him. "We end when you say so and not before." He drove deep inside her, focused, fierce and intense. "And whatever happens, I'll respect the hell out of you in the morning."

"What if I don't end it when you want me to?" Her voice was a whisper.

He plunged deeper, both of them desperate to get closer, heat steaming from their pores, sweat gluing their bodies together, and his heart pounding so hard his ribs hurt.

"You will," he promised.

She cried out, quivering in his arms, looking like some breathtaking angel. He didn't deserve her, but God help him, right now, he didn't care.

CHAPTER FOURTEEN

"I MISS MY DOG."

Nick's words rumbled through her hair, his chin rubbing the top of her head as they sat on the front step of her cottage watching dawn break over a clear October morning. It felt good to have his arms around her, good to connect after a night of mind-blowing, invigorating sex. The shame that usually rose up and choked her after being with a man didn't materialize. Somewhere, somehow, his confession last night had eased her. Dampened the fear inside her that enjoying sex would lead to her own moral destruction.

The knowledge that Nick had been abused, that he'd been raped at a young age made her insecurities seem petty and ill-conceived. She'd had sex at fifteen, she'd gotten pregnant and she'd given away her baby while in the throes of depression. Her baby was safe. She needed to move on.

"When will you get Rocket back?" She felt the pause of his breath and turned around as he stared at her.

"I can't believe I didn't tell you." He huffed out a laugh. "We arrested Judy Sizemore for the murder of Tracy Good last night. She also confessed to killing Chrissie."

Susie gripped her mug tighter as surprise rippled through her. How must he feel to know he'd finally found his wife's killer? She reached out to touch his face, but he drew back. She swallowed and reminded herself that this was not a relationship. It was sex.

"Did you tell Emily and Lily?"

Nick nodded, leaning over to the side to pick up his coffee from the stoop. "I went over last night before I came here. Emily took it badly."

That explained the desperation she'd seen in his eyes when he'd walked in the door.

"Because of me, she's been blaming Jake for years." He looked over to the Heathcotes' cottage, just visible over the hedge in the distance. "She didn't believe me when I told her it was Judy, not Jake. She insisted I'd made a mistake." Lines fanned out like a spider's web at the corners of his eyes.

"I spent all day yesterday conducting interviews." His eyes latched onto hers as if trying to reinforce the truth in his words. "I may not be good at relationships, but I did try to call you."

"Oh." The sun glowed like molten gold over the eastern horizon and there was a matching glow inside her chest. *Don't get sucked in*, she told herself. *Don't fall for him.* They were just two adults having a fling until she found someone better, someone more solid.

Even so his words soothed her disquiet.

"Maybe I should get a dog." She changed the subject and he let her. A gull hopped down from her chimney and eyed them with distrust from the nearby gravel.

"Dogs are more hassle than kids." His eyes sparkled, but she couldn't help flinching. She wanted kids and he knew it. He missed nothing and gave her a half smile of apology as he stood. "I've got to get to work."

"When do I get my car back?" Susie asked, standing.

Nick took her mug from her fingers and walked inside. She followed him.

"I'll give them a call today." He glanced over his shoulder as he washed the mugs and placed them on the drainer. "Even though Judy confessed, there's still a lot of work to do corroborating evidence." He dried his hands. "I'll give you a lift to work if you want."

She hid her surprise. It only took a minute to grab her flash drive and a couple of the more relevant papers she was using to write her review.

"You don't mind?" she asked.

"I pass right by the Gatty, why would I mind?" Confusion creased his brow until he got it. He laughed at her. "You think I don't want to be seen with you in public?" His hand curved over her shoulders. "Susie. How can someone so smart be so friggin' stupid?"

"Practice?" She grinned and allowed herself to believe the sincerity in those green eyes.

He shook his head, tugged her after him, holding her hand, waiting while she set the alarm and locked the door. They drove without talking, Radio Five-Live filling the silence with news stories covering everything from Manchester United to the G8.

At East Sands he pulled up on the embankment overlooking the sea, just yards from where poor Tracy Good had been viciously slain. Susie mumbled goodbye, climbed out and was already walking away when he got out.

"Hey, Susie!" He moved quickly and caught her hand. The wind tugged her hair. People were all around. Cars flashed by carrying her co-workers. Jake. Candace. Rafael sailing past on his bike with a shouted, "Olá."

Nick's thumb angled her chin, fingers sinking into her hair as he lowered his lips to hers for a brief kiss.

Then he raised his head, smiled a heartbreaking smile. "I'll see you later."

There was a flash of a camera. Nick spun to face the same reporter who'd crept into her lecture last week. Susie cringed.

"What do you want?" Nick's lips curled as he stalked the chubby guy. Susie called to leave it, but he didn't hear.

Did he even know who her mother was? That thought shocked her into keeping her mouth shut. Senator Darcy Cooper intimidated most people to hell and back. And although Susie knew she and Nick were temporary, the feelings that had blossomed between them were too precious to trample just yet.

Nick pulled the camera from the protesting journalist's hands and looked at the digital display.

Please don't break it.

He checked the image, called out to her with a wink. "You look great, but I've got a double chin." He thrust the camera into the guy's gut. "You've got your picture, now fuck off."

Susie only realized her mouth was open after Nick walked back to her and tapped it shut, then kissed her again.

"Yes, I know who your mother is. I'd be a useless detective if I hadn't worked that out, wouldn't I?" And he was gone. Leaving Susie standing watching him drive away, bewildered by the way he used the f-word so casually and by the fact he'd just declared in a public manner they were an item, however temporary.

The shame that had solidified inside her heart all those years ago split open and Susie felt a whole new person emerging. It wasn't just Nick. It was how she was starting to view herself as a stronger, better human being. And she was going to make the most of it.

Nick blinked against the sunlight pouring through Ewan McKnight's windows. Amy reached out a hand to grasp Nick's sleeve, the pressure on his arm like a butterfly dancing.

"I—I—I...hear...you have a new...girlfriend." She spoke slowly, each word requiring careful enunciation and a great deal of effort. She lay prone in a hospital bed that had been installed in the McKnight's sunroom a year ago, overlooking a goldfish pond and a barren rowan tree.

Nick squeezed her hand. "Is that what Ewan said?" It was impossible to lie to a woman who was slowly wasting away, her body eroding around a mind sharper than Toledo steel.

The muscles in her face didn't always work so her smile was hit and miss.

"It would...be good. Help you...move on now you've found wife's murderer."

"Putting a murderer away is good for everyone." Nick shrugged. So what if he'd been wrong about Jake? They had Judy locked up tight where she couldn't hurt anyone else. "Susie and I are just having a bit of fun."

Amy's eyes twinkled and he looked away with a reluctant chuckle.

Out the window five pumpkins were piled up, waiting to be carved into lanterns by Amy and Ewan's kids. It was peaceful here, the smell of damp earth masking the faint odor of antiseptic.

Ewan was making a pot of tea in the kitchen. With the case sewn up and the suspect behind bars they could relax a little, so he was working from home. Nick had agreed to meet him here to finish the last batch of reports before he re-interviewed Judy Sizemore that afternoon.

Amy's hand tightened on his sleeve. "I want Ewan to find someone else…after…I'm gone." Bloodshot eyes nailed him as he shifted his weight from one foot to the other. "It isn't easy…to think…I'm going to be dead…one of these days. To leave Ewan and my babies behind." Tears spilled over her cheeks and Nick opened his mouth to say something reassuring but nothing came out.

Amy never cried. She was so strong she scared the hell out of him.

"Promise me you'll be there for him, Nick." The light in Amy's eyes unnerved him. Big bad Nick Archer terrified of a bed-bound woman who couldn't even stand.

Finally he found his voice. "Don't talk like that, Amy, you've got years left." But his voice was harsher than he meant it to be.

"Oh God. I hope not!" She laughed but winced as her lips cracked. Nick wished he were the sort of man who knew how to ease her burden, but he backed away, uncomfortable with this sort of helplessness.

"I know Ewan seems strong." Amy wasn't letting him escape. Not today. So he stopped retreating and met her gaze. "But when I'm gone. He'll need help. You… understand." Her hand shook as she reached for her lip balm. Nick picked it up and pressed it into her hands.

"Thanks." She smiled and took a hoarse breath. "It's the kids I worry about most. To have a mother…so crippled." Anger gleamed in the depths of her eyes. "I want to watch them grow…but if I were dead…they could move on."

"They love you, Amy." He didn't know what else to say. Her love for her kids was the most powerful emotion he'd ever encountered, which made his own mother's treatment all the more damning. Amy saved him from saying anything else by starting to cough and not being able to stop.

"Ewan!" Nick yelled.

"Here we go." Ewan came into the room carrying a tray of tea and biscuits. "You having a bit of trouble?" he spoke directly to his wife, who was wheezing and nodding, her eyes wide with terror. He placed the tray on the chair beside the bed and leaned over, bending her forward to pound her back. She finally took a shuddering breath and he eased her gently onto the pillow. Sunlight drenched her flushed skin as her breath slowly eased away from that awful wet rattle.

"Better?" Ewan asked and held a straw to her lips to give her a sip of water. She swallowed and nodded, closed her eyes and lay back against the pillows, exhausted.

Shit.

Ewan caught Nick's eye. Although his colleague's face was impassive there was grimness in the back of his eyes, a terrible pain.

Losing Chrissie had felt like a sharp dagger ripping through Nick's chest. So how did Ewan deal with that agony every single day? Did it get duller? Did the blade lose its edge? From the look in his friend's eyes, Nick didn't think so. Ewan led the way into a sun-soaked living room that was painted green and filled with effigies of frogs in all their forms. He looked knackered, deep pockets of purple flesh padding the circles beneath his eyes.

"Are forensics in?" Ewan asked. There was a catch in his voice that they both ignored.

Nick nodded. "Everything except DNA."

"Anything on the hammer?" Ewan cleared his throat.

"Just Tracy." Nick slumped onto the floral love-seat. "There's no evidence to tie Judy Sizemore to the hammer, or the body, or the murder scene." He rubbed his hands over his face. "I don't like it."

Ewan stood beside the gas fireplace. "Judy's a smart lady, maybe she knew enough about forensics to cover her tracks."

"Aye, but there's no blood in either of their cars, or on any of her clothes. No fingerprints or DNA on the murder weapon." Nick realized he was grinding his teeth when his forehead started to throb. "Did she really love that bastard enough to kill two women? Because I sure as hell didn't feel the love during the interview."

"The only blood trace found was in Susie's car."

Nick gave Ewan a challenging stare. "From my shoes because I drove it the night of the murder, remember?"

"You don't think it's a little coincidental that both blood trace and the murder weapon were found in her Mini?"

Nick felt every muscle inside his body coil. "God help me, Susie had nothing to do with this…if someone says she did—"

"A couple of woodentops thought *you* might have done it to set up Sizemore—"

"What?" Nick blinked in shock at his fellow detective.

"I'm just telling you what was said in the break room."

"And what did you tell them?" Nick had been so focused on Tracy's murder he'd missed the possible connotations.

"I told them if you'd wanted to frame Sizemore for murder, the girl would have died in the man's office, and he'd have been found holding the murder weapon and covered in her blood."

Nick didn't know if that was a compliment or an insult. "I wouldn't kill an innocent girl just to set him up."

"No. Nothing so underhand. You'd just beat him to a pulp."

He'd already tried that.

Ewan's face sagged and Nick wondered if he was a huge disappointment to his sergeant.

"Judy said she killed the women in a jealous rage. Why else would she confess?" Ewan asked.

"I don't know." Nick rubbed both hands over his face. His own lack of conviction grated on his nerves.

"It must piss you off to know you were wrong about Jake Sizemore all these years."

"Not really. He was still screwing my wife."

Ewan frowned at the teapot. "But you don't think Judy did it, do you?"

Nick picked up the files he needed. "I *want* to believe she did it. But maybe I want to believe it a little too much. There isn't any physical evidence."

Ewan snorted. "You're just scared of not having an excuse not to get on with your life."

Nick held back an expletive. "This isn't about my life, and I get on with it just fine."

"This has been your entire life since your wife died. Now it is over you've no excuse to be miserable anymore."

Temper sizzled through Nick making his skin hot and his fists clench.

"You could actually be happy with a nice girl like Susie Cooper. Wouldn't that be a bloody miracle?"

Christ. Each heartbeat thudded through Nick in slow

motion. Only the fact Amy lay in the next room stopped him from going for Ewan's throat, even though the D.S. looked as if he wanted to go a few rounds. Ewan didn't usually pick fights.

"Don't," Nick warned, raising his hands and holding back words that could never be taken back. "Just don't."

The doorbell rang and Ewan stalked off to answer it. Nick peered through the glass and cursed. Superintendent Pamela Richardson, the boss.

"Ah, thought I'd catch you both here." She walked across the green carpet, spick-and-span in her uniform, and held out a file for Nick. "DNA is in."

Nick reached out to take it, but she sensed the atmosphere and held on to the file for a moment longer than necessary. "Problem?"

"No," Ewan and Nick said in unison.

There was no problem as long as people kept their nose out of Nick's business. Ewan sent him a small smile and flashed his brows up in apology. Nick wondered if Ewan had any clue he might one day be in Nick's shoes.

Of course he did.

That's why he'd picked an argument in the first place.

Nick flicked open the file. Tracy Good had sperm from two different men in her vaginal vault, neither of whom were Jake Sizemore. Students—Tony Scott, who'd admitted a fling with Tracy, and Rafael Domenici, who hadn't.

"Bugger."

"What is it?" The supe asked, watching him carefully.

The feeling that he'd missed something skittered around his mind like a cockroach. "A witness who lied, boss."

Pam shrugged, her corkscrew curls bouncing on her shoulders. "People lie to the police all the time. Is it relevant?"

Nick was still expecting a call from the Brazilian authorities following up on Rafael Domenici's background. And the guy had an alibi for the murder he still needed to confirm. "I think I'll check it out, remind him of the inadvisability of lying to a police officer during an investigation." He smoothed his expression into one of conscientiousness. Not easy for a coldhearted bastard.

"Right." The supe shook her head and shot Ewan a smile. "I'm taking an hour for lunch and thought I'd visit Amy. If it's a good time…?"

"It is." Ewan nodded and smiled, though his eyes still looked drawn and tired. "You know how much she appreciates your visits, ma'am."

The supe stood as straight as a soldier on parade. "Are you kidding? I don't come for Amy. I come for a bit of sanity away from the station."

Nick looked away. If she hadn't had his respect before, she had it now. Pamela Richardson was a better human being than he would ever be. He liked Amy, he really liked her. But he hated being trapped in that stifling bedroom prison.

"Right then." Nick snatched his jacket off the back of a dining chair. Ewan looked at him and raised his brow in question. "You finish the reports, mate. I'm off to the pub. Police business." He slapped Ewan on the shoulder.

Ewan narrowed his eyes. "Dirty work."

"Some of us were born to suffer."

"You've got that right."

SUSIE WAS FEELING PRETTY DAMN good and found it hard to concentrate on work no matter how much she told herself not to moon over Nick Archer. She printed out forms for Lily and Rafael to attend the animal handling course in Dundee next week and decided to walk the paperwork up to the main office for Jake's signature. She couldn't believe he was in after his wife had been charged, but maybe staying home was worse. She ducked through the coffee room, smiling at the chief technician who was brewing coffee. She didn't want to chat because she didn't want to be grilled or teased regarding her fledgling relationship with the man holding the department head's wife for murder. It was guaranteed that news of her and Nick kissing outside the lab that morning would have spread like the crown-of-thorns starfish over a coral reef.

She headed up the stairs toward the admin office, paused when she heard raised voices, wondering what she'd got herself into. Marine labs were close-knit communities. But if she wanted to make a life for herself here, and she did, she needed to deal with Candace and her boss.

Steeling herself, she raised her chin and walked into the office where Candace was typing at warp speed. Susie stood quietly waiting until Candace looked up. The woman's eyes narrowed, but Susie smiled determinedly and handed her the forms.

"I need Jake to sign these ASAP, please, so I can send them off in the afternoon mail."

Candace tilted her head to one side like a raptor deciding whether or not to eat a mouse. She pursed her scarlet lips and took the forms from Susie with none of her usual banter, but at least she wasn't hostile.

Jake heard Susie's voice and came to the door of his office looking like an escaped convict. His clothes were rumpled, hair taking off in all different directions, pudgy lips pressed together as if containing sobs.

Sympathy welled up inside her. The poor man must feel terrible about what had happened.

"Susie. You need to call your mother. My wife is an American citizen. This whole situation is outrageous."

She kept her voice neutral. "Your wife confessed to two murders."

"My wife didn't kill anyone. She was bullied into a confession." He ran his hands through his hair, sweat staining his shirt. As he turned, Susie caught sight of a young woman in Jake's office. Jake's daughter, Callie. Callie was tall and lanky, long bones and perfect skin, mousey-colored hair and big, otherworldly eyes.

"Have you called the embassy?" Susie suggested, looking away from the girl's intense stare.

"I tried, but no one will take my calls." Jake's expression turned ugly, as if the emotions inside him were eating his face from the inside out. "Why did I hire you if you won't even make one lousy phone call?"

Susie blinked at the unexpected attack. *Okay.* "I seem to recall an entire committee hiring me, not just you, Jake. And you hired me because I'm good at my job."

"You and plenty of others," he jeered.

"Are you telling me I was hired because my mother is a politician?" Susie needed to know she'd gotten this job on merit, but Jake Sizemore wasn't in the mood to assuage her ego.

He said nothing, but Callie spoke up, her voice as thin as her body. "Don't trust her, Daddy. She's screwing that detective."

Susie's jaw dropped. Why would this young woman

be so rude? Susie wasn't the one who'd admitted to killing two of Jake's students and neither was Nick.

"My private life is none of your business and that policeman is just doing his job." Susie took a step into Jake's office and lowered her voice. "Maybe you should examine your own behavior." She looked straight at Jake. "If you hadn't acted inappropriately with students, maybe your wife wouldn't have killed anyone."

Jake's eyes glittered and he stepped toward her. She smelled the testosterone in his sweat and felt the heat of his anger.

"Watch your mouth, Dr. Cooper. The university has given me its full support in this matter and those allegations are unfounded. Repeating them will earn you an official reprimand and a slander suit in court."

Even though everyone knew it was true? Why would the university support this man?

She drew a tight breath. She thought she'd escaped politics. "What about the dead girls? Who's supporting them?"

"Who cares?" Callie's eyes were hard as flint. Her dad put a hand on his daughter's shoulder. "They were both lying sluts."

Outside the sky was blue, the sun blinding, the cathedral sitting high on the hill like a ruined temple. But the perfection was ruined and the balance of Susie's world shifted, revealing a malevolent shadow.

CHAPTER FIFTEEN

"WHERE'S NIALL?" Nick asked a young woman working behind the bar. She was pretty. Midnight hair, young, slim, with a smile that should have moved his blood and didn't. He glanced at his watch and considered calling Susie. But what would he say? *I'm looking at a pretty girl and thinking of you?*

"He's in the back. I'll go get him for you." Her eyes lingered with interest, but he shifted his gaze away.

"Get us a pint of 80, first, would you, love?" Nick needed a drink, needed to wash away the taste of slow death and friendship. He looked around. The pub wasn't busy, just a couple of barflies and one table of students.

The silence of his phone was beginning to piss him off. He was waiting for a return call from the Brazilian Consulate in Edinburgh. He pulled it out of his pocket, made sure he had a signal and put it away again.

"Hiya, Nick." Niall came out of the back room. "Don't see you in here very often."

They played on the same Sunday league football team and Niall had worked in this bar even when Nick was an undergraduate. Niall started stacking beer bottles on low shelves, and let the pretty girl deal with the customers.

"I hear you've arrested someone for that murder."

Niall pulled a face. "Gave me a fright when I heard about it, what with Lily working there."

Nick nodded. It had given him a fright, too, and he still couldn't shift the apprehension.

"Lily worked here on Saturday night, right?" She'd said Rafael was with her on Saturday night, which meant the guy had to have been here, too.

Niall hesitated. "She did. I put her in a cab around two."

"What about a Brazilian bloke? Tall, blue eyes and black curly hair." Nick tapped his beer-mat on the bar. "Was he here?"

Niall's mouth tightened and he hefted a crate up onto the granite surface. "There was a guy like that in here talking to her."

Nick released a deep breath. Shit. He'd been sure he was onto something. He didn't trust Rafael Domenici's smart mouth or pretty face.

"I found him in the back room with her around eleven. I kicked him out of there and he left. I'm not even sure he bought a drink, come to think of it." Niall took up a cloth and started wiping the bar, a frown of concentration on his face.

Nick felt a current of excitement zip along his nerves, but he was confused. "So Lily left with him? Or he came back later?"

"No, no." Niall shook his head. "She never left the bar and that nancy-boy never came back."

Shock rocked Nick. The world spun even as he stood motionless. Lily had lied to him. Even after everything he'd done and experienced, he'd never expected Lily to lie to him. His mobile rang and he nodded to Niall, leaving the bar to take the call. It was the Brazilian Consulate. And although the charges had been dropped, Rafael Domenici had once been arrested for rape.

By LUNCHTIME, SUSIE WAS STILL too disconcerted to get any work done. She steadied her hand on the wooden banister, pressing her temple to the cool plaster wall. Should she believe her whole career had been shaped by the fact her mother was a politician? Why even bother to turn up and put in the hours if that was all that mattered? She should just put her feet up and ride the nepotistic wave. Angry tears blurred her vision as she hurried to the ladies' room in the basement. Passing her CT room she heard bangs and crashes from inside. *Hell.* She was hanging on to her professional credibility by ragged fingernails—the last thing she needed was one of her students causing trouble.

She raised her face to the heavens and paused with her hand on the door handle of the restroom. The metal latch was worn smooth beneath her fingers, polished by a thousand female hands. Women in science had always fought discrimination. She wasn't the only one trying to balance life and work. Life was lonely, work was hard, but she was damn well doing it.

She took a deep breath, turned and opened the door of the CT room to deal with another situation she didn't need. But she stopped, stunned by the scene that confronted her.

Jake was demolishing her plumbing, throwing pipes on the floor, twisting PVC joints violently until they split or cracked. Pipes her hard-won research grants had paid for.

"What are you *doing?*" she yelled, rushing into the room.

He whirled. "I just got a phone call from the principal. He told me he'd received a complaint about my conduct from one of my staff." He snapped another gray pipe over his thigh.

"I never made a complaint!"

"I want your equipment out of this room now. You had no right to move into this space."

"Are you *nuts?*" From the dull glitter in his eyes she was afraid he might be.

He glanced over her shoulder and lowered his voice. "You got this job because I thought you might be useful, and if that failed at least I might get a good fuck." His eyes raked her body as he advanced a step. "But you aren't worth the effort."

Fear hit first and she backed up a step. His eyes catalogued her reaction and satisfaction flared in their depths.

Son. Of. A. Gun. He enjoyed frightening her. She had been warned.

"Break one more piece of equipment and I will file a complaint." Susie was known for her calm temperament, relied on for her tactful diplomacy, but right now her emotions were being trampled and she was done with being nice, composed or tactful. "I will not tolerate this sort of threatening behavior from someone who should know better."

He bared his over-bleached teeth. "You'll never get anywhere at this university. No secretarial support, no space, no funds, no promotion, no tenure." He ticked the list off his fingers. "And once your two years are up I'm going to bury you so deep in teaching and admin you'll never get another paper written. Better start looking for another job, bitch."

Everything inside her crystallized as she drew in a quick breath and squared her shoulders. She was sick of being treated as if she was a worthless piece of trash. She advanced on her boss, drilled her finger into his chest. "I have had it with your over-inflated male ego and bullying tactics."

He shoved her and she stumbled. Rage ruptured inside her, obliterating her logical temperament. Her fist started low, traveling in a wide arc as she swung from the hip and carried it through to his nose, pain exploding through her knuckles as she connected. But it was worth it.

Jake cupped his bleeding nose, looking more startled than wounded.

"Aye, aye, what do we have here then?" Nick blocked the doorway, smiling dangerously. The chief technician stood behind him, interest flashing across his face.

Susie's chest heaved as fury slowly settled into a pool of horror. Had she really just assaulted her boss—in front of witnesses? Nick's eyes narrowed in critical assessment.

"Are you all right, Susie?" He moved to stand beside her, picked up her hand, blew the skin of her knuckles to soothe the sting. Then he raised them for a kiss.

It helped.

"Do you want to press charges?"

"Yes," Jake spluttered through blood.

"Not you, asshole." Nick touched her face. "Are you okay?"

She hid her face in her hands, extremely embarrassed she'd used violence on another human being.

The technician came in with a mop and bucket of water to clean up the blood. Jake ripped off a bunch of tissue from a blue roll and tipped back his head, a crimson moustache staining his upper lip. "You're ruined. I have witnesses."

What the hell had she done?

"I didn't see anything." One side of Nick's lips tugged into a cold grin.

"Unfortunately, I didn't see anything either, boss." The technician shrugged his shoulders in apology, but when she caught his gaze the amused gleam connected to something deep inside her and she remembered to breathe. The passionate nature she'd forced into a box as a teenager had again exploded out of control, and the usual chaos had resulted. But the results weren't terrible or heartbreaking. Somehow, despite everything, she'd handled herself and possibly made an ally.

Jake stormed out, muttering obscenities. She looked around to assess the damage.

Nick stepped away. Gone was the concern. His eyes turned hard and flat. "I need to talk to Rafael Domenici and Lily. Any idea where I can find them?"

"Lily's working at home, looking after her mother." Susie thought for a moment. "I think Rafael is in his office. Want me to get him for you?"

Nick shook his head, pressed his lips into an uncompromising line that closed off all communication. "I'll find him. Thanks."

There was a distance about him she recognized as cop mode. He hesitated for a moment at the doorway, but didn't turn back. The new assertive Susie decided she wasn't going to give a damn that Nick hadn't said goodbye.

But why was a cop looking for her students?

She started picking up pipes and reassembling the jigsaw that was her aquarium. After a few moments the technician started to help.

Nick took the steps up the spiral staircase two at a time, the structure creaking under his weight. Heads turned, students visible in the open-plan offices and desks, but he ignored everyone, searching for a mop of curly black hair. Posters of marine life were blue-tacked to the walls and embarrassing photos were pinned to a message board; a new generation of students, the same old goofy humor. He strode across the platform, found what he was looking for flirting in the middle cubicle.

"You." He pointed his finger at Domenici then hiked his thumb over his shoulder. "Outside, now."

The girl's eyes widened at Nick's tone. Rafael flashed her a reassuring smile, but there was a tenseness about him, as if he knew what was coming. Lying little tosser.

Nick led the way, shoving out the front door, glancing into Susie's office windows. Christ, what was he doing with a woman like Susie Cooper? The guilt of using her warred with an attraction that just wouldn't dissipate. She was going to get hurt and he was the one who was going to do it. But he couldn't help grinning remembering how she'd punched Sizemore on the nose. Who'd have thought it?

The day was bright, a nice sunny October day, the sea a dark rippling blue. But it wasn't dark enough to match his mood. He jumped onto the beach, all thoughts of Susie wiped away by what was to come. Lily was his family and she'd lied to him. He needed to know why.

Rafael thudded onto the sand behind him and stopped twenty yards from where they'd found Tracy Good's battered body.

The boy lit a cigarette right-handed. "What can I do for you, Detective?"

"You lied to me." Nick wanted to punch the insolence off his face.

Rafael rolled one muscular shoulder. "*Talvez.* Maybe," he corrected.

"You were shagging Tracy Good." Nick controlled his temper because he wanted to shred skin and that never looked good in a police report.

Rafael looked away and expelled a deep breath. Shrugged again as though it didn't matter. "*Sim*. We had sex if that's what *shagging* is." He looked back at Nick, his face carefully blank of expression. Too blank, too controlled. "She like sex. I like sex."

"You lied during a police investigation, Romeo. That's obstruction of justice and I can bust your balls onto the next flight to Rio just for that."

Rafael's face bleached beneath his tan and a nerve ticked in his jaw. "I didn't hurt her. I just want no trouble with the *policía*." He appealed to Nick with those pretty eyes, but they didn't work on him. Nick knew what hid behind the shiny façade. A rapist. It must have shown on his face because Rafael's expression closed up as he looked away.

"Ah, you've found out my *mau* past." The words were punctuated with a hard expulsion of air. The Brazilian crushed the cigarette beneath his sneakers and picked up the butt, staring up at the sky like a martyr. Nick hoped a seagull shat on his face, but neither of them was *that* lucky.

"Why don't you tell me what happened?" Nick invited.

Rafael's lip thinned and he didn't look so pretty now. "I no care to discuss it."

"Then you'd better pack your bags, sunshine, because I don't have time to fuck around." With feigned indifference Nick started back up the beach. "I'll have your case file in half an hour anyway. Go say goodbye to your boss because—"

"*Não!*" Rafael stood rigid, his eyes burning with what looked like tears.

Poor baby. Nick stopped walking and stared at the young man, waiting.

"I had sex with the wrong girl!" Rafael's fingers constricted into fists as if to contain his emotions. "I was nineteen and stupid." He stared at the sand, then back at Nick, his eyes a curious mixture of beseeching and pissed. "I picked up a girl in Copacabana and we went dancing and had sex." He closed his eyes and raised his face to the sky. "I was drunk."

He muttered something in Portuguese that sounded like a prayer, opened his eyes and looked straight into Nick's eyes. "She was fourteen and the authorities would have done nothing except the little *puta* found out my family was rich and cried rape."

Anger settled low in Nick's stomach. "You had sex with a fourteen-year-old and expect me to feel sorry for *you?*"

Rafael spat. "Feel sorry for her if you want, she said she was legal, and I was drunk enough to believe her." Rafael peered down his arrogant nose. "I didn't ask her to *chupar meu pau.*"

Nick didn't know what *chupar meu pau* was, but figured it wasn't a peck on the cheek. "The charges were dropped?"

Silently Rafael drew a line in the sand, stood looking down at it. The wind was getting up, cooling the temperature, cooling Nick's temper.

"My father paid her off." The self-loathing on the boy's face made Nick pause.

"There is a saying in Brazil. Prisons are for BPPs— black people, poor people and prostitutes." Rafael's lip twisted. "My father was proud of me that day."

"So you came over here to screw older girls?"

Rafael laughed, his eyes traveling slowly down Nick's length as if to disconcert him, but Nick was too old for that crap. "Perhaps. I like sex, but I am not a violent man, Detective."

"Then why did Lily lie to me about being with you on Saturday night?" Nick's voice shook with renewed rage, except it wasn't rage, it was betrayal and it caused a pain in his chest that was new and frightening.

"I not know." Rafael stuffed his hands in his pockets and frowned. "Lily and I are friends. *That* is not easy, but it is…interesting," he admitted, his eyes softening. "She thought I needed an *álibi*. You must tell her everything, I suppose?"

Nick stared at the cocky bastard and didn't know whether to ignore him or flatten him. "Where were you after you left the bar?"

"With a woman." Rafael's eyes turned opaque, impossible to read.

"Name?"

Another self-depreciating smile tugged the corners of Rafael's lips. "I didn't ask her name. Just her age. She liked my accent." His eyes twinkled, saying just how much women liked his accent, the arrogant, smarmy, little shite.

"So what will it be Detective? Will you make my father proud again and throw me out of the country for *shagging?*"

Nick took a single step toward Rafael, tension spiking. There was nothing Nick would like more than to rough up that pretty face. But he stopped and they stared at each other. One with dirty secrets. The other with secrets as dark as sin.

The beat of Nick's heart was heavy in his chest. "If

you had anything to do with Tracy Good's murder, deportation will be the least of your worries. And if you touch Lily with that overactive dick of yours, I'll rip it off and stuff it down your throat. Daddy won't be able to get you out of this one, pal. Got it?"

Rafael nodded, clenching his jaw against whatever response he wanted to make. Nick strode away, kicking up sand. Vaulted the seawall and climbed the embankment, glancing to where Tracy had taken her last agonized breath. It was easy to forget about Tracy. There were no relatives baying for justice. No friends weeping with grief. Just men who'd used her for sex and no one who really gave a shit. He looked back at Rafael Domenici, who stood smoking yet another cigarette. The worthless sack of...

And Nick shouldn't give a damn because he had Tracy's killer in custody, but Lily, closer than blood, had lied to him.

Why?

He glanced at the Gatty building and checked his watch. Two o'clock. He hovered uncertainly beside his SUV, unnerved because he wanted to go see Susie for a few minutes before he headed off to question Lily. But he was working and only had an hour before he was due to re-interview Judy Sizemore. And although he could make the accused wait, it wouldn't go down well with the Crown Office.

His stomach churned as he unlocked his car door and got in, Rocket jumping over the seat to lick his face. Nick gave the dog a quick rub under his chin and started the engine. Right now, Susie was an indulgence he couldn't afford.

CHAPTER SIXTEEN

RESTING HER CHIN IN THE PALM of her hand, Lily dragged her fingers over her face, stretching down her lower eyelids as she read a review paper outlining the developmental stages of octopods. She sipped her coffee, trying to clear her blurry vision and fuzzy mind. She needed to call Niall and quit her job. She didn't have time for it anymore, not with her mother's illness and trying to do her Ph.D.

If she could just get her mom stable, she'd be able to concentrate on her studies and achieve more than even Saint Chrissie had been able to do. A car pulled up outside and Lily craned her neck to see who it was.

Nick!

Grinning, she ran out the kitchen door, closing it quietly behind her so as not to wake her mother from her nap. The drugs the doctor prescribed made her tired and woozy. Rocket nearly bowled her off her feet in the rush to say hello.

"Hi there, boy. Long time no see." Lily laughed and hunkered down for a stroke while avoiding a good licking. "No tongues. I know where it's been!"

She stood and reached to give Nick a hug, but he pulled away.

"What is it? What's the matter?" The stern set of his features told her he was angry. Despite what Susie had told her on the beach yesterday, Lily knew there was something going on between the two of them. She'd spotted his car there when she'd gone jogging that morning.

Had they already broken up?

"Let's take a walk." He inclined his head toward the path in the marram grass along which he'd rescued her mother just a couple of nights ago.

"Okay." It wasn't too cold so she didn't bother with a coat and Nick was wearing a leather jacket she could always steal. She picked up a slimy tennis ball Rocket had brought along for his own entertainment and slugged it over the dune. Rocket took off, the grass whipping behind him like the swish of scissor blades.

They followed the dog to the beach where the surf played tag with the gulls. She'd dyed her hair last night, blond with pink streaks, and even though it was just her and her mother in the house she wore full battle makeup.

Nick stopped on the soft sand, his countenance severe and unfriendly. "Why did you lie to me?"

What was he talking about? "I never lied." She frowned. Despite the blood connection, she'd always preferred Nick to Chrissie and this was the first time he'd been anything but friendly. She didn't like it.

"Rafael Domenici." Nick's eyes were the same green as the sea glass she'd picked up the other day on the beach, but right now they held less warmth.

"Oh. That."

"You lied to me during a murder investigation. I could charge you with obstruction of justice."

"Oh, come on." Lily couldn't believe his tone. He was her rock, her anchor, her ray of hope in a world dominated by a ghost. "Rafael didn't kill Tracy. You've got your murderer, why are you making such a big deal out of this?"

Was it a coincidence he hooked up with Susie after years of not getting involved with anyone, and then treated Lily like crap? Resentment rose inside her against a boss she'd wanted to worship. "Is this because of Dr. Cooper? Did she say something about me?"

Nick cut her off with an impatient exclamation. "This has nothing to do with Susie. Shit, Lily, if you don't think lying to the principal investigator in a murder inquiry is bad enough—" his lips stretched taut "—what about lying to *me?*"

"I don't know why you're getting all pissy with me. It wasn't that big a deal."

His fists clenched at his sides. "Since when did you get so good at reading men? Since when do you *instinctively* know some guy isn't a killer?"

She didn't know if it was the sarcasm or the derision that hurt the most. Humiliation crawled up her spine and made her feel very, very small. *How dare he?* Nick, more than anyone, should understand she wasn't some stupid little twit. "He's a Romeo, not a killer. Come on. I know him, I work with the guy."

"You know him, aye? Well, did you know he was charged with rape back in Brazil?"

Tension bit into her stomach. "Bullshit."

"He had sex with a fourteen-year-old girl who cried foul and reported it to the police."

"Did he force her?"

Nick shook his head. "I don't think so."

Relief hit her solar plexus. "Well then—"

"She was fourteen, for God's sake!" Nick retrieved the ball Rocket had dropped at his feet and sent it flying into the air.

Lily jerked a shoulder. "Plenty of girls I know had sex at fourteen."

"Did you?" Nick's eyes narrowed as he asked the question and she knew he'd switched from cop to brother-in-law.

"No." She put her hands on her hips and shot him a glare. "But I could have. Girls use sex to control boys at that age. Boys are just too stupid to know it."

The disappointment in his eyes hurt more than she could have ever imagined.

"And you think boys are stupid." This time he kicked the ball for Rocket and she watched it run for miles across the hard-packed sand, the dog in flat-out pursuit. She wished she could run away, too.

"What happened to you, Lily? I trusted you." Nick's voice dropped away and shame rolled in her stomach like nausea. "What happened to the little girl I used to carry around on my shoulders?"

She wiped at the eyeliner she knew would be running down her face.

"And why do you wear all that crap on your face?" His expression screamed *freak* and suddenly she couldn't catch her breath. He put his hands on her shoulders and she tried to jerk away, but he was stronger than she was. "Why, Lily? Why do you hide behind all that shit?"

He turned her to face him, but she refused to look up. He knew why she wore so much makeup. He was the only one who understood exactly why she wore any makeup at all. She wanted to kick him in the balls, but Nick wouldn't take that from anyone and though he might love her, he might also leave, and that thought made the air in her chest freeze with fright.

Everyone left. Chrissie, her dad, and now her mother. She didn't want to be alone. Lily scrubbed her cheek against her shoulder to wipe the tears away. They were both breathing hard. She stared at Nick's shirt buttons, not wanting to see the expression on his face.

Please don't leave...

All her mother cared about was Chrissie. Her sister hadn't been perfect, but Lily had loved her, too, and now she wanted to forget she'd ever existed—except whenever she looked in the mirror all she saw was her sister's reflection.

"Do you think I *like* looking like her? You think I enjoy seeing the pain in Mom's eyes when she calls me the wrong name or the disappointment when she realizes her mistake?" Lily gripped his jacket with both hands and shook. "You're just as bad as she is. You always blamed yourself for Chrissie's death, but you never blamed her! She was screwing somebody else, for Christ's sake." Her knees buckled as she tried to pull away but he wouldn't let go. She collapsed against him and he wrapped his arms tight around her.

"I'm sorry." Nick stroked her hair the way her mom used to. "Don't cry. It's all right, Lily."

He jammed her against his chest to comfort her and suddenly her anger evaporated and the great gaping hole of truth stared back. It wasn't all right. It would never be all right, but maybe she knew a way to make him stay. She lunged for his lips, crushing his mouth to hers and had her tongue down his throat for one second before he thrust her away.

"What the fuck do you think you're doing?" Nick stalked away in a tight circle. He wiped his sleeve across his mouth and looked as if he wanted to spit. "What the hell was that?" His green eyes were furious and blazing.

What have I done?

Tears flooded her eyes and she spun away, running

through the dunes. He didn't follow and she knew that, to him at least, she was nothing like her sister.

Nick was late for the meeting he'd set up. He gave the guy from the Crown Office a shit-eating grin and followed him into the interview room. Judy sat talking to her lawyer, the wariness in her eyes exposed by the harsh assault of fluorescent lights. Nick sat, started the recorder and reeled off the time, date, people present and purpose of interview.

Lily had kissed him and it tasted like incest.

He wiped his mouth again and pushed her out of his mind. Then he noticed how hard Judy was staring at him. How hard she was concentrating. He paused mid-word and stared back.

Killers usually relaxed after they confessed, opened up as if they were in therapy. They either regretted what they'd done and wanted absolution, or they got a thrill out of reliving the moment and shocking their audience. Nick had outgrown shock years ago, except for Lily friggin' kissing him.

He took a sip of coffee to try and blot it out.

"I need you to talk me through the murders, Judy. Everything you did on those days, starting with last Saturday."

Her fingers played with the swollen arthritic knuckles, which trapped her wedding band on her finger.

"I told you I killed her. *Them.* Why do we need to go through all this again?" Her eyes were weak on contact, her voice big on determination.

Nick leaned forward, fighting his growing sense of unease. "How did you get into St. Andrews last Saturday night?"

She flicked him a glance, frowned at him as though he was an idiot. "I drove my car."

"The Peugeot?"

She nodded and he looked at the report in his hand. His toe still throbbed, but it helped him concentrate on the here and now. "Okay. There are a few things I don't understand. One of them is why we didn't find any of Tracy's blood in your vehicle."

Watching her face he noted the way her eyes swung toward her lawyer and back again to him.

"I washed off in the sea after I killed her." She took a quick breath and released it. "I couldn't stand feeling the blood on my face and clothes so I ran in and washed it all off."

It sounded like the ideal way to thwart a police investigation.

"Must have been cold?" he queried. But Judy was a diver, like him, Jake, and Chrissie had been. Like Susie. Cold water wouldn't bother her that much.

Judy shrugged. A muscle ticked on her face, tugging her right eye in a garish wink.

"What happened when you first got to the Gatty? Did you go into the building?"

She sipped her water, looked straight through him to the wall behind his head. The guy from the CO fidgeted in his chair.

"I hid behind the Dumpster and waited for Tracy to come out of the building. Jake had been working that day, when he got home I could smell her on him." Her nostrils flared, but her tone was crisp. "I left him drinking in his study, knew he'd fall asleep." Her fingers moved in a weird knitting motion. "She always worked late. God, I wish I hadn't given up smoking."

Smoking would be the least of her worries in jail. "So you hid behind the skip and then what?" Nick pressed.

"She came out and walked past me."

"Did she cut through to the gate or walk all the way around the car park?"

"I—I don't remember," she stuttered.

How could you not remember? Unease slipped through him and his gut clenched. "What happened next?"

Judy looked relieved to have gotten off so easy, but Nick wasn't done with the details.

"I crouched down when I saw her coming. She passed within a foot of me, but it was dark."

Nick kept his face impassive, but foreboding grew with each word Judy uttered. No mention of the haar that had enveloped the beach that night, providing ample cover.

"I remember now. She went through the gate. I sneaked behind her and hit her over the head, and then she turned toward me and I hit her again."

Either Judy was running a double bluff or she was making the whole friggin' thing up, which potentially left a killer loose in his city.

"Let me get this straight, you hit her once from behind."

Judy nodded, her eyes bulging.

"And then? Was she still standing?"

Judy nodded again.

The pathologist had said the first blow had probably driven Tracy to her knees.

"Then she turned around toward you and you hit her in the face?" Nick prompted.

"That's correct." Judy pursed her lips and crossed her limbs, neat, tidy, well pleased with herself.

Nick pulled a color photograph out of his file and slid it in front of Judy. The blood drained from her face as she looked at the back of Tracy's head gleaming with blood.

"You did a lot of damage. What did you use by the way?"

"A hammer." Judy looked smug with knowledge, but the media had leaked that information.

"And then you hit her in the face?"

She nodded.

A shiver crawled up his spine as he pulled another photo from the file, slid it across the smooth wood beside the first one. Tracy's pale, dead, perfect face.

"Funny, you didn't leave a mark."

Panic and fear widened Judy's eyes and mouth. The pulse in her neck throbbed as she shoved the photo away. "It's hard to remember everything as it happened."

"Who are you protecting, Judy? Your husband? He's had affairs for years. Why the hell would you protect a man who can't keep his pecker in his trousers?"

Her face contorted. "That bitch you married was no better."

Which brought Nick to his second line of questioning.

"Jake was going to leave you for Christina, wasn't he?" Nick had finally figured it out. The vital ingredient that had made Chrissie unique enough to kill.

The bony cartilage of Judy's knuckles stood out against her skin. The muscle below her eye ticked faster. "She made him do things he'd never done before."

"How did the kids react? I mean, you can't have hidden that sort of tension for long." Nick sipped his coffee, looking at her from beneath his lashes.

"They didn't know." Her eyes flicked right. Her

hands rubbed her thighs as she uncrossed and crossed her legs repeatedly.

She was lying. Again. Confess to murder but lie about the kids knowing their dad was shagging his student? Didn't make any sense.

"Where are your kids now, Judy?"

Her agitation turned to fury. "Don't you dare go after my children, you sonofabitch!" She bared her teeth and looked as if she might physically attack him. Her lawyer touched her arm and whispered in her ear.

"They're going to get brought into this anyway when their mother stands trial for murder, don't you think?"

Judy had no more killed Tracy than he had. An emotion he didn't recognize stabbed him in the chest but it wasn't pain. It felt uncannily like relief and Nick wondered if Ewan was right. Maybe he had hung his entire life on finding Chrissie's killer and wouldn't know what the hell to do with himself if he found them. But he had made a vow to his dead wife and he wouldn't let anything, not even his own pathetic inadequacies, get in the way of that promise.

He scanned the files for information. Finally found what he was looking for.

"Brady and Molly are studying abroad?" He'd get someone to check the passport office and airlines for travel details.

Judy tapped her finger against the desk. Stared at the table, not looking at him, not cooperating anymore.

"Callie's the only one living at home now, isn't she?" Nick asked.

Fear flashed in her eyes. "If you touch my daughter, I'll—"

Nick leaned closer and laughed in her face. "You'll

what? You'll kill me?" He jerked to his feet, stuffed all the pieces of Tracy Good's death back into the file. "I don't think so."

SUSIE SURVIVED THE DAY. It hadn't been easy and her hand still throbbed from the punch she'd landed on Jake, but it throbbed gloriously. She let herself into her dark cottage, keyed off the alarm system and threw her bag to the floor.

Images of Nick filled the space. In the bedroom. The living room. The kitchen. And it stung like salt in a wound that he hadn't called. Stupid, stupid woman.

She walked over to the couch and straightened cushions, trying not to remember how they'd got jumbled in the first place. She was falling for him, that rough charm and unexpected compassion, even though she knew he would break her heart.

Rafael had gone AWOL after his meeting with Nick and late this afternoon Jake Sizemore had been escorted from the building by uniformed police officers.

Susie frowned. She had called her mother. "Not even the president could get that woman out of that mess if she murdered two women in cold blood. The most he could do is get her extradited to serve time back in the U.S. But if her family is in Britain, what's the point?"

What indeed?

Her muscles ached, from stress, from sex, from assaulting a fellow biology prof. She rolled her head around her shoulders, energy fizzing inside her like a shaken can of Coke. She needed a shower but decided a run first might work off the tension in her muscles and clear her mind of Nick Archer fever.

She changed into workout gear, reset the alarm and locked the door behind her, hanging her keys on a cord around her neck along with a whistle. It was full dark now but the moon was on high beam, lighting her way like a giant personal spotlight. The Heathcotes' house was dimly lit as if someone inside was watching TV or reading a book. She'd drop in on them tomorrow before work, make sure they were okay. But right now she wanted to avoid Lily's all-knowing gaze. Nick might not mean to hurt anyone, but he was damned good at it.

She jogged along the path to the beach, the sand stretching east for at least half a mile. Shadows raced over the shore as clouds billowed overhead. The sand gave slightly beneath her feet until she reached the harder packed surface of the intertidal zone. Her heart rate rose. Her breath became deeper, her lungs stretching in that first response to the increased need for oxygen. It was an easy pace, a kick-back-and-cruise pace. *Sensible. Steady.* Just like her. For some reason it irritated the crap out of her, so she pushed harder. Kicked her legs faster against the beach, pounded the sand, pumped her arms until her breath came in deep bellows and her leg muscles began to burn.

Running was like sex without the fireworks. Images of Nick rose again in her thoughts, but Susie blocked them out and pushed harder, nearing the end of the beach in an all-out sprint. Suddenly she tripped and sailed through the air. Plowing through the sand, skinning the palms of her hands a split-second before she collided with a boulder. The smell of the incoming tide and the scream of gulls chased her into oblivion.

CHAPTER SEVENTEEN

EVER SINCE LILY HAD KISSED HIM with something other than brotherly love, the earth's axis had felt dislodged and out of whack. Now Nick sat across from Callie Sizemore and wondered if he'd finally lost it. But who else would Judy Sizemore protect except her children?

Callie had only been eleven years old when Chrissie died, but he'd once threatened his mother with a knife and he hadn't even been nine.

He started running through the structured interview questions, monitoring her responses for what she said and how she said it.

"Do you know why I've asked you here today, Callie?" He forced himself to smile, but his fingers were squeezing his notes so forcefully the paper crumpled. "You don't mind if I call you by your first name, do you?"

She shook her head, her thumbnail never leaving the slight gap between her front teeth.

"I need you to answer the questions out loud so the recorder can pick it up. Think you can do that?" Nick watched her closely, looking for a clue this scrawny young woman was a cold-blooded killer. It seemed absurd, but his mind couldn't let go of the idea now he'd latched onto it. Judy wouldn't lie to protect her cheating, worthless prick of a husband. And though Nick had never experienced a mother's love, he'd seen the depth of the emotion in Emily Heathcote and Amy McKnight.

Callie's lips tugged into a pink pout. "Yes, you can call me Callie, and no, I don't know why you want to talk to me."

"Who do you think might have committed this crime?"

"That's your job. I have absolutely no idea." Looking bored, she stared up at the darkened windows.

"Why do you think someone would do this, Callie?"

She shrugged, obviously not giving a damn about the victims. His teeth locked as anger began to grow inside him. All her responses pointed to a guilty woman and despite his need to find Chrissie's killer, to solve this decade-old mystery, he didn't want his wife to have been murdered by a kid.

Chrissie had loved kids. They'd planned to start a family just as soon as she'd written up her Ph.D., but Jake Sizemore had beaten him to it.

Nick pinched the bridge of his nose. Maybe she hadn't died alone. If God and Heaven did exist, maybe Chrissie had her child with her for eternity.

Callie nibbled the skin of her cuticle until it bled. She shifted, braced her hands on the table as if to stand. "Can I go now?"

"No. You can't, not yet." Nick forced his voice to be gentle. Warm. "Tell me why you wouldn't do something like this?"

"Me?" Her eyes flashed with surprise. "I thought we were talking about Mom."

Nick leaned forward. "I'd appreciate your take on things. I need to understand exactly what happened. Can you tell me why you would never have done this?"

He kept his expression mild even as something dark shifted inside his belly.

"I couldn't do something like that. My parents are highly respected in our community. We go to church." She sat back as if that were an alibi etched in granite.

Nick imagined throwing the door open and yelling, "They go to church for God's sake! Let them all go!" But the BTK killer in Wichita had been a church deacon. "Where were you the night Tracy Good was killed?"

"I don't know why you even care about that cheap little slut." Loathing filled her eyes as she switched fingers to chew her other hand.

"Your mother confessed to killing Tracy Good because she was having an affair with your dad." He felt irritated and unsettled, by Lily's kiss and thoughts of Chrissie being murdered by an eleven-year-old kid. "You must have met her?"

Callie shrugged, silent and sullen, as if he was wasting her time.

"You didn't like her?" he persisted.

"What was to like?" The twist of her lips was scathing. "Spreading her legs so my *dad* could fuck her?" She laughed. "Come on. She was a stupid cow in a long line of stupid cows." She held his gaze with her oversized eyes and he glimpsed answers he didn't want to see.

He tried a different angle.

"What do you do, Callie?" He looked at his notes even though he knew the information by heart. Let her think he was slow and didn't recognize a sociopath when he saw one.

"I go to university here and help Mom at home."

"But your attendance record says you haven't been to a single lecture or practical class this term?"

She shrugged. "I don't need to go to class. I always ace the exams." Her eyes held sparks of defiance.

Maybe she did. Her records at the university said she had an IQ of 146, but she hadn't finished the first year of her undergraduate degree yet, because she was lazy, unmotivated.

Was murder a challenge? Just to see if she could beat the judicial system? The law?

"How's your girlfriend, Detective?" Callie asked. Her smile turned glacial.

A shiver of something he didn't recognize passed through him. Fear? He kept his face expressionless. Susie was fine and he wasn't so easily played.

Callie picked up her water with her right hand and sipped, sending him a flirty smile. It settled in his stomach like sulfur.

"Do you remember the night Christina Archer died in South Africa?" He let the silence hang, listening to the tick of the clock on the wall. He waited for her to fill the silence, but even though he was the one experienced at interrogation she didn't say a word. "You were only a kid. You probably don't remember."

"I remember." She gave him a wide smile as if they shared treasured memories. "The police there were hopeless, couldn't find their way out of a paper bag." She rapped her fingers in an incessant tattoo on the desk. "Must drive you mad not knowing what happened to her." There was more in her eyes now. Amusement. Knowledge.

Something violent lurched inside him, but he held himself still, not knowing exactly who was the cat and who was the mouse in this little exchange.

"It must be hard knowing she was going to leave you for a man old enough to be her father." Her foot tapped in time to her fingers. "Doesn't say much about you, does it? You must have been a piss-poor husband and a shitty lover."

Piss-poor husband he would concede.

"She was going to have a baby." He lowered his voice, forcing her to lean forward and pay attention. "Your daddy was going to replace *you* with Chrissie's little bastard. Would have been a cute kid too. Chrissie was better-looking than that old hag you call a mother."

Callie raked at his face and he jerked back to avoid being scratched. Vicious little bitch.

"Not after the sharks finished with her she wasn't."

"How would you know?" he goaded. "You'd have been tucked in bed like a baby."

"And you're just as stupid as those South Africans." Her eyes narrowed, her lungs pumping tiny breasts against the sheer fabric of her sweater.

He had her. He knew he had her. "Did you kill my wife, Callie?"

"Wouldn't you like to know?" she taunted.

"Did you kill Christina Archer? Yes or no, Callie, for the record."

Her eyes shot up and to the right. "No."

Liar…but proving it was another thing. He let out a breath.

"Where were you the night Tracy Good was murdered? I know you weren't home." It was a guess, but he knew he was right when her eyes shot to his.

"That bitch was ruining my life, making Mom miserable, making Dad behave like a friggin' moron—again." She rolled her eyes, twitched her foot beneath the table. "Why do women chase after him like that? He's an old man. It's disgusting." She started working the nail on her index finger. "At least you look like you might be worth the effort—if you can get it up."

With her big eyes she looked slightly amphibian. He leaned back in his chair, his legs stretched out beneath the table. It took her a moment to take the bait, but she ran a foot up his calf and back down again.

Hatred slithered in his stomach like eels.

"What were you doing last Saturday night between 11 p.m. and 1 a.m.?" he asked, ignoring the insidious sensation her touch aroused.

"Hmm…" Her cheeks formed tight little apples when she smiled. "I was in the Student Union doing, I believe, a Brazilian." She slipped her tongue out and touched it to her top lip.

Defeat roared through him and his body felt as heavy as lead. After all these years, he was never going to nail Chrissie's killer. He was never going to be able to make things right.

Nick reached out from a long way away and clicked off the recorder. Time stretched out like the moment before death. Blood slipped through his veins like barbwire.

He'd never get a conviction in a court of law.

But he could kill her. Right here in this room he could reach out and seize Callie Sizemore by the throat, crush her windpipe and watch her slowly suffocate. He could be the avenger. He could deliver justice.

His life would be over, but it would feel good. It would feel really, really good.

Sound amplified in the small room. His breath rasped through a sandpaper throat as Callie mutilated her fingernails. He shuffled papers in his files, avoided looking at Sizemore's daughter who sat oblivious to her fate, watching him with soulless eyes. She looked like a waif, a fawn. But he knew she was a monster.

An image of Susie flashed through his mind.

He recited the rosary in his head. In Latin. Reached out and grasped the trailing edge of his humanity before it disappeared forever. He went to the door, opened it and found his boss standing there, her chest heaving as if she'd sprinted all the way there.

They exchanged a long silent look before he slipped out of the room.

Nick ignored occasional greetings from his colleagues and sat in front of his murder board. Tracy Good's photograph was surrounded by pictures of suspects. Jake Sizemore, Judy Sizemore, Rafael Domenici, Callie Sizemore. It went round and round in circles and he couldn't tie it down. Christina's murder board would have the same people, except for Domenici. Nick pressed his hand over his face. He was on a bloody merry-go-around where all his prime suspects alibied one another.

He needed proof.

Rage burned inside, but he ignored it, the way he'd ignored it for years so he could do the job. Eleven-year-old Callie had something to do with his wife's murder. But proving it without a confession would be impossible. Had she acted alone? Or had all the Sizemore kids ganged up to get rid of the threat to their family?

Jake had no alibi for Tracy's murder. But there was no physical evidence to tie anyone to Tracy Good except the DNA of Rafael Domenici and Tony Scott, the latter who claimed to be in Glasgow the night of the murder. Officers had done a preliminary check with the kid's parents to confirm the guy's alibi but now he needed them to follow up with something solid like a surveillance photo from a street camera. They had Tracy's recording of sexual intercourse with her boss—more damning than his sperm. It provided motive, which no one else appeared to have.

Tracy Good hadn't meant enough to anyone else for them to kill her.

Nick ran his hands over his scalp, glanced at his phone and knew he should call Susie. He wanted to hear her voice. *Leave her out of this.* Instead he stared at the list of suspects and wondered what he was missing. Skinny narcissist Callie Sizemore, the classic sociopath. Judy, wild-eyed aging wife and overprotective mother. Jake Sizemore, the blackmailed boss, and Rafael Domenici, addicted to sex.

Tracy hadn't been sexually assaulted. Her murder had been clinical and cold.

Judy hadn't killed anyone, he was as sure of that as the pope was Catholic. But she'd perverted the course of justice and made him believe, however briefly, he'd fulfilled his vow.

Okay, Archer. Do the job.

He needed to find out exactly what time Callie and Rafael had been in the Student Union, and he needed to request polygraph tests for each of the Sizemores and Rafael Domenici, and a psych evaluation while he was at it. He scrubbed a hand over his face and glanced at his watch. Ewan would be tucking his kids in bed and making sure his wife didn't choke to death on her own spit. That left Nick with a lot of legwork and not a whole lot of chance to sleep.

He picked up the phone and dialed Susie. The dial tone droned in his ear and after thirty seconds he laughed. He'd imagined her sitting home waiting for him to call. *What an ass.*

WATER HIT HER WITH A BLAST. Susie reared to her knees, shocked into consciousness as another wall of water crashed over her head and sent her under. The current gripped her body and started to drag her out to sea. Dela's face flashed through her mind—dead at the surface, blood on her lips from a ruptured lung. Susie choked back the panic rushing through her limbs as she scrambled for purchase.

She clawed harder into the sand. It anchored her enough so that the next wave thrust her forward. She would *not* die in the sea. She would not let that giant entity suck her up and spit her out like flotsam. She staggered to her feet and whirled in a disoriented circle. The moon was gone. So was her flashlight. Mist cloaked the beach in an icy glaze, visibility reduced to a few feet. Confused, she oriented herself to the waves and stumbled out of the water.

Wet clothing clung to her body like saggy skin. The wind seemed to come direct from the Arctic and stabbed into her skin like knives.

A cry came out of the darkness and Susie froze. Was it an animal? Or a woman crying for help? Survival instinct had her crouching in the sand like a beast. Lightheaded, she spread her fingers on the cold sand, restrained a whimper as yet more icy water soaked her skin.

Silence echoed through the sea mist as if someone or something listened attentively. Hysteria and panic welled up, the pounding of her heart resounding through her ears like drums. Desperately she drew in one slow deep breath, and then another. She ignored the way her heart fluttered and the panic eventually receded. The woozy sensation stopped whirling inside her head. The cry came again and she looked around, trying to stare through the fog.

Was it a wild animal she'd heard? Maybe the fox they'd seen on the road the other night? Or could it be Emily out for another deranged ramble?

Susie swallowed, torn between the need to go home and get warm, and the knowledge she should check to see if Emily was hurt.

But the last time the fog had crowded the shoreline Tracy Good had been bludgeoned to death. Fear crawled over Susie's body like scarab beetles and she couldn't shake the terrible sensation that someone was watching her.

Even though Judy Sizemore had confessed to murder and was in jail, adrenaline warmed her muscles, readying her for flight as she edged through the fog in the direction of home. Because maybe Judy hadn't killed Tracy? Or maybe Jake was angry enough with Susie to stage a copycat murder to get his wife out. Or maybe Nick had been right and it really had been Jake all along. The hairs on the nape of her neck sprang to attention and she silently scanned the darkness. Tingles shot along her spine as she heard *something* moving in the night.

Fight or flight? The age-old response to fear.

She wobbled slightly and gripped her head as more dizziness hit. She felt as fragile as a brittle star. Fight wasn't an option and she didn't think she'd get far with flight either. There was another option. Concealment. She held absolutely still, hardly drawing breath as she cowered in the sand and tried to disappear.

NICK CUT THROUGH THE MERCAT WYND onto Market Street and strode along the pavement as cars rumbled over ancient cobbles. Students were out playing, but not in the numbers that hailed a weekend. A young couple, arm in arm, gave him a wide berth as he approached, the woman's eyes flickering over him nervously. Nick caught sight of his reflection in a shop window and didn't blame her. He hadn't shaved in days, his shoulders were hunched and his fists armed and ready.

Tomorrow was Halloween and he'd fit right in.

Briefly he wondered where Susie was. He'd try her number again in a few minutes.

A couple of boy-racers tailgated along the street, suspensions bouncing dangerously close to the stone cobbles. A memory hit. Being taught to drive by a priest who'd spent most of the time swearing and praying to God Almighty for safe deliverance.

Nick had always ragged on Father Mike. Why was he so worried about dying if he really believed in Heaven? Father Mike had replied that if he survived Nick's adolescence without committing murder, he would have passed God's ultimate test and be fast-tracked to a halo and wings.

Nick grinned.

A car alarm went off, jolting him back to the present. His eyes narrowed, but the owner pressed his key fob and jogged to catch up with his buddies.

Nick was back to square one in the investigation. An aide was going through the security camera data from Market Street, looking for Callie Sizemore and Rafael Domenici. He crossed Greyfriars Gardens and looked up at the poorly lit concrete block that had been the students' domain since 1973. The building was never going to compete with the grandeur of the rest of the town, but students didn't give a damn about the décor when they were dancing at the Friday night bop.

A bouncer stood at the door. She was beefy, but only came eye-level with his chest. Her hair was cut in a flat-top and if she wasn't a dyke he'd eat her dungarees.

"ID," she demanded, unsmiling and professional.

He pulled out his police badge in one hand, alumni card in the other. "Take your pick."

Her brows lifted and her lips rose in a smile that made her plain face pretty. She waved him inside to wait, checked another couple of student IDs while he stood and absorbed the scent of sour beer and disinfectant over the subtle hint of vomit. Plastic skeletons dangled from the ceiling, witches and spiders crept over the walls.

A camera covered the main doors—exactly what he'd been hoping for.

The bouncer turned to him, earrings piercing her right ear from tip to lobe. "What can I do for you?"

"Were you working last Saturday night?"

The light danced off her hair as she dipped her chin. "I was."

Nick pulled two color photos out of his pocket. "Recognize either of these two?"

She took the picture of Rafael. "Yeah. God's gift to women." One side of her mouth turned ugly. "He pinched my ass, and I would have decked him, but he moved fast. Next time." Her eyes glinted retribution.

"The girl?" he prodded.

Her mouth thinned into a sneer. "Yeah, she's the same. Another delusional piece of work." She handed back the photos. "They were both here on Saturday night, and Friday night too, I think. Not together as far as I know, but I only work the front door." She shrugged and waved three more students inside.

"Can you still get out the other door?" Nick nodded

toward an entrance at the end of the car park that was locked from the outside.

"You can get out." Her eyes lifted. "But they can't get in without me seeing them."

He didn't need to ask if it were possible to have sex in this place without being spotted. The building was enormous with different levels and offices, closets and storerooms. Dougie had once scored with a German exchange student in the bathroom stalls. The romance of it. Leanne would kick his ass if she ever found out.

He glanced up at the surveillance camera. "Do you have the security tapes for last weekend?"

"Sure, but I need to check with my boss before I can hand them over."

"No you don't." He handed her a warrant.

"You came prepared." She shot him a grin and shouted to someone to come and take over for her.

Nick followed her dungarees through the building and up the stairs. A shiver ran over his shoulders as he recalled walking these same halls with Chrissie when they'd gone to buy her air-ticket to go to South Africa. She'd been so excited to be going abroad…so vivid, so blindingly special. A few months later she'd walked out on him and he'd let her. Jake had seduced her and shattered the fairytale Nick had been living.

Anger churned in his stomach. He was so close he could taste the answers like ink on his tongue. He'd promised to bring Chrissie's killer to justice. But for the first time he wondered, what was he going to do if he couldn't get results? What if he found out who killed her—and he believed he already had—but couldn't prove it? What sort of man would he be if he just let it slide?

CHAPTER EIGHTEEN

SUSIE STAGGERED UP THE soft-sided dunes, the sand shifting beneath her feet, making her trip. Her flesh was numb with cold and beginning to burn. Her breath came in hoarse gasps through her raw throat. The fog dissipated as she climbed farther up the shore away from the sea. She risked a glance behind her, but there was no one there, no sinister figures. She stood and slammed straight into a hard male chest and screamed in terror.

"*Merda!* Dr. Cooper, stop, stop!" Rafael grabbed her shoulders. "Calm. What is the matter?"

Susie tried to rear back, gulping for air as Rafael's grip dug into her triceps. "I was running. I fell and hit my head."

Suddenly exhausted, she dropped her forehead in her palms and leaned against him for support as energy flowed from her limbs in a rush. His arms engulfed her, supporting her weight, and she was grateful.

"What are you doing here?" Her voice was thready.

"I needed to speak to you about the detective."

"Nick?" Trying to clear her vision, she blinked. Remembering Emily might be lost on the beach, she jerked out of Rafael's arms and took a step toward the Heathcote cottage. "I need to check on Lily's mother."

"I just see her." He grabbed her elbows, put his thumbs under her chin and angled her face to the moon that had reappeared from behind the mist. "She is fine, but you, I think, are not." He swung her up into his arms and she grabbed his shirt, her head whirling like a Catherine wheel on the Fourth of July.

Rafael carried her over the dune and set her on the gravel lane running between the cottages. His handling was clinical, not intimate or inappropriate the way he'd acted before Tracy Good had been murdered. Stars twinkled against midnight velvet, but Susie was pretty sure it was her eyesight and not the solar system.

"Thank you," she said, grabbing on to his arm as she swayed.

"*Nenhum problema*." Those usually laughing eyes were flat, the mobile mouth a slash of formality.

But she didn't care as long as she could get warm and change into dry clothes.

"I have made errors in my life, Dr. Cooper."

"Susie," she corrected. She could barely concentrate on what he was saying, but she was glad his conscience had picked this precise moment to bring him out here because she didn't know if she'd have made it otherwise. "Call me Susie and we can talk later."

He half carried her along the footpath and she was grateful to see her cottage with Rafael's car parked outside. She wanted to get home, sink into a hot tub and succumb to misery.

"Were you on the beach?" she asked. They were almost at the door. She could taste safety, Percocet and solitude.

"No, I just get there when I find you. Give me your keys." He held out his hand as they crunched along the gravel path.

Susie grappled at her chest and realized the lanyard with her keys on it was missing. It must have fallen off when she took a head dive into the rock.

"I must have lost them." Her voice got all high-pitched as if she was about to cry. She glanced toward Lily's cottage, but remembered Nick had swiped the spare set she kept there. Stupid tears flooded her eyes.

Rafael hugged her and maneuvered her to the passenger side of his car. "I take you to the hospital. They check your head, *sim?*"

Susie laughed, wiped the tears from her eyes. She needed her head checked all right. And she'd contact Nick in town and get her keys back. It would be okay. Everything would work out. Rafael grabbed a blanket from the backseat and draped it over her shoulders.

"You need to *se secar...merda*. I no find the words." He waved his hands in frustration. "Get dry."

Susie frowned at her wet clothes, her brain sluggish. "But I don't have any clothes."

He tucked the blanket carefully over her lap, ran around the car and jumped in the driver's seat. "No worry. I know where to get some." The headlights came on when he started the engine. He slammed his foot on the accelerator and the car jerked forward with a machinegun spray of grit. Susie should have been scared. As it was she just smiled.

Hospital lights never flattered, but right now Susie Cooper looked like the It girl for battered women. The absence of makeup was glaring, her skin pallid except for a massive bump on her forehead.

Lily pressed her lips together and swung her legs beneath her chair. She'd needed to get out of the house, even if the hospital's A & E at midnight was not her idea of a good time. She'd left her mother in a drug-flavored sleep, but she needed to get back soon just in case she woke up. They'd been here for hours. She might have been sympathetic if she hadn't been choking on her own personal humiliation. Why had she kissed

Nick? How could she ever face him again? Hot nausea roiled through her belly whenever she thought of losing him.

Rafael sat beside her, muscles on show in a form-fitting T-shirt, his beautiful bronze skin looking warm even though it was freezing outside. He was annoyed with her, too. She'd got him into serious bother with the police. Damn. Nothing in her life was going right. Her eyes felt gritty when she closed them.

"I'm sorry I lied to Nick and got you in trouble." She covered her mouth with her hand, not used to being wrong. When she opened her eyes Rafael was staring down his nose at her with an expression as frigid as a clear arctic day. Flirty-boy was gone, replaced by a stone-faced Adonis with a social conscience. He turned back to watch Susie as she answered more questions at the A & E desk, like some Labrador pup watching its master.

"Look." Lily's voice rose in temper. "I lied because I didn't think you killed Tracy." No reaction. He went on ignoring her, so she raised her voice even more. "And I'm sure you didn't rape that girl in Brazil."

Heads jerked in their direction as he swiveled around. "*Merda*, Lily! Why you say that?"

Most of the girls she'd known at fourteen would have found Rafael highly fuckworthy. But he hardly needed the reassurance of words when hot and hungry eyes followed him everywhere.

"Tell me what happened," she urged him.

His eyelids drooped and he slouched back against the uncomfortable chair. "*De noite todos os gatos são pardos.*" He laughed, but it was a small bitter sound. He translated the idiom. "At night all cats are gray." He shrugged again, searching for words. "It is easy to make mistake."

"Did you know she was jailbait?"

His eyes flashed like the sun glinting off the ocean. "*Não*. Her mouth was much, much older." Anger faded into a dissolute edge.

"Was she a hooker?"

Rafael's eyes crawled over her with a slow probing look that wasn't at all flattering. She shivered.

"In Brazil, girls can be sold into prostitution by their parents. Others do it to eat." He looked toward Susie. The stubble darkened his jaw, turning the boy into a man. "I no go with prostitutes, but I make *one* mistake and the last three years have been the *diabólico*." His eyes jabbed her. "And it was only after I meet *you* I figure out what was wrong with me."

"What?" Stunned, Lily met his gaze. What could she have taught a guy like Rafael Domenici?

His voice dropped to softness. "I use sex as punishment."

Lily stiffened, but Rafael touched her cheek in a petal-soft caress.

"Not physical punishment. But inside me." He picked up her hand and pressed the palm to his heart. "Every time I had sex it was for revenge, not because I wanted it, but because I needed to get rid of the—" he lifted his hands in the air, still holding hers as he searched for the right words "—anger? Pain? *Merda*."

Lily bit her lip and pulled her hand away, glad she hadn't succumbed to the obvious temptation of Rafael's red-hot Brazilian flesh.

"I had no one to trust. No friends. Until you." Rafael's eyes shone with sentiment, and Lily swallowed and looked away.

Susie sent them a punchy smile from across the waiting area, leaning against the desk wearing black sweats that reached her calves and a hooded sweatshirt with Black Sabbath plastered on the front. Lily winced. She'd been acting like a bitch because she'd screwed up her own relationship with Nick and wanted someone to blame. The problem with Susie was she was so bloody nice Lily wanted to kick her.

She sighed. It wasn't Susie's fault Nick had given Lily grief. Knowing Nick's M.O., Susie Cooper was heading for a nosedive into heartbreak any day now. Lily had been dumped by enough lesser men to know it stung. That's why she usually did the dumping herself. And why it was better she and Rafael stayed just good friends.

Susie wobbled unsteadily toward them and Lily stood. "I should have brought my car." She frowned because now Rafael would have to drop her back home and it was late and he looked knackered.

"You take my car." He put a hand on her shoulder, his fingers absently massaging her tense muscles. "Dr. Cooper can stay at my house tonight and we find her keys *amanhã*. Tomorrow."

Lily raised a brow and he eyed her narrowly.

"I have another room," he declared. The expression on his face was so earnest, so eager to do the right thing, Lily smiled.

Rafael was trying to prove something by taking care of their boss and it made her feel sad—as if one of them was growing up.

"Fine. Whatever. I'll drop you guys off." She shrugged as he handed her his car keys. And though neither of them said anything, they both knew if he mucked this up, his fledgling career as a scientist was over.

NINE HOURS LATER, SUSIE WALKED into the police station on North Street feeling as if she'd been beaten over the head with a baseball bat. She wore a Quiksilver T-shirt of Rafael's under a zippered moss-green chunky cable sweater that smelled brand new and hung to her knees. The ensemble was finished off with Lily's black Lycra pants that rested just below her knees. She wore no underwear, no makeup and her sneakers felt damp. Her usually well-groomed hair was a straggly mess that she'd straightened as best she could without a brush. At least it disguised the mottled bruise that covered one side of her temple.

Altogether she looked very, very unattractive, but strangely she felt stronger and more confident than ever before. Her mother would have a fit if she saw her now, but Susie was finally breaking the mold she'd squeezed herself into years ago. Leanne would jump with glee and even Dela, who must be up in Heaven, would be proud.

Poor, darling Dela. They'd gone on vacation to get over being dumped by the men in their lives. Events that seemed so important at the time, but one week later had turned out to be insignificant.

She walked up to the glassed-in desk. "Can you page Detective Inspector Nick Archer for me, please?" Her accent stood out and marked her as a stranger here. But St. Andrews was her home now and she was determined to make it work.

The woman P.C. behind the security window eyed her with the hint of a smile. There was a plastic pumpkin on the shelf that reminded Susie it was Halloween.

"I'll let him know there's someone here to see him, just go through and take a seat."

The woman pointed to a small waiting area and Susie

walked inside and sat, settling her head against the cool wall at her back and closing her eyes.

A moment later there were footsteps and the rustle of a newspaper.

"You look better in print."

Susie half opened her eyes and saw a police officer standing before her. She frowned as he handed her a copy of a tabloid newspaper, and saw a grainy black-and-white photograph of her and Nick kissing.

"Great." She thrust the paper away. "Why would anyone care about my love life?" Pain throbbed as she shook her head; she must be due another pain pill soon.

"How long have you been seeing D.I. Archer?"

Susie rubbed her eyes. "Not long." And it struck her that she wasn't the only one in that photograph. "Who are you?"

The man smiled, but despite the curved lips his eyes were wintry. "I'm P.C. Mosel."

"So you work with Nick?" Susie sat up, not liking the other man's calculating expression.

"That's correct." P.C. Mosel picked up the paper and read aloud. "*Top police detective embroiled in murder investigation still finds time for romance with daughter of United States senator.*"

Susie closed her eyes as a shiver ran across her shoulders. Damn.

"I'm just wondering why you haven't been questioned given we found blood and the murder weapon in your car?"

Susie felt welded to the spot under the weight of the man's suspicious gaze.

"Is it the fact you're sleeping with the lead detective or the fact your mother is a high-ranking politician?"

The shiver bloomed into a full shudder that worked

its way down her spine. She frowned, confused. "I thought you had Tracy's killer locked up?"

"The investigation is ongoing." The man's lips tightened and he looked away. They heard footsteps, and Nick walked into the waiting room and caught sight of Susie.

"What the hell happened to you?"

Susie touched her hand to her scalp. She'd forgotten about her bruise. "It's nothing."

Nick shot the uniformed officer a look from beneath lowered brows. "Why do I get the impression my ears should be burning?"

The P.C. held up the newspaper and pointed to the photograph.

Nick snorted. "One of these days you'll learn to read and then we'll really be in trouble."

Indignation twisted the man's features, but Nick ignored him, maneuvering Susie through the inner doorway into the heart of the police station. "I was worried." He supported her with a hand around her waist, up the stairs into an empty, tightly crammed office. He closed the door and they were alone.

She pressed a hand to her stomach. "That officer said there was blood in my car—"

"There were traces from the bottom of my shoes the night of the murder. I intend to get it valet cleaned as soon as they release it from evidence."

Oh. Susie sagged into a chair, too exhausted to process the information.

Last night Rafael had woken her every time she'd drifted off for more than thirty minutes and while she appreciated the sentiment, she needed sleep and needed it badly. Otherwise she was going to collapse.

"I just came for my keys." Her sore throat made her

cough, and coughing sent pain shooting in a million different directions behind her eyes.

Nick was silent. She squinted at him. She might not look good, but he wasn't cutting the Hollywood auditions either. His eyes were bloodshot, the stubble on his cheeks darkening his jaw and making him look rough and not just dangerous, but deadly. His features were cut too deep, blond hair standing up in ragged spikes.

"Where were you? I called, but there was no reply." He raised a finger to her bruise, but she flinched away.

"I stayed at Rafael's house." His expression shifted and she knew she'd go to hell for baiting him. But as anger seeped into his green eyes, she laughed. It was inappropriate—like smiling during a cremation. She wasn't going to play games. "Nothing happened, Nick. He's my student, for heaven's sake. I went for a run, tripped and hit my head on a rock." Disorientated by the injury, she'd also managed to scare herself silly on the beach afterward, but she wasn't going to admit that to anyone. "When I came around, I crawled home and found Rafael on my doorstep."

"What was he doing there?"

So much for sympathy. Maybe Nick didn't realize she was being literal.

"I've no idea and, frankly, I don't give a damn."

Nick's trust issues were as wide and deep as the Atlantic and out-competed basic human emotions like compassion or sympathy. It was one more reason they'd never work out. She was a wuss. A softy. He was… something else entirely.

His eyes moved over her features and, by the way his features tightened, he was obviously trying to suppress anger or jealousy. Or maybe she was deluding herself?

Maybe he wasn't feeling anything at all. Octopi demonstrated more emotion.

"Look Nick, I just came by because I lost my keys when I tripped. I'll search the beach for them later, but with the tide…" She shrugged. She'd never find them. "Rafael and Lily took me to the ER last night and then Rafael let me sleep at his house and checked on me throughout the night because I had a mild concussion." She forced her lips into a smile. "He was a real sweetheart."

She expected fury but got the sort of frozen stillness that reminded her of a predator armed with long sharp teeth poised to strike. His eyes glittered—busy trying to figure out if she'd screwed her student while she'd had the chance. Trying to work out just how big a slut she really was.

Nice.

Her eyes watered and she curled her fingers into her palm because finally she knew she was worth more than that. "Look, we aren't working out. I'll just grab my keys and say goodbye."

"Don't." Something unreadable flickered across his face and he took a step toward her. "Don't."

He moved closer, brushing past her to open a drawer. Keys jingled as he stepped away.

"Let me drive you home." A small dimple punched the corner of his mouth even though the light in his eyes dimmed.

"No," said Susie. Nick had already seen her weak and exposed. It was time to reconstruct the barriers, to end it before she got her heart broken. Obliterated. She opened her mouth to speak but he interrupted her.

"Look, Susie…" He ran his hands through his hair, flattening the tufts. "I'm sorry you had a rough night.

I called you a few times, but then I got caught up in work."

Work was important. She understood work. But it only emphasized all the reasons they were wasting their time together. They'd never have time for a relationship. They just squeezed in sex—fantastic sex—but just sex and she shouldn't kid herself it was more. And she wanted more. She wanted a baby. The last few days had made her realize she should grab life and wrestle it kicking and screaming into the shape she desired.

It was humbling, but she finally conceded she didn't even need a man to get pregnant. She seemed to have a flaw inside her that was attracted only to the "love 'em and leave 'em" types. But she had a good job to support herself, and even though her mother would never approve of her being a single parent, it wasn't Susie's problem. She'd call some fertility clinics and arrange an appointment as soon as her head stopped rotating in the opposite direction to the earth.

Voices echoed down the corridor.

"Come on," Nick urged her with a glance at the door. "Rocket needs a walk and I want to check up on Emily." He smiled and Susie felt a funny little twist somewhere in the region of her chest.

Nick's colleagues were just outside the door. She stood awkwardly, clutching the desk behind her to stop swaying. A group of police officers opened the door and squeezed into the tiny office.

"What happened to you?" Ewan held two mugs of steaming coffee. He put them both on a desk then swept aside her hair and checked out her bruise. He whistled. "That's a stoater. How d'you do it?"

"I fell on a rock."

"That'd do it." Ewan squeezed her shoulder.

"Beating up your girlfriend, Nick?" Another officer shot her a smile and a wink.

"I only hit real men," Nick said without taking his gaze from hers. "You're safe."

They huffed out laughs.

"I'm driving Dr. Cooper home. I'll be back in a few hours." His eyes dared her to refuse him.

God, she wanted to, but the words evaporated in her throat because there was this gossamer-thin thread of hope inside her that maybe she could have everything she wanted—if only for a short time.

"Good idea. Make sure she gets home safe." Ewan patted her arm and Susie swallowed back tears. Why would this man's awkward attempt at comfort make her weep?

Nick took her hand, his fingers gently entwined with hers as he pulled her away from the support of the desk. "Let's get you home, Susie Q."

Susie was hyperaware of all eyes on her. How many others had the same suspicions as P.C. Mosel? She straightened her shoulders and tried not to show how uncomfortable she felt being in the spotlight.

"Oh, I nearly forgot." Ewan's eyes crinkled. "Your car is due back today. I'll arrange to have it cleaned and drop it off this afternoon."

Gratitude overwhelmed her. "That would be fantastic, Ewan, thank you." Her car meant freedom and she needed that.

Nick hustled her out of the building. Sunbeams streamed over St. Salvator's clock tower as they turned east and somehow they were holding hands. It took a moment to register and when she glanced at his face, he had a grim set to his mouth.

"Why, Nick? Why drag this on when we both know

it won't last?" They strolled along the sidewalk like real lovers, the smell of the sea teasing her soul like wishes and confetti.

"We're not done, Susie." He turned to her with a smile and lifted her off her feet, his body solid against hers. She rested her sore head against his shoulder and breathed in his scent. She had a feeling by the time Nick was done with her she'd be nothing but a quivering, weeping mess. But maybe by then she'd have something else to hold on to.

Nick opened the door to his flat and a hairy bullet shot down the steps to cock his leg on a small patch of grass. Rocket took a leak with a resentful gleam in his black eyes.

"Sorry, boy." Nick herded the bouncing bearded collie back up the steps. Poor bugger hadn't been out since dinnertime last night. Nick should have taken him back to Dougie's, but he'd been foolish enough to believe this investigation was over.

Susie hovered at the bottom of the stone steps that ran up the outside of his house. The bottom floor was a workshop and storage area. He'd been thinking of converting the whole building into living space, but hadn't got around to it yet. She looked pale. Nick frowned at the bump on her head.

What had happened last night? And why had Rafael Domenici been there to pick up the pieces?

Professional distrust melded with male territoriality, but he wasn't jealous of the Latino prick. He wasn't *that* freaking juvenile. Domenici had been charged with rape, he was a suspect in a murder investigation and Susie had been alone with him all night.

But Susie was here safe and sound, so what did it matter?

He'd spent a useless night searching the Student Union surveillance tapes with nothing to show for it except pinning down separate arrival times for Callie Sizemore and Rafael Domenici. He didn't know when they left—they must have exited through the side door onto the street—but they hadn't been picked up on the Market Street camera, which left him exactly nowhere.

He'd already requested polygraphs from all his suspects, but he was skeptical as to whether or not they'd be any better than he was at revealing who was lying. But even asking for the polygraph might reveal something useful. Like who had something to hide. If Judy were innocent it left Jake wide open with no alibi. Or maybe Callie and Rafael were in it together? Some sort of lovers' pact?

Nick felt as if he was missing a vital piece of the puzzle, but was too tired to see straight.

"After you." Nick waved Susie up the stone steps and into his home. It was the first time he'd let a woman enter this sanctuary, except Leanne, who didn't count. He followed Susie and saw the apartment through her eyes. Sparsely furnished with solid oak pieces he'd gradually been restoring. French doors that led to a tiny balcony with the view of the harbor. A big-ass TV and a hairy couch. No pictures. If he wanted a seascape he opened the curtains. He didn't need a photograph of Chrissie to remember her. Her image was etched on his mind like an acid engraving.

The only thing on the wall was a wooden crucifix.

Susie pointed to the cross, a crease pulling at her brows. "I didn't know you were religious." She tried unsuccessfully to hide her skepticism and he smiled.

"It belonged to a friend." He shrugged. His relationship with the church had little to do with God and everything to do with a man he'd called Father Mike.

"Your family?" she asked.

"I don't have family." His relationship with Susie was getting complex and personal, and yet he was the one who'd refused to end it. He walked into the bedroom, flicked a glance at his bed where he hadn't slept in days, grabbed a change of clothes, picked up his shaving kit and came back into the living room. If he were honest he'd admit he'd considered getting Susie naked, but she was hurt and needed sleep and maybe he wasn't as big a bastard as he'd always thought.

She opened the curtains and stared out to sea, the sun flooding her skin with golden light, but her eyes looked distant and sad. Something about the image made words dissolve on his tongue. He couldn't speak.

"I saw your grave that day you had lunch with Candace," she said.

Her words registered somewhere in the dim recesses of his mind. He frowned. "My grave?" Then it clicked and he snorted. "Emily had that headstone made. I couldn't convince her I wouldn't rest next to Chrissie for eternity. Not after what she did."

And that still hurt, knowing that the promises he'd made before a God he'd believed in had turned to dust.

Susie faced him, big blue eyes shining with empathy. And something that looked suspiciously like love. Dammit. He knew he should leave her alone. Why hadn't he let her finish things between them? He'd told himself he wasn't finished with her yet. Not just sexually. There were those secrets of hers that intrigued him, and a need to make her realize she was a good person, better than him, that was for damn sure. But what would it do to her self-esteem if she found out he'd used her to steal her card and break into the Gatty the night Tracy was killed?

"Let's go." He jerked his head and Rocket shot out the door. Susie swept past him, but her now guarded expression tore at his conscience. He reached out, stroked the pad of his finger down the soft skin of her cheek. "It'll be all right."

The look in her eyes told him she didn't believe him and he sucked back a breath because she was right. She walked into the Fife morning, silent and brooding. But he didn't have time to deal with this emotional crap right now. He had a killer to catch and Susie needed a ride home. That was all.

He cared about her—so what? It didn't mean he was about to declare undying love. Nick never wanted to feel that soul-sucking sensation ever again. Susie deserved better than him, but he was addicted to her as certainly as his mother had been addicted to heroin. No doubt about it, withdrawal was going to hurt like a bitch.

CHAPTER NINETEEN

SUSIE OPENED HER EYES and stared at the vision of a clean-shaven Nick Archer sleeping soundly at her side. There was a jolt in the region of her heart. Light cut through the drapes and made his cheeks look as smooth as weathered granite and his hair as soft as ermine. He was naked, stretched out face-down on top of the white duvet. Planes of strong muscle covered his back, no hint of spare flesh, no soft edges. Beautiful.

It hurt to look at him.

Her brain was still a little fuzzy around the edges, but she was pretty sure they hadn't had sex. She checked and her pj's were carefully buttoned. They had definitely *not* had sex. So what was he doing here?

The scent of her shampoo drifted from his hair and stirred up a vision of domestic fantasy. The desire for that familial illusion closed her throat and threatened to choke her. She edged away from between the sheets.

She was falling in love with him.

He wasn't a man to commit. Loving Nick would get her nothing but loneliness and disaster. She bit her bottom lip, determined to stop hanging on to some bogus dream about falling for a guy who actually wanted to make a life with her. Artificial insemination was cold and sterile, but it wouldn't break her heart. And he would.

Looking at him sleeping made something twist inside her, an ache, a pain, a terrible sense of foreboding. They were running out of time. He hadn't even left yet, but already it hurt to let him go.

In the bathroom she stared at her reflection. She was pale but the lump on her forehead had disappeared, leaving the skin a magnificent purple. She washed her face and her head was clearer, the tenderness almost gone. She patted her face dry with a soft fluffy towel.

She walked through to the kitchen and the dog stirred. Then he stared at the door and started barking a second before someone knocked. Susie dashed for the front door, not wanting Nick to wake just yet. Grabbing the knob she yanked it open, forgetting the alarm, which started its countdown of irritating warning beeps.

Lily threw herself inside as the dog shot out. "I can't find Mom!"

Susie staggered under Lily's impact even though the girl was a good head shorter than she was. Lily gripped Susie's pajama lapels and started shaking. Damn, the girl was strong. The alarm was about to go off when Nick sauntered into the hall, pulling up his jeans, and punched in the code, even though she couldn't remember giving him the number.

Embarrassment washed through Susie, although her sleeping arrangements were nobody's business. But Lily was her student. It was all such a tangled mess.

"When was the last time you saw her?" Nick asked Lily.

"I checked her at 1 p.m., just before I went for my run." Lily let go of Susie and stood poised on the balls of her feet. After a moment's hesitation she threw herself at Nick and he wrapped his arms around her.

"Why didn't Ewan call?" Nick asked Susie with a frown.

The clock on the mantel said it was 2 p.m. Susie shrugged.

"I gave Mom her pills and went for a run. I just got back and poked my head in on her before jumping in the shower, but she wasn't there." Lily's hair clung to her face in darkened sweaty streaks. "What if she's hurt? I already looked on the beach." The girl gulped noisily, tears running down her face, her black eyeliner running down to her chin. "I should never have left her alone!"

Oh hell. Susie didn't want to think about the night they'd dragged Emily out of the sea.

"Maybe she just went for a walk?" she suggested, trying to calm the girl.

"And maybe she fell off a cliff looking for her dead bloody kid!" Lily drew back her lips as she bared her teeth. Susie took a step away.

Nick frowned over Lily's head and raised his eyebrows in question. Susie hugged herself—she didn't know what had warranted the change in her usually upbeat and open student. But the stress of worrying about her mother must be enormous. He pulled out his cell phone as Lily impatiently paced the hall.

"Ewan?" Nick spoke quickly. "Never mind that. Emily Heathcote's gone AWOL. I didn't tell you before, but she's been showing signs of dementia. I need a bulletin put out for officers to be on the lookout for a sixty-year-old gray-haired woman along the Crail coast road. Five-foot-ten, medium-to-heavy build."

Susie went into the kitchen and flicked on the coffeemaker. She needed caffeine. Nick angled around to keep her in sight. "*You* do it. The supe won't give a damn when the alternative is another dead body turning up when an officer was in a position to prevent it. Don't give me that crap, you'll be fine."

Nick closed his phone and looked up. "The boss is planning a press conference in an hour." He went into the bedroom and, to Susie's dismay, Lily followed him. Susie trailed them both, uncertain whether to get changed out of her pajamas or wait for privacy. Nick pulled a green T-shirt over his head and bent to pull on socks and shoes.

"They polygraphed the Sizemores after they agreed to non-binding voluntary tests."

Lily looked impatient enough to do up his laces. Susie hovered uncertainly.

"Jake failed on the sexual relationships and Judy failed when she repeated her confession of murder."

"What about Callie?" Lily held up his jacket, which he grabbed.

"She passed everything." The expression on Nick's face revealed nothing. "Doesn't mean anything. True sociopaths don't feel guilt, so the physiological readings that might tell us she's a liar don't always register."

Susie rubbed her upper arms, feeling cold. She knew she needed to do something so she went to her dresser and pulled out clothes. "I'll get dressed and help you search."

"No." Nick walked over and examined the bruise on her forehead, kissing it gently. "Stay by the phone and try to get some rest." He brushed his lips over hers.

"Nick, come on!" Lily's voice was impatient as she hovered in the doorway.

He shot her a glare and then looked back at Susie, the green of his eyes darkened by the olive shirt. "Lock up once we're gone, aye? Don't let anyone in except Ewan or me," he added.

Susie was still nodding like one of those wobble-headed dolls when they went out the door. She didn't even have the dog for company. Alone, she went to the living room window, the glass cold beneath her palm, and watched them jog up the gravel road toward the Heathcote cottage. A big man and a tiny young woman, both of whom had impacted her life in a major way. When she breathed out, the window misted with condensation, leaving a handprint behind.

It was Halloween, she remembered suddenly. And a real-life horror might be unfolding at this exact moment. Poor Emily. Poor Lily.

She rubbed the gooseflesh that pebbled her arms and hoped Emily was okay. She flicked on the TV to catch the world news but frowned. It made her antsy to be up but not to be working. She needed to finish that review article, needed to draft the NERC grant application due the beginning of December.

Susie walked into her office, booted up her PC and checked her email. There was one from Candace wanting to know when she should reschedule today's lecture for. Four messages from her mother in an escalating scale of worry and irritation. Remembering she'd unhooked her phone before going to sleep that morning, she went and plugged it back in.

The marine lab was caught up in a scandal that was probably making her mother squirm in pre–million-dollar-campaign jitters, though derailing her mother's run for office wouldn't be such a bad thing for Susie.

She sank her teeth into her bottom lip. That wasn't really fair. Her parents had forced her to give up her baby, but it hadn't been through malice. Darcy Cooper had believed she was doing the right thing at the time and had found a wonderful couple to adopt Susie's little boy.

Maybe it had been the right thing to do?

Susie shook her head, determined not to get distracted by thoughts and doubts regarding what might have been. That was the past. With a click she filled the oppressive silence with music.

She deleted a bunch of emails from the press. A message from the university reminded staff and students about tomorrow's memorial for Tracy Good. Poor Tracy. Tears welled in Susie's eyes and she couldn't quite make them stop.

Tracy had been in foster care. She'd had no blood family who wanted her. Had she ever really felt loved? Did Susie's child feel loved?

Hot tears streamed down her cheeks for a girl she hadn't known and the boy she'd abandoned. She clicked open a file a private investigator had sent her and looked into the blue eyes of a young man on horseback. Laughing, joking with the person behind the camera. All appearances suggested he loved his adoptive parents and had everything in life he could wish for. What if the press found out about him and destroyed that joy?

Every time she looked at her son, a huge yawning chasm opened up inside her chest. A sense of failure, pity and regret. But also pride that he'd turned out so well.

She'd been stupid. And yet there he was, happy and healthy. How could she risk tipping his world just because she wanted to get to know him?

But what if he wondered whether or not his real parents had loved him?

And what if he didn't?

She was caught between a rock and a hard place. She had to get over her own regret and let her son choose his future.

She searched for "Sperm Bank" and "Scotland" and

stared at the facilities listed on the Web. Not redemption for her past mistakes perhaps, certainly not forgiveness, but a way forward, a way to get on with her life. She'd also check out adoption laws in this country.

She picked up the telephone and made an appointment at a private fertility clinic in Edinburgh for the following week. As soon as she replaced the receiver, her head started pounding. Pushing away from the desk, she headed for the shower. The phone rang, but she ignored it. She stripped and shoved her head into the hot deluge of water. She'd deal with the world later.

NICK HADN'T FOUND EMILY. His body was sweat-soaked from jogging the coastal path to Crail and back. Lily had gone the other way, toward St. Andrews, but neither of them had seen any sign of the confused woman. Spray rasped his face as he looked out to sea, and coldness spread over his skin and seeped into his flesh as he realized how completely he'd failed.

It didn't seem fair that Emily might die like this. Alone. Bewildered. Perpetually grieving. She was just a fragile old lady, long broken by grief. But who knew what the tide, with its grasping currents and bitchy temper, would toss at their feet come morning.

Twilight thickened. Night came early this far north at this time of year, an irascible darkness that cut deep into life. Darkness was the enemy now. Search and Rescue had been called. The police force and local media had been alerted. There was nothing he could do except wait and hope. He turned and spotted Susie walking the length of the beach, skirting the wet sand. Her body was braced against the wind, her blond hair whipping behind her like a flag. He couldn't see her expression but had no doubt her forehead was pinched with worry, her mouth compressed with concern.

Why did he find that so alluring?

He was an experienced detective, used to getting his own way and wise to the ways of the world. Did he really think he wouldn't hurt her when he walked away? Did he really think he wouldn't screw himself in the process? He stepped down the dune to meet her. He couldn't do anything for Emily and he had to get back to work. The murder investigation wasn't over, the Sizemores had been released because of lack of evidence, and Tracy Good's killer was still at large.

As Susie got closer, he saw evidence of tears in her eyes. Something told him it wasn't Emily she was crying over.

Bloody hell. He didn't have time to deal with this, but he held out his arms even as his conscience screamed for him to leave her the hell alone. Then she was in his embrace, warm and sweet, her breasts pressed against his chest, her arms pinned tight around his waist. He nuzzled her hair, tasted the wildness of the sea on her skin.

"Did you find her?" Susie's voice was muffled against his shirt, her breath stirring both heat and lust.

"No. We didn't find any sign of her." He held Susie away from him and stared at her tear-stained face. "What's wrong?"

"Nothing." She avoided his gaze.

"Come on, Susie." He was getting impatient. He didn't have time to screw around.

"I'm not the person you think I am."

"Susie…" Nick smiled, exasperated. "You are *exactly* the person I think you are."

She flinched. And maybe that was why he bothered

trying to change her skewed perception of herself. Susie was as transparent as Edinburgh crystal. She was kind. Beautiful. Intelligent. Warm. Innocent. And definitely not for the likes of him.

He'd stolen from her, lied to her and gotten her naked every chance he got.

"You're uptight, overconscientious, hardworking and practical. You worry every little detail to death." Her eyes flashed, but he stalled her by brushing the hair off the bruise on her brow. "You are a *good* person, Susie Cooper. Christ knows I've dealt with some of the bad."

She pulled away, her eyes narrowing, her pointy jaw set at the sort of angle that told him she was pissed. God, she was pretty when she got that pain-in-the-ass look on her face.

"When I was fifteen I seduced an older man and got pregnant. I gave the baby up for adoption without even holding him in my arms." Her eyes turned opaque, holding on to the memories, her fingers biting into the sleeves of her jacket.

Nick laughed and her eyes burned with fresh tears. *This* was her big secret? This was what caused the self-reproach he saw in her eyes?

"Susie." He held her arms. "There are worse things than that. I already told you what happened to me."

She flinched and lost what little color she had left. "That was different. You were abused. I gave away my baby."

"If you expect me to despise you for what you did when you were a kid, you chose the wrong confessor." Nick found his patience vanishing. "What did your parents do when you got pregnant, your mother the senator?"

"They set up the adoption in secret." Susie avoided his eyes.

"And what happened to the guy who committed statutory rape?" He watched humiliation slide over her features. "Jack shit, right?"

Tears flowed down her cheeks as she nodded. "Nothing. He was a colleague of my mother's. He wasn't married at the time." She stared at the ground as if she deserved to be whipped. "I seduced him."

Nick grabbed her hands to stop her nails digging into her own skin. "So where's the kid now? Is he happy? Safe?"

"He grew up on a ranch in Wyoming."

It sounded fantastic to Nick. Memories of the tiny council house he'd shared with his granny flickered through his mind, edging out the squalor of his mother's flat. But Susie was still self-flagellating. He bet she spent every day beating the crap out of herself for one lousy lapse in judgment, a mistake most teenagers were capable of making.

A little fissure cracked in his heart. She took life so seriously. Cared too deeply. He wished he had more time. He wished he didn't have to track down a killer and a disorientated pensioner. He let out a slow breath and pushed Susie's hair behind her ear. "You were just a kid, Susie. The child was looked after. You need to forgive yourself."

She took a step back, the wind molding her clothes to her body like a second skin.

"That's it? That's all you can say?" Her eyes were wide with anger, but it beat the hell out of tears.

"You want me to tie you up and give you a good spanking, I'm game, but don't kid yourself it has anything to do with your past." And it shocked him that he wanted her, right here, right now. His hands started shaking so badly he stuffed them in his pockets. "There are plenty of kids who'd be grateful for a good home and people to love them."

"Like you, you mean?" Her words were ice against his soul.

One side of his mouth curled because Susie might be softhearted but she had guts.

"I lived." *Just.* After his mother had got hold of him it had been touch and go, and after Chrissie…well, maybe *existed* was closer to the truth.

What about now? The question taunted the edges of his mind.

Susie gazed at the rippling ocean. "I don't know how to forgive myself."

"Susie, people do worse things than that every single day and never give a monkey's." He rubbed the sting of salt from his eyes. "I've done things that would make you run screaming in horror. I'm not some hero who always does the honorable thing." And there it was, the perfect weapon to drive her away, even though he didn't want her to go. But he couldn't stay and he didn't want to hurt her.

"That night I drove you home from Dougie and Leanne's dinner party?"

"The night Tracy was killed?" She frowned, a tremor of emotion running through her voice. "What about it?"

"When I kissed you that first time on your doorstep?" He waited for her nod. "It was great, wasn't it? So damn hot I only just remembered to lift your wallet and steal your keycard."

Her mouth dropped open in shock. He held up his hand to stop her speaking, determined to finish this. To wreck the illusions that kept them afloat.

"I used your keycard to break into the Gatty and search Sizemore's office for evidence that he killed Chrissie."

"You used me? You...you lied to me and questioned me about that stupid card!" She thrust away from him, staring at him wide-eyed. "You sonofabitch. What about Tracy?"

"What about Tracy? You think I killed her?"

"Did you?" She bit her lip uncertainly.

"Bloody hell, Susie, I've spent my entire adult life looking for justice for one murdered woman. What makes you think I'd kill another?" He was breathing hard, guilt hurting his chest and thick emotion blurring his vision.

"I'm sorry."

He backed away. "No. It was a smart question, exactly the sort of question you should be asking. But if I had killed her, I wouldn't have told you about the keycard." The smile he sent her was wolfish as he strove to hide what he was really feeling.

"Is your wife's death the only reason you became a cop?"

"Yes. That's why I became a cop." Some cop—he couldn't even nail one lousy killer. "I promised Chrissie I'd get her justice." Twelve years of resentment reached out to suffocate him and he could barely breathe. "And I know who killed her. I just can't prove it." He'd failed. So where did that leave him?

"So." She took a deep breath. "I take it we're finally done? You got everything you wanted?"

Not even close.

Susie tucked her head down and started walking away. But he couldn't let her go without telling her the whole truth.

"Chrissie was pregnant with Jake Sizemore's child when she died."

Susie stopped walking and he caught up with her and grabbed her arm. "The last time I felt like this about a woman I married her." He turned her to face him, wishing he could hold back the words but needing her to know how much she mattered.

Damn, there were tears in his eyes again and she was crying. "I can't go through that again."

She flinched. God, she must hate him.

"Get out of my life, Nick. Leave me the hell alone."

There. It was over. They were done. He squeezed shut his eyes against the pain. He followed her back to her cottage in silence as the moon shone down with a malevolent gleam. Emily was missing, two women had been murdered and he was breaking Susie Cooper's heart.

Susie's Mini sat beside his Subaru, and Rocket was asleep in his backseat. Ewan had been here. Nick grabbed his belongings, unable to meet Susie's gaze. She deserved a man who'd support her and love her the way women were meant to be loved. And the thought that it wouldn't be him gouged his heart.

Bile rose in his throat as he shifted the car into gear, and shame slithered through his gut.

A helicopter buzzed in the distance. Search and Rescue looking for Emily out at sea.

Mick Jagger crooned a solemn lament as the tires crunched slowly over gravel. Nick's throat worked and his vision swam and he wished to hell he was out of tears.

CHAPTER TWENTY

EXPECTING TRICK-OR-TREATERS, Rafael opened his door with a bag of candy and a grin. Instead, he found Lily in tears. Exhausted. Incoherent. Dripping with sweat. She had no money, no keys, just her cell phone clasped in a tight fist. She stuffed it against her lips, trying to smother her sobs.

"Lily? What is it?" Rafael hugged her to his chest and rubbed his chin in her hair. "What is it, *gata?*"

He'd been angry with her yesterday, but now he was concerned. A helicopter sounded in the distance, the boom of rotors bouncing off the surface of the water. He maneuvered her inside until her knees hit the couch and she collapsed upon it.

"I can't find my mother, Rafael. She's missing." Sobs tore through her, rising from deep inside, big painful wrenching sounds that ripped into him like hatchets.

"I help you look for her." He went to grab his jacket but she stopped him.

She shook her head. "No. It's no good. I just spoke to Nick. We searched everywhere and there's no sign."

"Did you tell him you come here?" The policeman was a complication Rafael didn't need.

She shook her head, quivering in his arms, delicate, needy, a mess. Nothing like the girl he thought he knew. His *friend.* Her heart was shattering. He didn't know what to do. There was only one form of comfort he was good at.

He kissed her.

He didn't know what to expect but it wasn't her hands slipping around his neck as her legs wrapped around his waist. He'd expected her to slap him, to insult his *pinto* again. Because they were friends. The only friend he'd had in years.

He didn't expect her to ignite in his arms like a maelstrom and turn his comfort into a conflagration. Her lips slid along his skin as she pushed him back onto the couch. Her hands ran over him and he jerked and trembled when she touched him.

"Stop." He tried to grab her hands as she yanked the button of his jeans open and inched his pants down his thighs. Her eyes were brilliant with emotion.

"Lily. You are upset. We not do this." Urgently he tried to capture her hands.

She shook off his grip, yanked his pants lower. He tried to pull those lips away from his betraying *caralho*, but she was there, her hair soft as silk against his stomach, and her mouth sliding over him like one of the deadly sins. He groaned like an animal as she consumed him, pleasure screaming through his veins.

No! He came back to himself just as his body primed for release. He thrust her away, breathing hard, his lungs bellowing for oxygen. Then she stepped out of her panties and the small triangle of ebony hair was as dangerous as any steel trap. But he didn't want to fall again. Not with her.

She stopped and narrowed her gaze. Must have seen the reluctance fighting his arousal. The doorbell rang and he tried to get up, but she stopped him.

"I need this, Rafael. If not you, I'll find someone else."

Anger made his teeth lock. How could she do this

to him? She was the one person in the world who knew what this did to him. He looked at her tear-drenched face, furious blue eyes, and then between her thighs as she parted her legs almost in a dare.

Sweat broke out on his brow and he throbbed. How could he refuse? He could never refuse.

The doorbell rang again, but this time he ignored it. Holding her tragic eyes, he caught one of her knees and drew her to him, stretched her across his body and then shimmied down the sofa. Her hot tears fell on his face. He felt her impatience and irritation.

"It is my way or not at all, *gata*." He didn't wait for an answer, just buried his mouth in her soft dark curls and devoured as she bucked and writhed above him. He tasted heat and sweat and woman. Her scent filled him, the feel of her flesh beneath his fingers more precious than all his father's gold, silver and oil. She pulled away and he let her. Her eyes blazed fierce blue as she rolled a condom over him.

She was in control. The determination in her eyes as she guided him inside her made him ache. The chains that bound him were moist and volcano hot. The iron manacles that imprisoned his soul were soft floating breasts. She arched her back, stripping the rest of her clothes as she went. Took his hands and cupped her breasts, rubbing his fingers over perfect nipples as she pressed deep inside him. Deep. Inside. Him.

Oh, merda. It felt so good.

He finally began to breathe, finally began to enjoy it.

Reverence of her breasts took time. He had to force her to slow her frantic pace. Rafael Domenici knew all about making mistakes. Sometimes the best were the biggest ones, the ones that blew up and exploded in your face.

He took her nipple in his mouth and feasted until she writhed on top of him. With his other hand he slipped the belt from his jeans, grabbed her hands and pinned them behind her back, binding her wrists with thick leather.

"What are you doing?" Her eyes changed from fierce to fearful in a heartbeat.

"Giving you what you want." He cinched the leather tight and she flinched. Tomorrow there would be marks.

"I never said anything about bondage…"

"You want me to punish you, Lily." Just as he'd punished Tracy Good. "Otherwise you'd have gone somewhere else." The words hung suspended like tears on a lash.

He jerked on the leather and though she was above him, he was in control now. He smiled into her eyes and met her fury. But he was an expert at the exquisite balance between pleasure and pain, and knew exactly how hard to push before ecstasy became torture. Within minutes she was begging.

And he'd never felt so lonely in his entire damned life.

HEARTS DID *NOT* BREAK.

Susie had lived through terrible things. Depression. Giving up her baby. Holding Dela as she convulsed and died in her arms. Decompression sickness. And no matter how badly she'd hurt, her heart had always beat in perfect synchrony, all autonomic nervous control and physical precision.

Hearts did not break, but parts of you died. Little pockets of hope and light perished. And maybe that's what the aging process was? The destruction of hope and light.

It seemed an appropriate epiphany for All Hallows' Eve.

She'd always known Nick was a brief fantasy and it was time to get on with her life. But he was right, she did need to forgive herself, to heal herself, rather than expect some other person to make her whole.

She wasn't over him—the awful numbness inside her chest suggested it would be a long time until she was over him. But it was time to go to work, to throw herself back into research and forget she'd fallen in love with a man who knew all her secrets, who'd made her feel as good as she would ever feel, and who still wouldn't stay.

Her fingers grasped the handle of her laptop case as she headed to the door. A knock stopped her midstride and she stared, hope springing inside for one blinding instant. Then she remembered Nick didn't knock.

The lump of emotion blocking her throat was the size of a football. She strode to the door, pulled it wide open before she recalled that only a week ago a woman had been bludgeoned to death.

TWO SKULKING JACK-O'-LANTERNS guarded the portico of the Sizemores' home and reminded Nick it was Halloween. Tea lights cast fluttering shadows that danced within the gourds like evil sprites. Nick should have gone to the police station. He should have steered clear of the Sizemores' property. Pounding the large brass lion knocker, Nick knew all about shoulds, woulds and maybes. But he had to do something to stop himself from crawling back to Susie on bended knees and begging her forgiveness.

"Trick or treat," he called. Misery ate at him as though he was slowly being devoured by poison. He needed a distraction and he needed answers.

The door opened and a single apprehensive eyeball peered through the crack before Jake's angry face filled the gap.

"Who is it, Daddy?" Callie's high-pitched voice reached Nick. Breezy, unconcerned.

Why would she be worried when she'd gotten away with her crimes for so long?

"Leave us alone!" Jake hissed as he tried to close the door.

Nick's size-eleven boot somehow got in the way. "I just need a quick word with your daughter." Looking into Sizemore's washed-out eyes, Nick was startled by the lack of antipathy he felt for the man. No rage. No guilt. Just business. "I have a couple of questions to finish up."

Behind Jake, Callie smiled. Her oversized eyes in that gaunt face made it more expressive than it actually was. An optical illusion. Her glance swept him from head to toe, and her lips twitched slightly as if she held back amusement.

"Go on, Daddy, he can't do anything to us now." Callie touched her father's arm. "Fetch us a cup of tea."

"You're sure?" Jake took her by the shoulders and kissed her forehead when she nodded. "Don't say anything he can twist. Today has already been bad enough."

"I don't think D.I. Archer has come for a confession of murder, Daddy." Her laugh was sugary—and turned Nick's stomach.

Jake grunted and walked away, disappearing into what must be the kitchen at the back of the house.

"How's your mom?" Nick asked, stepping uninvited

into the hall. There was a rack of coats hanging on the wall, a shoe stand beneath, and an antique table topped by a vase full of dead roses.

"She's taken a sleeping tablet and gone to bed."

"I'm surprised your brother and sister didn't fly home?"

"I told them not to. There was nothing to worry about." Callie smiled and went into the parlor where he'd first talked to Judy.

He followed her in. She bent over to plug in a lamp, showing her skinny ass to its best advantage.

"I suppose you have a recorder in your pocket? Hoping to trick me into a confession?" Her laugh lanced his soul.

"You can search me if you like." He raised his arms and offered her a slight grin. She eyed him thoughtfully.

Everyone had a weakness. Even sociopaths. What was hers? The door banged open as Jake came in with a tea tray rattling in his hands. He glared at Nick, looked over at Callie as if to make sure Nick hadn't strangled her or nailed her against the wall. There was more than one type of revenge, but Nick didn't think he'd have the stomach for the latter.

"Just leave the tray, Daddy."

"How often did you watch them together, Callie?"

She blinked slowly, like a kid's doll tilted backward and forward.

"What the hell are you talking about now?" Jake grumbled, setting out cups.

"You and Chrissie, screwing each other's brains out." It didn't taste bitter anymore. He actually felt at peace because there was nothing left of his feelings for Chrissie, just the sadness she'd died so young. "Was it just once or did you spy on them regularly?"

One side of Callie's mouth curled in amusement as she leaned against the mantelpiece. Jake went beetroot red, squared his shoulders and took a threatening step toward him.

Nick straightened. "You know better than that, Jake," he warned. The older man hesitated and Nick felt the first measure of pity. "Are you telling me you didn't know your daughter was getting a biology practical from the two of you?"

Jake swung to face Callie, his features stretching with growing horror. The silence felt like an extra person in the room, but Callie killed that, too.

"They used to take me out in the cruiser with them." She smirked before walking over to the couch and sitting down, crossing her legs. "I think Mom thought I'd be their chaperone. But they couldn't keep their hands off each other."

The blood slowly drained from her father's face, leaving skin the color of used chewing gum.

"They'd set me up with a fishing rod and a book and trot into the cabin, all smiles. 'Just going to check the equipment.'" Callie huffed out a laugh as she poured herself tea. "Like being a kid was the same as being stupid."

Jake reached out a hand to the arm of the couch before lowering himself down. He rested his face in his hands. "Oh, God."

"I could hear them at it, and yes…" The look she slipped Nick was sly as a fox. "I admit I was curious. I peeked a few times."

"Oh, sweet Jesus." Her father's face crumpled. He finally seemed to appreciate that his libido had caused a cascade reaction that ended in disaster.

"That must have been difficult for you as a kid, watching your dad cheat on your mom."

"My dad was slumming." Callie's eyes went hard, and something sinister swam in their depths. "Your wife screamed like a whore every time she came, but I assume you knew that." She flicked her hair over her shoulder.

Jake stared at his daughter, slack-jawed, and Nick wondered if the man was going to have a heart attack.

"She couldn't seem to help herself, not even when Dad put his hand over her mouth." She narrowed her eyes. "She screamed. A lot."

It hurt but Nick had been playing with monsters since he was a kid. "Well, at least she enjoyed it, aye?"

He looked at the pathetic figure who'd made Chrissie scream. Jake's face muscles had lost their firmness years ago and gathered bags and wrinkles. Tears streamed down his face and he looked as if he was trying to form words but had lost the ability to speak.

"It would have pissed you off if your mom and dad had split up, wouldn't it, Callie?" Nick pushed her. "If you'd had to share Daddy with someone else's brat?"

"That was never going to happen." She tapped her toe with the self-assurance of God.

"The only thing I haven't figured out is how you got off the boat after you pushed Chrissie into the water? Was she conscious?"

Jake staggered to his feet. "Now just wait a goddamn minute!"

Callie's eyes gleamed with intelligence and a punishing smile curved her lips. "I always figured *if* your wife was murdered the way you said she was, the killers just towed another boat behind the cruiser, maybe a little tin boat with an outboard? Then returned before anyone knew they were gone."

Killers. Plural. "Your mother knew. She tried to cover for you."

Callie just blinked as her father blustered.

"Don't come in here trying to destroy my daughter with your wild accusations," Jake rallied. "First it was me, then Judy, now Callie? I had a relationship with Christina, I admit it. But you were the one who broke her heart. You tossed her out. She made one mistake and you wouldn't have her back!"

The rage reignited inside Nick. He didn't want to hear this shit. He stared at Callie. She popped her gum.

"In South Africa we fell in love." Jake plowed on, oblivious. "I was going to marry her, but she died—in an *accident*—I didn't kill her, and neither did Callie!"

Nick looked at the man who'd destroyed his life. Returning the favor was the least he could do.

"It was your wife who put me on to Callie actually, and the little bitch *did* do it, probably with the help of your other kids." He pointed his finger. "All because you couldn't keep your dick in your trousers. I mean, I knew Judy would lie to protect you, but confess to murder? Seemed a bit extreme given your lax interpretation of your wedding vows, but a mother's love for her child? That crosses all boundaries..." Nick stopped talking.

His heart stuttered and for a second he didn't think it was ever going to start again. He'd never experienced it, but he knew there was nothing stronger than a mother's love.

Bloody hell. A light switched on inside his head.

"Judy mentioned something about a break-in in your garden shed a few weeks ago. What did they take?"

Jake looked flummoxed by the change in conversation. Callie yawned.

"Some tools. I don't know. The place was trashed."

Nick would bet a hundred quid someone had stolen a hammer hoping for latent fingerprints. And suddenly he knew exactly who had killed Tracy Good and the adrenaline kick-started his heart with a rush of blood. And while Jake's lecherous appetite had put Tracy in the bull's-eye, it was Nick himself who'd gotten the girl killed.

Shit. Was Susie in danger? Indecision warred inside him. He was so close to finally getting a solid confession out of Callie Sizemore because she thought she was so frickin' clever. But Susie's safety was more vital than bitter promises or overdue justice. And it hit him like a wrecking ball that Susie was more important than anything: his pride, his vendetta, his fear of getting his heart broken again.

He tried to slip out, but Callie caught him at the front door and grabbed his arm.

"We chummed the water to draw them in." She spoke quietly. "Chrissie was conscious. Even after the first few strikes, she was wide awake. We had to force her away from the boat with an oar." Malice blazed in her eyes. "She was a fighter. A fighter and a screamer."

Icy shivers ran up his back.

"And she screamed like a fucking banshee when the sharks tore her apart."

Time was suspended as revulsion boiled in his stomach. He held her smug gaze as he pulled a tiny digital voice recorder from his pocket and showed it to her. His voice cracked. "I'm no expert, but this should give the South African authorities enough to reopen the investigation."

She lunged for the device but he towered over her and held it high. It might not be enough for a conviction, but it would throw the shadow of suspicion on the whole damn family for the rest of their miserable lives.

He opened the door to a chorus of little voices.

"Trick or treat!"

He edged past the miniature ghosts and witches with a shudder. The monsters lived inside that house.

"EMILY! COME IN! Everyone has been so worried." Susie smiled as she opened the door. No one had actually said it, but it was obvious everyone thought Emily was dead. Relieved, Susie propped her laptop against the wall, caught the older woman's arm and dragged her inside. "Did you see Lily? She's been worried sick about you."

Susie drew her into the kitchen, flicking on lights as she went. Emily's hair was tangled by the wind, frizzed by ocean spray, but apart from that she looked perfectly *compos mentis*. Her thick winter coat was wrapped snugly around her waist, her sturdy purse pinned beneath her arm.

"Do you want coffee? Tea?"

"Tea. I'd love a cup of tea. Milk, one sugar, please." Emily lowered herself into the kitchen chair, which creaked in protest. "I couldn't find the car keys so I got the bus into town to buy Halloween treats." Her eyes crinkled, forming confused triangles. "I left a note for Lily, but when I got home she wasn't there."

Susie frowned, reassessing Emily. Lily would not have been panicked if she'd seen a note. She wouldn't have called out the Search and Rescue teams if she'd known her mother had just popped into town for candy. Even now helicopters buzzed in the distance, running search patterns for Emily's body. Unless Lily hadn't spotted the note in her initial haste?

"Let me call her." Then Lily could call Nick, because Susie didn't want to speak to him and the feeling would be mutual.

She was still coming to terms with the fact that as much as Nick claimed to care about her, he'd used her and lied to her to avenge his dead wife. Susie forced a smile and picked up the phone from the counter, checked Lily's cell number from a neatly printed list she kept beside the phone. The call went through, but she got a busy signal and was bumped straight to voice-mail.

"Hi, Lily, great news. Your mom's safe and at my place. Give me a call and cancel the search party."

Grinning, Susie turned around. "She's going to be so relieved. They have helicopters and half the coun-tryside out looking for you."

Emily squeezed her fingers in her lap. "I don't know why she made such a fuss, silly girl."

"She loves you." Susie looked at the pallor in the old woman's skin and decided to opt for something stronger than tea. "Here, let's celebrate with a real drink." She pulled down a bottle of twenty-one-year-old Glengoyne and poured two fingers' worth into crystal tumblers.

She handed one of the snifters to Emily and took a drink of her own, letting the alcohol sear her throat.

Emily took a sip. "I'm not much of a drinker."

"Think of it as medicinal." Susie put down her glass and went into the hall to slip out of her jacket. She wasn't going anywhere until Emily was in safe hands.

"Do we actually get trick-or-treaters out here?" Susie called.

"We used to. Some of the kids from Kingsbarns

would wander down or get driven by their parents, but I always have sweets in the house for the girls. I don't like the idea of them walking the streets and knocking on strangers' doors. It seems so dangerous…"

She trailed off as Susie walked back into the kitchen frowning. Maybe Emily wasn't all right after all. Susie picked up her scotch and took a hearty swallow. God, she needed a drink after the day she'd had, and it beat the heck out of painkillers.

"Life is dangerous," Susie agreed. "Doesn't matter how careful you are, things can still go wrong."

Emily had a strange expression on her face. "Why don't you have any children?"

Susie held Emily's gaze but wasn't sure the woman was really seeing her. "I want to have kids, but I haven't found the right guy to settle down with." And never would, she realized now. She finished her drink and reached for the bottle to pour herself another one. One more wouldn't hurt.

CHAPTER TWENTY-ONE

SUSIE BLINKED HERSELF AWAKE. Wow, she'd almost nodded off.

"I see you, Susie Cooper." Emily's voice had a teasing quality, but there was a disconcerting look in the woman's eyes. "You're trying to steal Christina's husband for yourself."

Susie's dry throat convulsed. "No—"

"Don't lie to me!" Emily screamed, rising to her feet as Susie gaped in shock. "Don't you dare lie to me!" The old woman shook her finger at Susie, leaning over her, blue eyes wild.

Susie felt her heart thump woodenly, but despite the fact that Emily was scaring her, she actually felt as if she was about to fall asleep. Her lids drooped as heavy as lead, and the tips of her fingers tingled, turning numb.

"I'm not lying," Susie protested, trying to stand up.

"I saw you." Spittle flew from Emily's mouth and Susie flinched.

She tried to climb to her feet but they got all tangled up. She should remember not to mix scotch and pain pills in the future.

"I saw your picture in the newspaper. You were all over him!"

Ah...that.

"And I saw his car here earlier. I know what you were

doing with another woman's husband. You should be ashamed!"

"Was nuffing." Susie swayed, tried to use the table for balance but it screeched across the kitchen floor and she dropped to her knees. *Ow.* "I fink I need help, Emily."

Keeping her eyes open took all Susie's energy. The elderly woman just stood there looking at her.

"You should never have tried to steal my daughter's husband, you little slut." Emily took a step toward her and slapped her across the face.

Shock rippled through Susie's body like a stone thrown into a deep lake. Even though she knew she had to get up and get help, her limbs wouldn't cooperate. Her mouth was parched and her tongue too swollen to form words. Her eyes closed and no matter how hard she tried, she couldn't crack them back open. Then she felt herself being dragged across the floor like some rag doll.

After that she felt nothing at all.

CALLIE KILLED CHRISSIE, but she had no motive to kill Tracy because no way in hell was her dad going to give up his comfy life for an easy lay. Nick floored the accelerator, punching the brakes on the hairpin turns, screeching around corners while his mind screamed, *This can't be right.* He'd put away too many murderers. Knew the psyche, knew the signs. But Emily hadn't been herself for some time now.

He'd missed the clues. Maybe because that maternal bond was the one sentiment he had never experienced. It was a force beyond his comprehension.

Was the dementia an act? Or had mental illness let the need for revenge overtake social convention? Or had

Emily simply lost faith in the justice system and taken the law into her own hands?

Rocket whimpered as he slid on slick claws around the boot of the car.

"Sorry, boy." Nick slowed for a second before the panic roared back through his mind like a spark through an engine and he put his foot down again.

Susie.

She'll be fine, he told himself. Emily wouldn't go after Susie just because they'd slept together. Would she?

Emily was missing. Possibly dead. He should be mourning her, not worried she was running around town avenging years of injustice. But sweat ran down his spine and his gut told him Susie was in danger.

He'd give his life to protect her. She meant more to him than anybody ever had—so why had he forced her out of his life? Was Ewan right? Was he using what had happened with Chrissie as an excuse not to be happy? Was he such an emotional coward he wasn't willing to give their relationship another shot?

The circle of violence worked its evil through generation after generation. He'd seen it a thousand times and was scared he was already tainted. And he, big bad homicide detective, was terrified of passing it on, of perpetuating the vicious cycle.

But it didn't have to be that way.

Look at what he shared with his friends, look at what he'd done with his life. He'd always viewed himself as damaged, but maybe he was just scared. Maybe inside he was that defenseless little boy terrified of having his soul torn asunder.

Love was dangerous. For anyone in this uncertain

world brave enough to risk it, love was dangerous. And he loved Susie.

He didn't know when he'd realized it for sure—maybe the first time he'd kissed her and she'd tasted like hope. Maybe that moment on the beach when he'd driven her away with the bare bones of the truth, but hadn't had the balls to admit the very real emotions that swamped him every time he thought of her.

Now he might never get the chance.

He pulled out his mobile phone. Gritting his teeth in frustration, he was forced to pull over into a farm gate to dial because it was too dark to see the numbers.

He tried Susie first, prayed she was locked up nice and tight in her cottage, crying her eyes out over what a bastard he was. No one answered and he waited an age for the answerphone to kick in. Damn. He put the car in gear and started driving one handed. "Susie, this is important. Whatever happens, don't open the door to *anyone* but me. No one. Not even Emily."

He rang off and dialed Ewan's number, trying not to end up in the ditch. "I think I know who killed Tracy Good," he said when Ewan answered.

"Who?"

Nick heard Ewan's kids moaning in the background. "What are you up to?" Nick asked him.

"I'm about to take the kids trick-or-treating." The sound muted as if someone put their hand over the receiver. "Go kiss your mother before we head out."

Shit. Nick wished this whole nightmare was part of his imagination—unfortunately, Tracy was dead.

But every police officer in the county was already on the lookout for Emily Heathcote as a missing person. The Coastguard was combing the coastline for her body.

"Emily Heathcote. I think she killed Tracy Good to

try and set up Jake Sizemore because she believed he killed her daughter." That lay at Nick's door. He'd been the one to rant and rave about the man when Chrissie died. To vow revenge. Now he had to face the fact that he was wrong.

"Hell's bells." Ewan sucked in a breath. "You told me she was suffering from dementia."

"Maybe she is, or maybe she was conning us all along. I'm going out to her cottage to see if she's turned up yet, and then I'm taking Susie out to Dougie and Leanne's house for safety."

"You think Susie's in danger?"

Dread gnawed on the ragged edges of his nerves. Emily would have seen the photograph of them in the newspaper and she'd have seen his car at Susie's house over the last few days. The panic tearing up Nick's heart was serrated and hot-edged. "I don't know, but I can't risk it."

Don't let anything happen to Susie. Not because she'd been dumb enough to fall for him.

"The kids can wait an hour before we head out..." Ewan said.

Nick heard the chorus of moans from Ewan's kids, and disgust washed through him at stealing their father when their mother lay wasting in the next room.

And maybe Nick was wrong. Maybe he was imagining the whole thing as an excuse to go see Susie again. Payback for spending too many years living undercover with people who'd slit your throat for a cigarette.

"Don't worry about it. I'll call you from Dougie's house." He hung up and cut down a lane used by tractors, speeding across the flat eerie landscape toward the lights of Kingsbarns which shone across the fields. His heart steadied because he was almost there.

A hairpin corner rushed at him. He tapped the brakes but the back wheels started to slide and the car spun. The steering wheel ripped out of his hands as the car slammed into a stone wall. Rocket howled, the sound penetrating Nick's skull like a drill as the airbag smashed into his face, bashing his nose. Darkness swept over him, dragging him down.

The sensation of a wet tongue licking his face snapped him back into consciousness. He didn't know how long he'd been out. His lips tasted of blood but he didn't think he was seriously injured. He struggled with the white floaty airbag and tried to undo his seatbelt. The bloody thing jammed. Frustration and fear scrambled along his nerves.

He had to get to Susie.

A LOUD, PIERCING SHRIEK roused her. Rough carpet scraped her cheek with every labored breath she stole. Susie coughed, drawing in smoke that made her stomach retch and her eyes water. Instinctively she squeezed her eyelids together against the fierce throb, but even that small movement felt like torture. Pain hammered her skull and sweat poured off her body.

Only the smoke alarm kept her from closing her eyes and going back to sleep. Damn that thing. She tried to raise a hand but couldn't. It felt heavy, not enough oxygen in her system to fuel movement.

Her cottage was on fire.

Hell.

She should be scared but the thick throbbing in her head made it hard even to acknowledge fear. Flames crawled up one wall of her office, eating her wall calendar. Her drysuit hung beside it. Slightly battered, a little threadbare. Before Dela's death it had been Susie's most treasured possession. Electric pink and neon green. The heat was starting to melt the neoprene. She turned her head away, watched a flame dancing up the leg of her desk, a foot from her nose, heading toward her computer.

Had she backed up her files? She drew her knees up to her chest and groaned. She hadn't backed up that damned review she'd been working on, nor the one and only picture she had of her son... She rolled onto her front, onto her knees like a baby in the womb. Heat pressed against her skin, stretching it tight over her flesh.

Smoke filled the air, thick and black, flooding her airways, making her cough, making her head throb and tears stream down her cheeks. She touched the mouse and her computer came to life. She didn't have much time. Her email was open. Swaying on her feet she sent an email to herself, attaching the image, hardly able to stand. An ember fell on her bare arm and she flinched, rubbing the burn, her vision swimming, blackness swirling, but she fought it. If she passed out again, she was dead.

The crackle of flames was deafening. Dragging the telephone unit toward her she dialed 911. Then she remembered Britain had a different emergency service number, but couldn't recall what it was. She dropped the phone, couldn't hear above the flames anyway. The air was so hot it hurt her lungs, and she had to get out. She glanced to her left and saw her dive cylinders. Finally realized she had to get out *now* before they exploded. She staggered to the floor and crawled into the hall.

The hardwood hurt her knees, but the air was cleaner. She shuffled toward the front door, her breath coming in desperate gasps. Sweat dripping down her face. She couldn't remember what had happened. There was a noise behind her and she flipped onto her back just as a poker crashed into the wood beside her cheek.

"Oh no, you don't, you little whore!" Emily Heathcote loomed over her, her hair disheveled, soot streaking her face like camo paint. She looked wild. *Insane.* She raised the poker again, a look of intense concentration wrinkling her face.

"Emily. No!" Screams stuck in Susie's throat. The older woman took a swipe at Susie's head but Susie lunged away, kicking at her attacker's knee. The joint buckled and Emily howled with pain and fell backward as the roar of the fire intensified.

Susie couldn't believe she'd just injured an old lady. There was a blast in her office, windows cracking, and Susie tried to pull away, but Emily grabbed her ankle.

"What is wrong with you?" Susie yelled, pumping her feet, trying to get free, fending off Emily's poker-wielding hand with both of her own. Her head pounded and her energy was flagging. Emily seemed to sense it, forcing her back against the floor, hate and determination blazing from her eyes.

"You shouldn't have seduced Christina's husband. You shouldn't have tried to take her place!"

Gathering all her strength, Susie punched Emily in the nose and her head snapped back. Susie wondered if she'd go to hell for socking a senior. A voice rose above the noise of the fire and the alarm. Susie thought she heard a dog barking.

"Dr. Cooper! Susie!" It was a terrified, high-pitched yell. Female. Emily's startled gaze shot to the front door as the handle turned and there was Lily on the threshold of the cottage, shielding her face from the heat and bending low to avoid the billowing smoke. She stared at the poker in her mother's hand.

"Mom?" Lily's horrified glance shot between Susie and the woman holding her. "What are you doing?"

"Get us out of here!" Susie shouted. Lily ran inside, yanked the poker out of her mother's hand, flinging it along the hallway into the flames. She grabbed Susie's wrist, hauling her along the slippery floor, dragging her mother along, too. Suddenly male fingers clamped Susie's wrist and hauled her out the door and into the beautiful cool air.

Susie drew in oxygen like a black hole sucking in stars. Relief rose up inside her so big, so enormous she thought her brain might explode. Someone swept her off her feet, carried her away from the heat and the flames. Laid her on the grass well away from the fire.

"Jesus, Susie. I thought I'd lost you." It was Nick, holding her, cradling her head in his palms. Whispering words of comfort. She held him tight, filled with relief. She had almost died in there. Would have died if they hadn't rescued her. She was so happy to see him, so happy to have his hands stroking her hair.

"Did she hurt you?" he asked.

Rocket came over and licked her hand. Fresh tears flooded her eyes and she reminded herself murder was Nick's job. She was a crime victim. It didn't mean he loved her.

Blood trickled from his nose but he didn't seem to notice. He watched her with panic-stricken eyes, the harsh angles of his face backlit with flames from the burning cottage. Her home. *Dammit*. She struggled to sit up, glancing across at Emily, who was fighting with Lily and Rafael. Rafael held on tight with an apprehensive glance at Nick.

"She deserved to die! She was nothing but a cheap slut," Emily raged.

Susie flinched. *Sweet Jesus.*

"No one else cared about justice for Christina. I wanted that murdering bastard to rot in jail, but no one ever did anything. No one ever cared." Emily started sobbing.

"Wait here. I'll be back in a minute." Nick started to get up but Susie grabbed his wrist.

"My dive cylinders are in there," Susie warned Nick as he pulled away.

"Can't you hear her?" Emily screamed, still struggling against Rafael's grip. "Can't you hear her calling?"

Suddenly Emily smacked Rafael in the balls and shoved Lily to her knees. Then she dashed back into the inferno.

"Bloody hell." The look Nick sent Susie was as ancient as death. "I've got to go after her."

He started jogging toward the blaze, silhouetted against orange and red.

She grabbed Rocket's collar to stop him following his master. "No! Nick, please no."

The front windows shattered, but Nick never flinched, never slowed. Rafael stumbled toward her, dragging a hysterical Lily by the waist, urging them all farther away from the intense heat. Nick braced himself at the doorway.

A heavyset Grim Reaper shot past them, racing toward the cottage. The Reaper tackled Nick to the ground, covering his body with his own just as the house exploded, cylinders shooting through the roof like grenades, landing on the beach like spent bombs.

Ewan held Nick around the chest, pinning his arms,

struggling in a low crouch away from the flames. Lily stared at the blaze, tears streaming down her cheeks. Fire trucks shrieked in the distance. Ewan wiped his brow on the edge of his robe, smudging his face paint as he shoved Nick toward Susie.

"Are you hurt?" she asked. An ugly burn seared Nick's cheekbone. Her voice sounded awful and she hacked, trying to get a clean breath. She took a step toward him before she remembered they weren't lovers anymore. Beyond him, her home was a bonfire, reminiscent of an oversized jack-o'-lantern.

She didn't know how to begin to grieve for Emily or her home.

"I'm fine." Nick grabbed Ewan by his robe. "I should bloody thump you." His Adam's apple bobbed up and down as he swallowed. Then he hugged the other man hard. "You interfering bastard."

They laughed and Susie started crying.

Nick turned to her. "What about you? Are you hurt?"

"I don't know. I don't really know what happened." Susie wiped her cheeks. Then she started to sway. At least if she passed out she could avoid the embarrassment of being in love with the wrong guy. Memories drizzled back. "We had a drink and I fainted." She frowned. "She must have drugged me."

Nick took a step toward her, but she backed away with a funky little dance.

"Do you think she killed Tracy?" Susie asked.

"I think so." Nick nodded, looking at Rafael who rocked Lily in his arms even though she fought and struggled like a wildcat.

Susie looked at what was left of her home. There was no way Emily survived that, *nothing* could survive that.

"To frame Jake Sizemore because I'd convinced her

he'd killed Chrissie." Nick reached out to touch a strand of her hair. "If I hadn't been so blind, I might have seen it sooner."

The first fire truck arrived and men began rolling out hoses.

"Nobody could have predicted that, Nick. She seemed so normal." She tried to swallow but her throat felt raw and her mouth tasted like the inside of a barbeque. "She seemed to think Christina was still alive and that I was trying to steal you from her."

Nick nodded. No emotion. No grief. "Hardly worth it, am I?" He looked away as if to save her from disagreeing.

He had no clue that the few days and nights she'd spent with him were some of the best of her life. He'd taught her that her sins weren't as bad as she'd always believed and instilled in her some badly needed self-esteem.

Hoses started to spray water at her house but it was too late. It was completely gutted.

Tremors started in the back of Susie's knees and worked their way up each muscle block. Nick rubbed his palms on his thighs, looking as if he'd rather be on the moon.

"It's okay, Nick. You don't have to stick around and play nursemaid." She shot Ewan a grateful smile as he wrapped a beefy arm around her shoulders, holding her up. She could love this man, the man who'd saved Nick from sacrificing himself on the altar of his dead wife. But she'd never love Ewan the way she loved Nick Archer. Holding back annoying tears, she smiled up at Ewan.

"I need to get checked out by a doc, but I know you have work to do. Maybe Rafael can drive me and Lily to the hospital?" Susie glanced at Lily, who had finally quieted in Rafael's arms. Poor, poor girl.

A line of police cars and more fire trucks raced toward them, blue and red lights flashing over fields. "Or we could wait at the other cottage." Susie tilted her chin carefully toward Lily.

Nick looked uncertainly between the oncoming squad cars and Susie. She kept her smile bright even though it hurt, knowing he was torn between duty and guilt. Guilt seemed to be Nick Archer's middle name.

"Just send the ambulance over…" She ruined perfect logic by fainting in Ewan's arms.

CHAPTER TWENTY-TWO

SUSIE WOKE AND SAW LEANNE asleep in a chair beside her. She eased onto her elbows and reached over to take a sip of water from the glass on the bedside table. A large hand took the glass, cupped the back of her head and held the straw to her lips. Startled, she looked up and found Nick leaning over her. He wore clean jeans and a fresh rugby jersey, his face clean-shaven, green eyes grim but relieved.

The bed sagged as he sat down beside her, his hip brushing hers. He smiled, just a slight crinkling of the lines around his eyes. Probably because she was such a complete and utter mess.

"Emily?" she mouthed. He shook his head and sadness flashed through her. Grief had twisted Emily's mind, and though the experience had terrified her, Susie understood the power of that mother-child bond.

But what about Lily? Why hadn't Emily been able to overcome her grief for the good of her living daughter?

"Have another drink of water."

Leanne started to snore, looking extremely uncomfortable on the square-backed hospital chair.

Susie obeyed. The cold liquid helped to drown the smoky taste from her mouth. She reached out to touch him, but there was an IV in her right hand. *Ouch.*

"How's the head?" Nick whispered. "Can you talk or are you punishing me with silence for being such a stupid prick?" His breath caressed her cheek and his lips were only an inch from hers.

She knew she was staring when he leaned back, still holding the glass, and stroked her cheek. Her head didn't hurt at all. Her brain felt entirely disconnected from her body so she figured drugs were taking care of everything except the heartache.

"It's never going to work out between us, you know." Nick put the cup on the side and leaned close once more.

Tears welled up in her eyes. She nodded.

He smelled fantastic, she smelled like a chimney stack.

"You're a liability. Two near-death experiences in six months? I'll need danger money just to hang around you."

Her heart squeezed because he was talking in present tense, a difference in vernacular that branded her heart with pain all over again. He held her hands. "Susie, I can't get married again. Ever." He looked away quickly. She closed her eyes, squeezed them shut because surely she was imagining him here, hurting her all over again. "If that doesn't bother you, maybe we could...you know...date." He rose and paced the floor, the sun glistening in his hair like frosted gold. "See how things go."

"If that's your idea of a proposal, you *suck*." Leanne wasn't asleep anymore. She was wide awake and had a protective glint in her eye that strongly hinted at mama bear. "You should be *begging* Susie to live with you and bear your children."

Susie opened her mouth to speak.

"Why the fuck would she want *me?*"

The f-bomb sounded just a little too loud in the quiet of the hospital and even Nick glanced at the door with a wince. Leanne rolled her eyes and stretched out her arms in a catlike movement that made Susie feel as stiff as a brick.

"Don't be pathetic. Susie doesn't need pathetic. She's had enough of those losers. She needs a real man." Leanne shot her a look to tell her to keep her mouth shut and Susie complied. "*Why* can't you get married again? Just because it didn't work out with your first wife, more than a decade ago, doesn't mean it won't work out with Susie. Susie," she said with enough conviction to drill a hole in the wall, "deserves the full package. The whole enchilada, baby. A man big enough to deal with *his* mistakes and give her the family she's always craved. It's not her fault your first wife screwed around on you—and I'm pretty sure it wasn't your fault either." Leanne's voice dropped. "But Susie would never do that. Think about it." She headed for the door. "I'm gonna see if she's here yet."

Nick watched her leave, but when he turned back to face Susie there was fear in his eyes.

He was terrified of her.

A horrified laugh escaped. Just what she needed, to be another chain of responsibility around his neck. She held up her left hand. "You don't have to do this, Nick. I know you feel guilty about what happened with Emily, but it wasn't your fault."

"It *was* my fault, but that isn't why I'm here." The smile on his face was gentle and full of something that looked startlingly like love. It pierced her with tentative hope and she looked away.

She played with the bedcovers, too nervous to hold his gaze, too unsure of herself to trust her instincts. "Why are you here, then? For forgiveness? I forgive you, now leave me alone." Her voice dropped to a wretched whisper. "Please."

He crossed to the window, then back to the bed, running his hands through his hair until it stuck up in all directions.

"I'm damaged, Susie. I'm damaged *and* I'm scared. I held on to the anger and guilt of losing Chrissie for so long, I don't even know who I am anymore." He pressed his fingers to his temples. "When I fell in love with her, I was a kid who didn't have a clue about what he was doing." The fact he was talking about his feelings for his dead wife held her rapt. "She was the first person who ever loved me back. *That's* why I fell so hard. That's why I never got over it. That's why I'm so scared right now I feel like I'm having a stroke." He stepped closer and cupped her cheek. "You scare the hell out of me, Susie Cooper. Relationships scare the hell out of me because I always end up back where I started, with nothing."

Emotion crowded Susie's throat. He stroked her hair and she tried not to cry. She gripped his wrist with strong fingers because no matter what she said, she didn't want him to leave.

"I told you I don't do long term, Susie." His eyes focused on her and she wanted to look away but was caught by the intensity in those green depths. "But for the first time since I met Chrissie, I want to give it a shot. No secrets, no lies, nothing between us but the truth. I love you."

He kissed her, his lips moving over hers gently at first, deepening until she could taste the truth. Everything he felt was in that kiss. Hope. Fear. Desire. And love. He loved her. He did.

Joy burst through Susie like the birth of a new star.

"I can't imagine life without you, and if you want me, I'll do my best to be the man you want me to be."

Tears dripped down her cheeks and onto their joined hands. Man, she had to get control of herself. "I love you, Nick." The words were so often used casually, but had the power to heal and destroy in equal measure. "You're already the man I want you to be." He dipped his head to kiss her again but reality hit Susie square in the face and she drew back. "There is something that might make you change your mind, though."

"The fact your mother is running for president?"

She shook her head, although that would put off most people. "Something else." She squeezed his fingers, knowing he'd want to bolt. "I already told you I wanted a family. I don't care about a ring. But I do care about a baby and if you can't give me that, or don't want to be involved, I'm going to a sperm bank to take care of it on my own."

"What?" Nick's eyes widened in surprise. She didn't think she'd ever seen him taken aback before. "A sperm bank? You?"

She didn't need a man to have a baby, but she wanted one. She wanted Nick Archer. "I want to give us a chance, but I'm going to try for a baby. Either with you—" her voice broke "—or through artificial insemination, or maybe adoption. I'm not sure yet."

He pulled away. Stood up to go stare out the window.

She forced back the compromise that wanted to squeeze out of her throat. Words that would bind him to her side in the short term but destroy her in the long term. "I could pretend for a little while that having a child wasn't important to me." She cleared her throat. "But after a few months it would eat me up."

He looked petrified and she understood because

this was a huge step for anyone, let alone someone as isolated and independent as Nick Archer. But nearly dying—*again*—had reinforced her clarity about what she wanted, and why she shouldn't hesitate or pretend. She had one life and she intended to live it.

"I love you. I *really* love you, but—" Everything she'd been through in the last few days hit her with the force of a bullet and a sob ripped out. She sank her face against her drawn-up knees. She was pushing him for something he didn't want to give, and she was going to lose him all over again.

She didn't hear him approach but she felt the mattress give when he took his place at her side.

His hand rubbed her back, warm against the bare skin where her hospital gown gaped. "What if it all goes wrong? What if we have a kid and then we can't stand the sight of each other?"

Her heart hurt and pity welled because that was what had happened to him. She raised her head. "I'll love him or her anyway, Nick. I'll give them all I can and hope it's enough. And despite what you think, you'd do exactly the same thing."

He held her hand, playing with her fingers, not looking at her. The lines around her eyes were cut deep with exhaustion. She didn't even know what day it was. "I only know what not to do with a kid—"

"That's a start." She squeezed his hand hard. He seemed to be withdrawing into himself, his eyes losing focus and she didn't know how to reach him.

"You said I was a good person, on the beach, do you remember?" She waited for his curt nod. "You said I needed to forgive myself for giving up my baby." She took a quick breath. "Well, you're a good person too,

Nick, and you need to forgive yourself for all the mistakes you've made in your past."

Hope warred with insecurity in the depths of his eyes. "You'd risk it? With me? I almost got you killed once and there are plenty of things in my past—"

"I'd risk it." She bumped his shoulder with her own. "I don't intend to waste another minute searching for something I've already found." She waited for him to either run away or kiss her. They had the opportunity to try and build something together, but would he take the chance?

They stared at each other for long seconds, both searching for answers.

His Adam's apple bobbed rapidly. Then his eyes suddenly sparked with some inner light, as if he'd finally let himself believe he had a right to happiness. "Our daughter would be beautiful, just like you." He touched the end of her hair.

"Maybe she'd have her daddy's green eyes…" Emotion clogged her chest.

There was a knock on the door and Susie adjusted the shoulders of her hospital gown as Rafael and Lily came into the room, holding hands. Nick rose to his feet. No one said anything for a moment, the weight of grief palpable across the narrow confines of the room. Then Nick held open his arms for Lily.

For a half second she remained frozen and then she gave a wretched cry and threw herself into Nick's embrace.

Tears threatened again. Susie didn't know how she was going to cope with the overload of emotion that kept bombarding her today.

When Lily stopped crying she wiped her cheeks on Nick's shirt. She moved closer to the bed, her head bowed. "I am so sorry about what my mother tried to do to you, Dr. Cooper. I had no idea…" The raw anguish in Lily's voice, coupled with the vulnerability of her gaunt face, was enough for Susie to hold out her hand. It took a moment for Lily to respond, her fingers deathly cold to the touch.

"Your mother was sick, Lily—"

"But I should have known—"

"Let it go, Lily," Nick said firmly. "We're not responsible for what your mother did and thankfully Susie survived." And as he met her gaze, she realized he finally believed it. "It's time to move on from the past." Lily's gaze shot between them, reading the implication behind the words. Her smile was sad. "I'll find a new supervisor."

"You don't have to." Susie hadn't even thought about her students since this whole ordeal began. "In fact, I forbid it." Although Lily must know she could do no such thing. She bit her lip. "Unless you can't stand being reminded of what happened."

Rafael went to stand behind Lily and cupped his hands over her shoulders. Nick narrowed his eyes and clenched his jaw, but Rafael held his ground.

"Professor Sizemore, he resign." The Brazilian sent her an uncertain smile.

"Really?" Her eyebrows rose and she sucked in a steadying breath of relief. "That's the best news I've had in days. Thanks. So now all I need is a new home—" she tugged at her gown with disgust "—some clothes and something decent to eat." She was starving.

"*We* need a new home," Nick corrected as he sat back on the bed. "Or you can help me fix up my place." The heat in his gaze flashed over her skin. His voice dropped. "And you won't be needing any clothes for a while." He kissed her and she sank into him, knowing this was Nick's way of saying they had a chance of a future together. The door opened and she assumed it was Lily and Rafael leaving.

"My, my," drawled a familiar voice, "you must be the infamous Detective Inspector Nicholas Archer. I've heard all about *you*."

Oh, heck. They broke apart, both turning to face Senator Darcy Cooper, who was dressed to impress, backed by three dark-suited strangers. Susie's dad was there, too. Smiling at his little girl.

"Mom. Dad? What are you doing here?" Her voice sounded strangled. Susie was hallucinating. She couldn't believe it.

Leanne grimaced and ducked into the room, grabbing the chair next to Susie's bed. Guard duty. Her mother ignored Leanne, as always, and focused exclusively on Susie and Nick.

Nick made room for her parents. Darcy came over and sat on the bed, taking Susie's hand with perfectly manicured fingernails, careful of the IV. Darcy looked immaculate and powerful, but there was no disguising the catch in her voice or the glint of tears in her eyes as she looked over Susie's injuries.

"I was so worried about you."

"I'm fine—"

"You almost *died!*"

"I— Well, yes, I did, but—"

"I've hired bodyguards, Susie." Darcy jerked her head in the general direction of the door. "They come with the best recommendations. Your father insisted."

Susie exchanged a glance with her father whose raised eyebrows told her this was the first he'd heard of it.

"I don't need a bodyguard, Mom."

"Of course you do." Darcy swept her hand over Susie's forehead, overruling her objections. "Especially if I win the nomination."

Susie's pulse pounded, heat began to suffuse her skin as she struggled to sit up.

Nick stepped in, looking mean as a switchblade. "If she says she doesn't need a bodyguard, Senator Cooper, she doesn't need a bodyguard. Anyway, she has me."

Darcy Cooper looked him in the eye. "For how long, Detective?"

Nick didn't back down from her mother's diamond-hard gaze. "I guess that will be up to Susie."

"You're not the sort of man I'd choose for someone as sweet as my little girl."

"What?" Susie started to splutter.

Nick just laughed. "She is sweet, isn't she? And you're definitely not the sort of mother-in-law I'd have chosen, especially after what happened with the last one. But we're stuck with each other, so you'd better get used to it."

Darcy Cooper glanced at her husband. "Pushy. I like it. Maybe he'll do?"

"Damn right I'll do." Nick looked so indignant Susie started to laugh. It seemed she'd finally gotten what she wanted, even though Nick Archer was about as domesticated as the Loch Ness Monster. Settling down with this man was not going to be easy, but it sure as heck was going to be interesting.

It was time for a fresh start. Time to wipe all the slates clean. "Mom, Dad, this is Nick, the man I want to spend the rest of my life with. Nick, these are my parents and if you're brave enough to take me on, I've also got an overprotective older brother." She held his gaze. He wasn't the only one with baggage, only hers was star-spangled. "What do you say? Willing to take a risk on me and my crazy family?"

Her mother watched him expectantly. Leanne grinned.

"I'm staying, Susie. You're stuck with me, forever." He leaned down and whispered in her ear, ignoring the nurse, who shooed out her parents and was trying to clear the room. "Together we can do anything. Together we can make a family and have a real life." He rested his forehead against hers and closed his eyes. She placed her hand on his chest and felt the solid beat of his heart against her palm. She could still smell the smoke clinging to her skin, but the ordeal was over, a new chapter in their lives was about to begin.

Nick checked his watch and groaned. "Except right now I've got to go. Tracy's memorial service starts in thirty minutes." He rubbed his tired eyes. "I almost forgot." He climbed to his feet and Susie swung her legs over the side of the bed. "Where do you think you are going?"

She dragged the IV pole to the door. "To borrow a suit from my mother." The air was cool on her back as the gown flapped.

Nick stopped her by touching her arm. "Are you sure you're up to it?"

Every inch of her body ached but she nodded. "I can't not go, Nick." Tracy had no one and Susie had almost met the same end as the poor woman.

He ran his hand down to her wrist. "I'll get the clothes—" he looked at her IV "—and talk to the nurse." He didn't approve but he kissed her and went anyway. Because he knew how much it meant to her.